PENGUIN 🐧 CLASSICS

THE TURNIP PRINCESS

FRANZ XAVER VON SCHÖNWERTH (1810–1886) was born in Amberg, Bavaria. He had a successful career in law and the Bavarian royal court, rising to the post of personal secretary to the Crown Prince Maximilian. In the 1850s he began to explore the culture of the Upper Palatinate region of Bavaria, recording his observations and the stories of the people he interviewed. Eventually he devoted himself full-time to his collection and, between 1857 and 1859, published *From the Upper Palatinate: Customs and Legends*, cataloging the customs and folktales of his homeland in unprecedented detail. This work contained only a fraction of his total research, the rest of which was eventually discovered in an archive, forming an important addition to the canon of classic fairy tales.

ERIKA EICHENSEER discovered five hundred previously unknown fairy tales of Franz Xaver von Schönwerth in the municipal archive of Regensburg, Bavaria, in 2009. In 2010 she published a selection entitled *Prinz Roßzwifl* [Prince Dung Beetle]. She began her career as a teacher, then worked for the cultural department of the regional government of East Bavaria. An expert on fairy tales and on puppet theater, she has written numerous books on folk art and customs and has appeared on television, produced radio programs, and performed all over Bavaria as a storyteller. She is co-founder and director of the Schönwerth Society and initiator of the Schönwerth Fairytale Path in Sinzing, near Regensburg, and she wrote the libretto for a musical based on Schönwerth's "The Flying Chest." She has been awarded many honors for her services to Bavarian culture.

MARIA TATAR chairs the program in folklore and mythology at Harvard. She is the author of many acclaimed books on folklore and fairy tales, as well as the editor and translator of *The Annotated Hans Christian Andersen*, *The Annotated Brothers Grimm*, *The Classic Fairy Tales: A Norton Critical Edition*, and *The Grimm Reader*. She lives in Cambridge, Massachusetts.

ENGELBERT SÜSS is a well-known sculptor, glass-artist, and illustrator who was born in 1949 in eastern Bavaria. He created the bronze statue *King of Dwarfs* for the Schönwerth Fairytale Path in Sinzing, Bavaria.

FRANZ XAVER
VON SCHÖNWERTH

The Turnip Princess

AND OTHER NEWLY DISCOVERED
FAIRY TALES

Compiled and Edited with a Foreword by
ERIKA EICHENSEER

Translated with an Introduction and Commentary by
MARIA TATAR

Illustrations by
ENGELBERT SÜSS

PENGUIN BOOKS

PENGUIN BOOKS

Published by the Penguin Group
Penguin Group (USA) LLC
375 Hudson Street
New York, New York 10014

USA | Canada | UK | Ireland | Australia | New Zealand | India | South Africa | China
penguin.com
A Penguin Random House Company

First published in Penguin Books 2015

Maria Tatar's translation of "The Turnip Princess" was published in The Guardian, March 5, 2012.
Ms. Tatar's translation of "King Goldenlocks" appeared in The New Yorker, issue of April 2, 2012.

ISBN 978-0-14-310742-2

Contents

THE TURNIP PRINCESS

PART I: TALES OF MAGIC AND ROMANCE

PART II: ENCHANTED ANIMALS

PART III: OTHERWORLDLY CREATURES

PART IV: LEGENDS

PART V: TALL TALES AND ANECDOTES

PART VI: TALES ABOUT NATURE

Foreword

"I'm here. Why do you keep rejecting me?"
"Just pull on the nail."

—"THE TURNIP PRINCESS," P. 4

Fairy tales are that simple. All you need is a rusty nail, and something that is hidden away, spellbound, and beautiful can be transformed, disenchanted, and reanimated. In real life no one hands us a nail that can lift away all our cares.

The fairy tales collected by Franz Xaver von Schönwerth (1810–1886) seemed to have vanished into thin air. These tales from the Upper Palatinate, the eastern part of Bavaria, were hidden away for a long time.

In 2009, after searching for many years, I made the exhilarating discovery that there were about five hundred fairy tales among the Schönwerth papers stored almost like buried treasure in the municipal archive of the city of Regensburg. The enthusiastic nineteenth-century folklorist and collector of tales had recognized that his era was witnessing a rapid decline in oral storytelling traditions. For that reason, he and his friends made the rounds, asking for stories from plainspoken men and women within the confines of their native territory. At first there was some reluctance to tell tales, but that was followed by eagerness to share. This is oral history in the truest sense of the term.

The social standing of the tellers and the collectors varied widely. In the archival materials there are some linguistically sophisticated texts with romantic flourishes but also some terse and fragmentary drafts, and they all have proven valuable. The tales are particularly colorful and lively when told in the regional dialect.

This book will fill a gap in German-speaking countries and in the global fairy tales landscape, appealing to readers young and old. And it is also directed at scholars who will be able to evaluate, analyze, and honor this particular selection of tales from the archive of a collector and researcher who was something of a pioneer. The door has been unlocked, and now it can swing wide open.

"No one in Germany has gathered tales so thoughtfully and thoroughly and with such finesse." This observation about Schönwerth made in 1858 by Jacob Grimm can be seen as a tribute, an acknowledgment, and a commitment to pay attention to an important message about nature and how it is animated by marvelous creatures as well as about how the magical and the natural blend into each other.

Let me close with one additional thought. Storytelling is an ancient art that rarely receives the respect it deserves. Is it even possible to find someone these days with the time to give something precious to listeners, who understands stories at a profound level and can tell them without a book or a page in hand?

"A world without fairy tales and myths would be as drab as life without music."

—GEORG TRAKL

ERIKA EICHENSEER

Introduction

When the British press reported in 2012 that five hundred unknown fairy tales, languishing for more than a century in the municipal archive of Regensburg, Germany, had come to light, the news sent a flutter through the world of fairy-tale enthusiasts, their interest further piqued by the detail that the tales—which had been compiled in the mid-nineteenth century by a man named Franz Xaver von Schönwerth—had been kept under lock and key. Victoria Sussens-Messerer, the author of the article published in the *Guardian*, created an unanticipated sensation, reminding us of the powerful global and cross-generational reach of these tales. A fairy tale soon emerged about mysterious treasures locked up and released at last, but the tale of how Schönwerth's fairy tales came to see the light of day has more to do with determination and detective work than with magic. Erika Eichenseer, a resident of the city, opened thirty dusty cardboard boxes of Schönwerth's tales and turned them into fairy-tale gold by reading, sorting, transcribing, and providing context for them. She has labored tirelessly in the service of these tales to ensure that they find their place in the folkloric pantheon. And now, with this English translation, a broader audience will have access to tales that possess a uniquely local narrative energy and provide a strong comparative basis for understanding the quirks of stories collected by the Brothers Grimm, whose tales became the dominant player in the global fairy-tale market.

Franz Xaver von Schönwerth was inspired by the Grimms, less by their best-known compendium, *Children's Stories and Household Tales,* than by their *German Mythology*, which a friend gave to him in 1835. Born in 1810 in the small Bavarian town of Amberg, Schönwerth studied architecture before settling into his legal studies and becoming a high-level civil servant, working first as a secretary to Maximilian II of Bavaria, and then in the Bavarian Finance Ministry. A man whom the Brothers Grimm praised for his "fine ear" and accuracy as a collector, he published three volumes of folk customs and legends in the mid-nineteenth century (*Aus der Oberpfalz: Sitten und Sagen*), but the books did little more than gather dust in bookshops. Like the Brothers Grimm, Schönwerth was an equal-opportunity collector, less intent on finding a source close to the soil, as it were, than a story with real zest. The task was challenging in many ways, for as Schönwerth noted, few took his project seriously.

Why would a high-level government official pay any attention to frivolous storytelling pursuits? How could he possibly take them seriously? Schönwerth found the trivialization of folk culture in his Munich surroundings discouraging: "I did not have an easy task . . . since I had to search out compatriots here in Munich and subject them to something of an inquisition. At home, women and weavers were easy to bribe with small gifts and treats, and they regaled me with stories, gladly in large part because I was the first one to talk with them in the regional dialect."

Schönwerth needed vast amounts of patience to secure what he wanted from other informants: "These people can't seem to get it through their heads that a scholar might actually be interested in their 'stupidities' [*Dummheiten*], and they begin to worry that you are just trying to make them look like fools." Long before Disney, folktales were seen as lacking the kind of substance that might make them worthy of scholarly attention. They had already begun to make the great migration from the childhood of culture into the culture of childhood, now as tales of Mother Goose, old wives' tales, or, worse yet, fairy tales—what the Grimms called *Kindermärchen*.

Schönwerth's tales have a compositional fierceness and energy rarely seen in stories gathered by the Brothers Grimm or Charles Perrault, collectors who gave us relatively tame versions of "Little Red Riding Hood," "Snow White," "Cinderella," and "Rapunzel." Schönwerth gives us a harsher dose of reality. His Cinderella is a woodcutter's daughter who uses golden slippers to recover her beloved from beyond the moon and the sun. His miller's daughter wields an ax and uses it to disenchant a prince by whacking off the tail of a gigantic black cat. The stories remain untouched by literary sensibilities. No throat-clearing for Schönwerth, who begins in medias res, with "A princess was ill" or "A prince was lost in the woods," rather than "Once upon a time."

Though he was inspired by the Grimms, Schönwerth was more invested in the local than in the global. If the Grimms wanted to preserve remnants of a collective pagan past and to consolidate national identity by preserving in print rapidly fading cultural stories, Schönwerth was committed to documenting the oral traditions of his beloved Bavarian homeland. This explains the rough-hewn quality of his tales, many of which were written down in the native dialect. Not one to dress up a tale with literary flourishes or to make it more child friendly, Schönwerth kept the raw energy of the tales, resisting the temptation to motivate surreal plot twists or to smooth out inconsistencies. Oral narratives famously neglect psychology for plot, and these tales move with warp speed out of the castle and into the woods, generating multiple encounters with ogres, dragons, witches, and other villains, leaving almost no room for expressive asides or details explaining how or why things happen. The driving question is always "And then?"

Our own culture, under the spell of Grimm and Perrault, has favored fairy tales starring girls rather than boys, princesses rather than princes. But Schönwerth's stories show us that once upon a time, Cinderfellas evidently suffered right alongside Cinderellas, and handsome young men fell into slumbers nearly as deep as Briar Rose's hundred-year nap. Just as girls became domestic drudges and suffered under the curse of evil mothers and stepmothers, boys, too, served out terms as gardeners and servants, sometimes banished into the woods by hostile fathers. Like Snow White, they had to plead with a hunter for their lives. And they are as good as they are beautiful—Schönwerth uses the German term *schön*, or *beautiful*, for both male and female protagonists. And time and again they are required to prove their mettle by sleeping in a Gothic castle of horrors. Here, too, we suddenly find clustered together the giant-killers and dragon slayers missing from the Grimms. The rescue of sleeping beauties after slaying nine-headed dragons and outwitting giants is repeated with mantra-like faith in the possibility of the little guy triumphing over the colossus.

Why did we lose all those male counterparts to Snow White, Sleeping Beauty, and the girl who becomes the wife of the Frog King? Boy heroes clearly had a hard time surviving the nineteenth-century migration of fairy tales from the communal hearth into the nursery, when oral storytelling traditions, under the pressures of urbanization and industrialization, lost their cross-generational appeal. Once mothers, nannies, and domestics were in charge of telling stories at bedtime, they favored tales with heroines. Schönwerth's collection may have appeared in print later than the Grimms' *Children's Stories and Household Tales*, but it gives us in many ways a culture of oral storytelling that is pre-Grimm.

The Brothers Grimm may have been wary of telling stories of persecuted boys, having suffered much in their own early lives. It is no accident that we refer these days to Jacob and Wilhelm Grimm almost as if they were a couple. The brothers lost their father at a young age and worked hard to educate themselves and to keep their fragile family intact. They studied law together and worked side by side for decades, taking notes, copying manuscripts, editing texts, and famously creating index card entries for their monumental dictionary of the German language. Is it any surprise that they might have found tales about quarreling brothers or male-sibling rivals less than congenial? Schönwerth's collection reminds us that fathers are constantly sending no-account sons into the world to seek their fortune and that they are generally relieved to rid themselves of an extra mouth to feed. Brothers stand in a relationship of rivalry, fighting over farms or kingdoms and betraying each other in ways that hark back to the Biblical

cruelties of Joseph's brothers. Schönwerth gives us unvarnished versions of these tales, uninhibited in their expression
of parental indifference and cruelty and of fraternal rivalry
and hatred.

The briskness of Schönwerth's style becomes clear in a tale
like "King Goldenlocks." The adventures of the fair-haired
prince bring together bits and pieces from "The Frog King,"
"Snow White," and "The Water of Life" to create kaleidoscopic wonders. The tale reminds us of the wizardry of words
in fairy tales, and how those words create worlds of shimmer-
ing beauty and enchanting whimsy. Who can avoid feeling the
shock effects of beauty when Prince Goldenhair enters "a
magical garden awash in sunlight, full of flowers and branches
with gold and silver leaves and fruits made of precious stones"?
Or when a dung beetle turns into a prince after a girl spares
his life and invites "creatures small and large, anything on
legs" to dance and leap at the wedding? Equally charming is
the story about Jodel, a boy who overcomes his revulsion to a
female frog and, after bathing her, joins her under the covers.
In the morning, he awakens to find himself in a sunlit castle
with a wondrously beautiful princess. Here at last is a transformation that promises real change in our understanding of
fairy-tale magic, for suddenly we discover that the divide between passive princesses and dragon-slaying heroes may be little more than a figment of the Grimm imagination.

The term *fairy tale* has not served the genre well. Often dismissed as an infantile confection, the fairy tale in fact rarely
contains the sprightly supernatural creatures featured so prominently in its name. It was the French, more specifically Mme
d'Aulnoy, who gave us the term *contes de fées*, leading us to
frame the stories as if they turn on the lives of diminutive
woodland folk (of which there are quite a few in Schönwerth's
collection) rather than ordinary people. In English, the term
was first used in 1749, casually by Horace Walpole, and with
self-conscious purpose when Sarah Fielding called a story em-
bedded in *The Governess*, published in 1749, "The Princess
Hebe: A Fairy Tale." The German term *Märchen* points to the
origins of the stories in the notion of news, reports, tall tales,

rumors, and gossip—in short, of talk and social exchanges. Fairy tales hover somewhere between tall tale and high fantasy, anchored in the real world, but with embellishments and misrepresentations that turn their lies and confabulations into higher truths.

There is magic in these tall tales, and the presence of enchantment is perhaps the defining feature of the genre.* We are not so much in the realm of fairies as in the domain of what J. R. R. Tolkien referred to as *Faërie*, that "Perilous Realm" where anything can happen. A plain girl puts on a necklace and belt and turns into a beautiful young woman; a boy swims on the back of a golden fish and enters an enchanted castle; elves teach a girl how to keep house and heal the sick. Again and again we witness transformations that break down the divide between life and death, nature and culture, animal and human, or beauty and monstrosity. Fairy tales take up deep cultural contradictions, creating what Claude Lévi-Strauss called "miniature models"—stories that dispense with extraneous details to give us primal anxieties and desires, the raw rather than the cooked, as it were. They use magic, not to falsify or delude, but rather to enable counterfactuals, to move us to imagine what if or to wonder why. And that move, as both Plato and Aristotle assured us, marks the beginning of philosophy. While fairy-tale heroes and heroines wander, we track their moves and wonder, in both senses of the term, at their adventures. It is no surprise that the term *wonder-tale* has been proposed and embraced as an alternative to the misleading *fairy tale*.

Fairy tales, like myths, capitalize on the three concepts the Greeks captured in the term *kaleidoscope*: sparkling beauty, austere form, and visual power. Once told at the fireside or at the hearth, with adults and children sharing the storytelling space, they captured the play of light and shadow in their environment, creating special effects that yoked beauty with horror. Imagine a time before electronic entertainment, with

---

*As Stephen Swann Jones puts it, "fairy tales depict magical or marvelous events or phenomena as a valid part of human experience." See his *Fairy Tales: The Magic Mirror of Imagination* (New York: Routledge, 2002), 9.

long dark nights around campsites and other sources of heat and light, and it is not much of a challenge to realize that human beings, always quick to adapt, began exchanging information, trading wisdom, and reporting gossip. "Literature," Vladimir Nabokov tells us, "was born on the day when a boy came crying wolf wolf, and there was no wolf behind him."* And that boy's story was no doubt both compact and vivid. Once the conversation started about that wolf, it was easy enough, in subsequent versions, to begin exaggerating, overstating, inflating, and doing all the things that make for lively entertainment. Fairy tales are always more interesting when something is added to them. Each new telling recharges the narrative, making it crackle and hiss with cultural energy.

At a time when some scholars have contested the vibrancy of oral storytelling traditions, claiming that fairy tales were literary confections, urban and urbane, rather than rooted in the popular culture of the unlettered, Schönwerth's collection reveals just how comfortably the tales inhabit a world that values spontaneity, improvisation, rough edges, and lack of closure. Much as there may be lively traffic between the oral and the literary, these tales, unlike stories written down by the Brothers Grimm or that other prominent collector, Ludwig Bechstein, have few literary fingerprints on them. We cannot go back to nineteenth-century nooks and hearths to learn more about the tales that were told for entertainment, but we do have Schönwerth's extraordinary archive, one that showed respect for oral storytelling traditions and did not work hard to turn hard-won fairy-tale silver into literary gold.

Schönwerth's collection of tales may lack some of the charm of other nineteenth-century collections, but it gives us a crystal-clear window into the storytelling culture of its time. Earthy, scatological, and unvarnished, these tales give us primary process rather than edited and embellished narrative. Where else will we find a woman who moons a scoundrel of a tailor, or a fellow who relieves himself in the woods much to

---

*Vladimir Nabokov, *Lectures on Literature*, ed. Fredson Bowers (New York: Harcourt Brace Jovanovich, 1998), 5.

the dismay of his pals? Schönwerth recognized the value of remaining faithful to his sources and refused to pull punches.

In a tale that is more anecdote or joke than fairy tale, Schönwerth recorded the story of a man who searches in vain for the right reading glasses. Frustrated by the fact that no matter how many spectacles he tries out, all he sees on the page are black squiggles, he learns, much to his distress, that the glasses will do him no good unless he first learns how to read. Written down at a transitional moment, when oral storytelling cultures were being replaced by print collections, the tale is a subtle reminder, among other things, that the dead letter is a poor substitute for the living word. It is to Schönwerth's credit that he had faith in the power of black squiggles to capture the letter and spirit of what he had heard from women, weavers, and all those folks who were convinced that he must be joking when he asked them for their stories. Many of his contemporaries possessed neither glasses, books, nor the ability to read, but Schönwerth nonetheless recognized that a time would come when we would rely on those artifacts and skills to discover a literary heritage that might otherwise have been lost.

Like fairy tales, translations are collaborations, and I want to thank, above all, Erika Eichenseer for undertaking the labor of love that rescued these tales, let them return to and breathe the fine air of the places they were once told, and brought them into the orbit of English-speaking cultures. Her tireless championing not just of Schönwerth's labors but also of the world of folklore went far toward inspiring me to re-create the tales in ways that made manifest the magic of the German versions. Doris Sperber, a genius at tracking down sources, flagging errors, and attending to devilish details, provided steady and steadying support. I am deeply grateful to John Siciliano at Penguin Classics for his faith in Schönwerth, in the collaborative work carried out by Erika and me, and in the sprinkling of fairy dust that animates these stories and ensures that they will thrive on both sides of the Atlantic and beyond.

MARIA TATAR

Suggestions for Further Reading

Cristina Bacchilega. *Fairy Tales Transformed? Twenty-First-Century Adaptations and the Politics of Wonder*. Detroit: Wayne State University Press, 2013.

Bruno Bettelheim. *The Uses of Enchantment: The Meaning and Importance of Fairy Tales*. New York: Knopf, 1976.

Robert Darnton. "Peasants Tell Tales: The Meaning of Mother Goose." In *The Great Cat Massacre and Other Episodes in French Cultural History*. New York: Basic Books, 1984.

Donald Haase, ed. *Fairy Tales and Feminism*. Detroit: Wayne State University Press, 2009.

Maria Tatar. *The Classic Fairy Tales*. New York: W.W. Norton, 1999.

Hans-Jörg Uther. *The Types of International Folktales: A Classification and Bibliography*. 3 vols. Helsinki: Academia Scientiarum Fennica, 2004.

Marina Warner. *From the Beast to the Blonde: On Fairy Tales and Their Tellers*. New York: Farrar, Straus and Giroux, 1994.

Charlotte Wolf. *Original Bavarian Folktales: A Schönwerth Selection*. Mineola, NY: Dover, 2014.

Jack Zipes. *Why Fairy Tales Stick: The Evolution and Relevance of a Genre*. New York: Routledge, 2006.

———. *The Irresistible Fairy Tale: The Cultural and Social History of a Genre*. Princeton: Princeton University Press, 1999.

Further Reading in German

Erika Eichenseer, ed. *Franz Xaver von Schönwerth: Prinz Roßwifl und andere Märchen*. Regensburg: Morsbach, 2010, 2013.

Roland Rörich (Hsgb.). *Der oberpfälzische Volkskundler Franz Xaver Schönwerth*. Seibn Leben und Werk: Kallmünz: Lassleben, 1975.

————. *Das Schönwerth-lesebuch*. Regensburg: Pustet, 2010.

Franz Xaver von Schönwerth. *Aus der Oberpfalz—Sitten und Sagen*. 3 vols. Augsburg: Rieger, 1857–59.

————. *Aus der Oberpfalz—Sitten und Sagen*. 3 vols. Hildesheim-New York: Olms, 1977.

————. *Aus der Oberpfalz—Sitten und Sagen*. Bed. I, II, III. Gesamtausgabe, bearbeitet und ergänzt von Harald Fähnrich. Pressath: Bodner, 2010.

Julia Weigl. *Der rote Zwerg: 12 unbekannte Märchen aus der Oberpfalz*. Regensburg: Niedermayr, 2000.

Karl Winkler. *Oberpfälzische Sagen, Legenden, Märchen und Schwänke*. Kallmünz: Laßleben, 1935, 1960, 2009.

The Turnip Princess

PART I

TALES OF MAGIC
AND ROMANCE

THE TURNIP PRINCESS

One day a prince lost his way in the woods. He found shelter in a cave and slept there for the night. When he woke up, an old woman was hovering over him. She had a bear by her side and treated it like a pet dog. The old woman was very kind to the prince. She wanted him to live with her and become her husband. The prince did not like her at all, but he was unable to leave.

One day the prince and the bear were alone together in the cave, and the bear said to him: "If you pull that rusty old nail out of the wall, I will be set free. Then take the nail and put it under a turnip out in the meadow. Your reward will be a beautiful wife." The prince yanked the nail so hard that the entire cave began to tremble. There was a sudden clap of thunder, and the nail popped out of the wall. The bear rose up on its hind legs and turned into a man. He had a long beard and on his head there was a crown.

"And now I am going to find the beautiful maiden," the prince shouted after him, and he ran out the door. Nearby he discovered a field of turnips and was just about to put the nail under one of the vegetables when, out of nowhere, a monster appeared. The nail flew out of the prince's hand, and he braced himself on a hedge. Thorns pierced his hands, and his fingers were bleeding so badly that he fainted.

When the prince came to, he found himself in an entirely different new place. Touching his chin, he discovered that he had grown a blond beard. That's how he knew that he must have slept for quite a while. He stood up, crossed the meadow, and passed through the woods, all the while searching for a place where turnips might be growing. But he searched in vain and found nothing.

Some time passed, and one evening he decided to lie down on a grassy knoll near a shrub. The shrub was a blackthorn bush in full bloom, and one branch of it had a red blossom on it. The prince snapped off the branch. He found a big white turnip growing in the fields right next to him, and he stuck the branch with the red flower into the turnip and fell fast asleep.

When the prince awoke the next morning, the turnip had turned into a gigantic bowl, and the nail was lying right in the center of it. The interior walls of the turnip bowl looked just like a nutshell, with the imprint of the nut still on it. He looked carefully at the imprint and saw little feet, tiny hands, fine hair, and then the entire body of a wondrously beautiful maiden.

The prince left to search for the cave in the woods, and he had no trouble finding it. It had been abandoned. The rusty nail was lying on the ground. He picked it up and hammered it back into the wall. Suddenly the old woman and the bear reappeared. "Tell me now, and don't try to deny that you have the answer!" the prince shouted at the old woman. "What did you do with the beautiful maiden?"

The old woman just giggled: "I'm here right now. Why do you keep rejecting me?"

The bear nodded in agreement and looked at the nail in the wall. The prince said to him: "At least you are honest. But I won't be fooled by the old woman a second time."

"Just pull on the nail," the bear growled.

The prince tugged at the nail and managed to get it halfway out. He turned around and saw that the bear was partly human and the disgusting old woman was half-ugly and half-beautiful. He pulled the nail all the way out. Lo and behold, man and maiden stood there, completely unharmed. He flew into the arms of the beautiful woman, for the spell had been lifted. The two of them took the rusty old nail and destroyed it.

The prince and his bride had no trouble finding their way back to the castle. The king was elated to see his son again and to meet his beautiful bride. The jubilant wedding guests held a feast for the couple, and the two lived a long, happy life.

THE ENCHANTED QUILL

A man on horseback fell fast asleep while riding, and the horse began grazing in a meadow. A crow flew down from a tree and pecked the horse so that it reared up suddenly and woke the rider up. "Why did you peck at my horse?" the rider asked angrily.

"So that you would finally wake up!" the crow said. "You've been asleep for three years now!" The rider looked at his beard, which was several feet long, and realized that the crow had spoken the truth.

"Tell me, how can I thank you?"

"By giving me one of your three sisters in marriage. Take this picture of me with you." The crow gave the rider a little picture of himself and flew off into the distance.

When the man returned home on horseback, he told his sisters about the crow and its request, and then he showed them the picture of the bird. The eldest of the three sisters wrinkled her nose, the second shrieked, "No way!" and the youngest just blushed. She took the picture and went to her room.

The next day a splendid carriage drawn by four horses appeared. The sisters were filled with curiosity, for they imagined a prince might be calling, and they raced to the door. A black crow stepped out of the carriage, and two of the sisters went right back in the house. Only the youngest of the three invited him in. Still, the crow asked all three sisters to visit his castle.

Together they traveled through a dark, gloomy forest. They

were all convinced that they must be traveling on the road to hell. After a while it grew light, and the path took them through a forest of lemon trees and then on to a beautiful castle. The crow said to the two sisters: "Just watch out, and don't get too curious about things." He took the youngest into another room in the castle. The two sisters tiptoed toward the door and peeked through the keyhole. They saw a handsome young man sitting at a table, having a cozy conversation with their sister.

All at once everything changed: The castle and the carriage disappeared, and the three young women were standing under a fir tree. The crow was up in the branches, scolding them: "Now only the youngest can save me. She must walk to the city in rags and accept whatever work she is offered."

And so the youngest walked to the city in rags and was about to be turned back by the constable when a tailor appeared to ask if she could do some cooking and cleaning for the prince living there. She assured the tailor, somewhat haltingly, that she could do all those things, and he walked over with her to the place where she would be employed.

Before long it became obvious that she had none of the skills she had claimed to have. The food was constantly burned; the silver was dirtier than ever. Gardeners, huntsmen, and servants all made fun of her, insulting her and calling her names. She wept bitter tears. Suddenly the crow appeared at the window, turned his wing to her, and said: "Pull out one of my feathers, and if you use it to write down a wish, the wish will come true." With a heavy heart she pulled a feather out. Before the noonday meal, she wrote down the names of the very finest dishes with the quill. The food appeared on the table in bowls that sparkled and glowed.

The prince and the princess were thrilled, and the servant girl was given beautiful garments to wear. She had such an exquisite face and figure that the caretaker was soon enamored of her and wanted her to be his. He tiptoed to her room and peeked in. When she didn't order him to leave, he ran over to her. "Shut the door!" she said. And just as he was turning around, she wrote with her quill: "Let him spend all night opening and closing the door." And that is exactly what happened. In the morning the caretaker, deeply humiliated, could be seen slinking away.

The next evening the huntsman came to the girl's room while she was lying in bed. He bent over to take his boots off. She wrote: "Let him spend all night taking his boots off and putting them back on." And that's exactly what he did. At daybreak, he left in a huff. On the third morning one of the servants appeared. He had a strange neck, twisted from constantly watching doves, and the fool looked deep into her eyes. While he was asking for her favors, he suddenly remembered that he had left the door to the dovecote open and asked if he could go back to close it. The girl nodded with a laugh and wrote down the words: "Let him spend all night opening and closing the door to the dovecote."

That's how she got the suitors off her back. But they were determined to have their revenge, and they made three whips that they planned to use on the cook. When she caught on, she wrote down the following words: "Let them whip each other with those devilish switches!" And that's exactly what happened. The prince and the princess tried to help them, but they ended up receiving more lashes than anyone else.

The time had come. The crow arrived, and now he had turned into a prince. He rode with the beautiful cook to his magnificent castle.

THE IRON SHOES

A man was working in the service of the king as a groundskeeper, and he had a son who was a real burden. One day he flew into a rage with the boy and said: "Why don't you just beat it, and let's hope that you learn some sense by going out into the world!"

Hans left home for the wide world. One evening he discovered an old castle in some overgrown woods. Thrilled, he walked up to the entrance, crossed the threshold, and walked through its many rooms. He heard not a soul, and he saw no one at all. Exhausted, he sat down in one of the rooms. A woman dressed in black came in, put food and drink on the table, pointed to a bed, and left without saying a word. At midnight a vicious man in black walked in, and he tortured the boy and tried to choke him.

The next morning, the woman appeared again, this time dressed in gray, and she brought him food and drink for the entire day, without saying a word. That very night two men appeared and tortured him even more cruelly than the man from the night before had. The boy made up his mind to leave and packed up his belongings in the morning. Just then the woman, this time dressed in white, entered the room. She asked him to spend just one more night there. It wouldn't hurt him to do that. But the midnight hour brought even harsher torture. This time there were three men, and they beat him, punched him, and tossed him up in the air and caught him. An hour passed and the luminous woman in white reappeared with thunder and lightning in the air and drove the brutes away.

It turned out that the woman was a princess who had fallen under a spell, and the curse was now broken. She gave her hand to Hans as a reward. He was dressed up in magnificent clothes and given as many servants as he wanted, as well as untold wealth.

Even in the midst of all this joy Hans did not forget his father, and he asked his wife to let him leave for a short time. She gave him a ring in case anything might go wrong. All he had to do was turn it, and she would be there to help him.

"Be careful, and don't use it to summon me if it's not necessary," she advised him.

Hans left for home with his attendants. He found his old father, who was still working hard on the king's grounds. The man did not recognize him. Hans introduced himself to the king, who arranged a feast to honor the noble guest.

At the ball all the knights danced with their wives. Hans was not allowed to dance with anyone, because all the men were jealous of his good looks. The knights made fun of him when he claimed that his wife was more beautiful than all the others. Hans was so annoyed that he turned the ring. Now the stunned crowd watched stylish carriages roll in, and Hans, or rather the prince from foreign lands, took his wife's arm and led her into the hall. She was more beautiful than anyone else there.

The morning after the feast, Hans was abandoned. His old clothes were laid out on the bed, and on the floor was a pair of iron shoes. A note was attached, and it read: "I'm punishing you by leaving. Don't try to find me. You will never discover where I am, even if you wear out these iron shoes." He picked up the ring and tried to turn it, but it was no use. He was so humiliated that he left the castle at once and began searching for traces of his runaway wife, but he could not even find the castle where they had lived together in such happiness.

His travels led him to a mountain, where he discovered three fellows fighting over three precious objects: a sack that was always full of money, a pair of boots that took you a hundred miles at a step, and a cloak that made you invisible. Hans offered to help settle the dispute, but first he wanted to make sure that everything was fair and square. He took the sack and emptied it out a few times, and each time it filled back up again with gold. He put the cloak on, and no one could see him. Then he quickly put on the shoes and fled with the sack. After a while he noticed that a little man was running right next to him. It was the wind, and it had to be in the next town within the hour so that it could dry the freshly washed clothes of a princess, who was planning to get married that day. Hans said: "Wait a moment; we'll go there together!" Since the wind was always behind him, he put it on a long leash, so the two of them could no longer be parted.

As soon as the wind reached the town, it began to send gusts into the clothes hung up to dry. Hans was not very well dressed, but he went right into the first inn he saw and sat down at a table. The innkeeper paid no attention to him. When Hans tossed some coins at him, the whole place swung into action to take care of him. From what he overheard, it became clear that the princess who was to be married the next day was his wife. During the ceremony, Hans stood behind the altar in his invisibility cloak and knocked the parson's book out of his hands. Every time the groom was about to say, "I do," Hans slugged him in the mouth so hard that the sound echoed in the chapel. The ceremony could not be completed, and so everyone went off to dinner.

Hans mingled with the beggars waiting for scraps, and whenever the servants walked by with food or drink, he would grab something and divide it among his starving neighbors. At one point his ring fell on the ground. A servant noticed it, picked it up, and took it to the princess, because her initials were engraved on it. The princess summoned the stranger to her side. He showed her the iron shoes and how worn down they were from his search. She was overjoyed to see her husband again. The two of them made up, and then they had a real wedding.

THE WOLVES

A wealthy prince was married to a beautiful woman. The two had no children, and that was a source of great sorrow for the prince. As for the princess, she was consumed with envy whenever anyone in the kingdom gave birth to a child.

One day the prince and the princess were visiting a village, and they looked on as a festive group made its way into the local church. A farmer was having his triplets baptized, and everyone in the village had gathered to celebrate. The princess was planning to put a stop to the festivities, but the prince made fun of her, mocking the fact that she was aching to have something that a mere peasant possessed. It was her own fault that she had no children, he added. The princess flew into a rage right then and there and accused the farmer's wife of infidelity, claiming that a woman could never have more than one child at a time with her husband. When the prince returned home, he held a mirror up to the princess's face so that she could see how ugly she looked. To her horror, she saw in the mirror the head of a shaggy wolf, red-eyed, baring its teeth.

It turned out that the princess, without knowing it, was actually pregnant at the time. She gave birth to seven boys in seven days, one after another. She remembered what she had said earlier to the farmer's wife. The prince was not at home, and she decided to send the midwife out to a wolf's lair, with the seven boys wrapped up in an apron. It happened that the prince was hunting right in that area, and he ran into the midwife. "What are you doing here?" he asked. She immediately owned up to her evil intentions, and the prince rewarded her by running her through with a sword. He had the boys raised by a loyal subject.

Eighteen years went by, and the prince was planning a grand feast. Seven boys with long hair, all equally handsome and dressed alike, appeared at the feast. The princess could feel her heart pounding when she set eyes on the boys, and she began to tremble.

During the meal the prince jokingly asked how to punish a mother who throws her sons to the wolves. "She should dance to death in red-hot iron shoes," was the answer. And so the princess condemned herself to that very punishment. The prince acknowledged the boys as his legitimate children, and they became known as "the wolves."

THE FLYING TRUNK

 A carpenter who had landed in jail sent word to the king: "If you spare my life, I will make something the likes of which the world has never before seen!" The king agreed to the bargain, and the carpenter presented the king with a trunk. When the king sat down on it, the trunk began to roar and lifted itself off the ground. Then it flew out one window and in through the other. The king kept the trunk and put it in his private museum.

The king had a son who liked to wear red boots. He was always getting new toys and breaking them. One day someone decided to give him the trunk as a plaything. The boy used his hammer on the trunk because he wanted to turn it into a carriage. A servant tied a cord to it, prepared it for an outing, and hauled the little rascal around in it. The boy had not been in the carriage for long when it lifted itself up to the window, and even though the servant was shouting loudly and pulling on the cord, it flew up in the air like a shot and vanished from sight. Everyone rushed around in a panic, and some horsemen tried to catch up with him, but it was no use.

The flight lasted for a long time. When its cord finally got caught in the branches of a tree, the trunk came to a stop. There was a stork's nest at the top of the tree, and the boy rested up there for a while. He left the trunk in the tree and decided to climb down and take a look at the town that he had spied from his perch. There he met a shoemaker looking for an apprentice. The prince with the red boots decided to take the job, and he worked there for many years.

A king with no children was living in that very town. There had been a prophecy that he would have a daughter, and it was said that she would bring disgrace upon him once she was grown up. That would happen at the moment when she set eyes on a stranger for the first time in her life. When the queen gave birth to a daughter, the king worried for a long time about what to do. He decided to build a tower as high as the skies and to lock the princess up in a room at the very top. And that's what he did.

The young apprentice with the red boots heard from another fellow about the princess locked up in the tower. He learned that she had been up there in the clouds for many years, pining away. She was said to be very beautiful. One day he returned to the tree that had a stork's nest in it, climbed back up, got into the trunk, and decided to see the princess by flying through the tower window. He spent all his free time there, and soon enough, word got out about what was going on between them.

The father was absolutely beside himself. He smeared some tar on the windowsill in order to catch the birdman flying in through the window. Before long a red boot was found stuck on the sill. The boot made the rounds, as the king had ordered, and it went from hand to hand and foot to foot. The reward set aside for the person whose foot fit the boot was still to be had. One day the old boot arrived at the place where the shoemaker's apprentice was living. He did not realize he was falling into a trap and pulled the boot on. It fit perfectly. The scoundrel was arrested at once and put in jail.

The princess was supposed to reveal the name of her beloved. "If you tell us his name, you can marry him. Listen carefully, and you will hear workers sawing boards to make your marriage bed!" the king told her. But in fact he had ordered the building of a funeral pyre, where both of them would be burned to cinders. The princess refused to reveal the name, and the fate of both was sealed.

Everyone in town gathered around to weep for the two

unfortunate souls and bemoan their fate. They were standing right on a stack of firewood, embracing and looking calm and collected when smoke and flames began to engulf them. The apprentice pressed down on the trunk concealed beneath them. It roared away like a winged horse through the smoke and flames, high up into the air. All the king and his people could do was stare at them as the two flew away.

When the prince with the red boots arrived back home and was reunited with his parents, he had become wise to the ways of the world. He married the beautiful princess, and in the end, he ruled over two kingdoms.

KING GOLDENLOCKS

 A king had a son with hair of gold. One day the king went hunting in the woods and encountered a giant of a man leaning against a tree. He blew his hunting horn, summoned his men, and they caught the wild man. The king was thrilled by the capture and decided to hold a celebration. He invited many neighboring rulers to the festivities.

Goldenlocks, the king's only son, was playing with a ball one day, and it landed in the wild man's cage. The wild man tossed it right back. But the next time around, the giant kept the ball and said that he would not return it until Goldenlocks agreed to set him free. While his father was sleeping, the boy tiptoed over to him and took the key from the chain around his neck. He set the wild man free and put the key back on the chain. The festivities were just about to begin, and the wild man was supposed to appear before all the monarchs gathered in the hall. But he was nowhere to be found. The king flew into a rage and swore that he would punish the crime, even if it had been committed by his own flesh and blood.

One person at the court knew exactly what had happened, and he betrayed Goldenlocks. The king was so upset that he tore at his garments, but he ended up condemning his own son and ordered him to be killed in the wilderness. As proof that he was dead, the servants were supposed to bring back tongue, eye, and finger of the boy.

The men who took the prince into the woods were so moved by how young he was that they decided to find a way out. They hailed a young shepherd who was in the woods with his dog and said: "Do you like this fellow's fine clothes? You can have them in exchange for your dog and your little finger."

Right then and there, the shepherd boy bit off his finger and exchanged clothes with Goldenlocks. The servants cut out the dog's tongue and eye, took the shepherd's finger, and brought them all to the king. Goldenlocks had nothing left but a piece of white cloth, which he used to hide his hair. He traveled to a distant land, where he met a gardener, but the man had no interest in hiring a boy dressed in rags. Still, he finally agreed to let him stay on and even took a liking to him.

Every day the gardener would cut flowers and make bouquets for the three daughters of the king ruling over this distant realm. Goldenlocks would bind the flowers together and bring them to the girls. The youngest of the three was also the most beautiful, and so he always tied her bouquet with some strands of his golden hair. She liked that, and soon she liked the gardener's helper as well.

One day it was announced that the eldest of the king's daughters was to be married and that she would wed the man to whom she gave her bouquet of flowers. Suitors came from all over the world, and she chose one of the princes. She handed him her bouquet and traveled home with him. Later, the same events came to pass with another prince and the second daughter of the king.

When the youngest of the three princesses had come of age, the king arranged the festivities. The young woman had a bouquet with golden hair wrapped around it, and she looked at the many princes gathered around and said: "There's no one here for me!" The king summoned knights and nobles, but once again the princess said: "There's no one here for me!" Then citizens and artisans were summoned. The princess moved through their ranks until she set eyes on the young gardener, and to him she gave her bouquet. The princess married the young gardener and moved into his hut.

Not much later the king became ill, and word was put out that the only way to heal him was with apples from paradise. Everyone left to search for the apples, even the young gardener.

He traipsed around in the woods, and there he met the wild giant a second time. "I already know what you are looking for," the giant said. "Take this club and strike the rock over there with it. Move fast after that; otherwise you will die."

The gardener took the club, went over to the rock, and struck it. He found himself in an enchanted garden awash in bright sunlight, full of flowers and branches with leaves of gold and silver, and fruits made of precious stones. The tree of paradise was growing right in the middle of that garden. He dashed over to it and picked two apples from its branches. Just then an aroma was released, one so powerful that he nearly swooned. The entrance to the rock began to close behind him with a crash, and he raced out in the nick of time.

On the way home he stopped at a tavern and saw his new brothers-in-law. They were eager to have the apples from paradise. "Why not?" said the gardener. "As long as you're willing to be marked on your backs with the gallows." They agreed, made the trade, and the gardener returned home.

Before long the king fell ill again, and this time it was said that snake's milk might be able to cure him. The gardener went back to the wild man and managed to get two drops of snake's milk in the same way he had acquired the apples. He received them from the radiantly beautiful snake queen in the palace of the enchanted garden. When he stopped at the tavern, the brothers-in-law wanted the drops as well, and he handed them over, but only on condition that they let themselves be marked on their backs with the rack.

The king recovered, but a terrible war broke out. The people rallied to the king's side to drive out the enemy. His sons-in-law appeared with their armies, but for a long time the battle was undecided.

The gardener's wife did not want her husband to join up. She feared for his life and allowed him to observe the conflict only from a distance. He used that chance to run off and return to the wild man, who gave him armor, a horse, and a sword. He flew off to battle. But the conflict was still not settled, and a weeklong armistice was declared. After that, war broke out again, and the wild man sought out the gardener, armed him, and told him that victory should still not be decisive.

War broke out a third time, and this time the wild man told the gardener that it was time for a real victory. The gardener took his invincible sword and struck down his enemies. In the heat of battle between friends and foe, the king accidentally injured the gardener's foot.

Once the battle was over, the king tore a kerchief from his neck and bandaged the wound of the gardener, whom he didn't recognize: The gardener was covered up, from head to toe, by his suit of armor.

Not much later, the king decided to host a banquet and wanted to invite all of his sons-in-law. He went over to the garden where his daughter was living. Looking over the fence, he could see the gardener bandaging his injured foot with the king's own kerchief. He was mystified, but did not let on that he knew anything and persuaded the gardener to attend the banquet.

When the gardener arrived at the banquet hall, he was wearing ordinary clothes and still had on the white head covering. He was given a seat between his two brothers-in-law.

"I will not sit between two fellows who have been marked by the rack or the gallows," the gardener declared, and he described what they had done with the apples from paradise and the snake's milk. After the uproar, it was decided that the two should be broken on the rack. But the gardener pleaded for mercy, and it was granted.

The king wondered why the gardener was wounded, and he also wanted to know how he had come by the kerchief. "I wounded a brave young soldier during the battle and bound his wound with my kerchief. I'd also like to know exactly why you are wearing that strange head covering."

Messengers from a distant land suddenly crowded the great hall and announced: "Our king has died, and we are seeking a new king, his son, Prince Goldenlocks. By using wisely the sorcery of the wonders in the garden, the charms of the snake queen, and the powers of the invincible sword, Prince Goldenlocks liberated the wild man and lifted the curse on him. And all the while he has been toiling here in humble service." The gardener blushed, took off his head covering, and his long golden locks fell down to his shoulders.

He was declared king in his homeland and true heir to his wife's fortune.

THE BEAUTIFUL SLAVE GIRL

A wealthy merchant had a son named Karl, who was the silent type. He decided to send the boy to live with his uncle to learn the ways of the world.

The uncle owned a beautiful garden. The boy loved visiting it, because a slave girl whom the uncle had acquired spent a good deal of time there. She was a woman of exquisite beauty and kept herself busy with all kinds of tasks in the garden.

Karl fell madly in love with her, and when he decided to return home, he was not satisfied with the valuable gifts the uncle had given him. "My dear uncle," he said, "you have given me many lovely gifts, but I would like to ask for an even more generous gift. Give me your slave girl!"

"You are the son of my brother and very dear to me, but I can't give her to you. She cost me far too much." The nephew carried on and said: "I'll pay for her. I'll send you the money right away." The uncle finally agreed, and the slave girl was his. The two made their way to Karl's home, elated to be leaving together. And Karl was relieved to be returning home. On the way they stopped in a city in a kingdom that seemed familiar to Karl's beloved.

The slave girl had a secret plan which she did not reveal to Karl right away. "Let's go to the market together," she said, "to a place where no one is allowed to transact business. We can sell things that are worth no more than twelve kreuzers or twenty-one at the most. Before long someone will come along and chase us away."

That's what the two did. An official appeared, as predicted, and made them leave. For a few coins he let the two off. A second official came, took his bribe, and left. The next day, the king himself sent a personal official. The slave girl gave him an envelope and put a letter inside it. The official brought the message to the king and he immediately recognized the handwriting of his beloved daughter. He had been searching for her for a long time.

The king raced to the marketplace that his daughter had named in the letter. When he found her, he took her home with Karl and said: "I have no other heirs. As the husband of my only child, you shall become vice chancellor and then, after I'm gone, king."

The king's marshal was filled with envy and wanted more than anything else to become the future ruler. He asked Karl: "Would you like to go hunting with me? Do you enjoy the sport?"

"Oh, yes, I am passionate about hunting!"

The two left for the hunt, and the marshal sent Karl ahead of everyone else. Then he shot him from behind, hitting him in the leg. Karl fell down, and he appeared to be dead. The marshal was sure that he was finished, and he threw the body over a cliff into a river. But Karl was able to swim until he reached an island.

Karl lived on the island for nearly half a year and survived by eating roots. He used herbs to heal his wounds. One day he saw a ship in the distance and thought: "If only that ship could see me and take me on board." He waved a white cloth, which the sailors saw, and they took him on board.

Karl returned home to his parents and became an artist. He was a skillful painter and traveled to his wife and her father, the king. When he arrived, they did not recognize him, since they believed that he had died long ago. He told them he was a painter, and of course that's what he was. The king gave Karl a room and asked him to decorate the walls with pictures. Karl let no one into the room while he was working, and he painted the little hut in the garden where the princess had once washed clothes as a slave. She was the first one to take a look at how his work was going, and she clapped her hands in delight when she saw the scene and recognized him. She threw her arms around Karl and brought the news to her father. Karl described all the adventures he had experienced.

The marshal was sentenced to death, and Karl was restored to the position he had once held. The loving couple lived happily together for many years.

THREE FLOWERS

Schönwerth's note: *Wood sprites, or forest sprites, are tiny creatures that make their homes near hearths. Their clothing is made of spun moss that hangs in ropelike strands from trees. We think of them as enchanted beings hounded by phantom hunters. They live together as married couples and bear children. Their enemies are the phantom hunters, who rage through the lands like wild beasts during autumnal storms. The wood sprites' only protection against them is to take refuge on a tree stump that has three crosses carved into it.* ✗

 Three huntsmen went in search of their sister, who had been abducted by a witch and hidden away in the woods. They traveled deep into the forest and managed to survive by killing game and sleeping beneath trees.

One day they discovered a cozy little cottage, where they were able to sleep more comfortably. The first night they watched a spark leap up from the hearth, and a tiny little woman began cooking milk in a thimble. The huntsmen forced the wood sprite to leave the hut. Now and then she could be seen perched on the fence post, singing a mourning song and weaving a brushwood crown into her hair.

When the men caught the unhappy woman and put her to

work as a maid, she trembled and wept, repeating the words: "Don't jail me; don't slay me. I can bring your little sister back to you." The huntsmen were overjoyed, and in a few days Katie, white as milk and red as blood, appeared in the hut. She told the brothers that a little gray man had been visiting her. He frightened her with his teasing and forced her to suck on his little finger. The brothers ambushed the little man, murdered him, and buried him in the garden. Before long three flowers with long stalks began growing on his grave. Katie marveled at the splendid colors and the sweet aroma of the bright blossoms. Whenever she bent the stalks down toward her nose, the wood sprite cried out: "Don't break the stalks!"

One day an adorable little white dog found its way to Katie and would not leave her side. The dog barked three times and a tall handsome stranger appeared in the woods. "What a beautiful maiden!" he exclaimed, and he walked toward her to take her hand.

"I want you to be my wife," he said. "My castle is just beyond those mountains in the distance, and I'll come to fetch you in three days." The young woman was astonished, but she nodded her agreement. The hunter left.

The brothers warned their sister about the stranger who was courting her, but she threw caution to the winds. Three days later the fair-haired hunter arrived in a splendid carriage, and their marriage was celebrated. The brothers came running up to the carriage, but their sister had already rushed down into the garden and picked the flowers. When the stems snapped, the brothers froze right in place and turned into deer. Katie stood there, as pale as snow and cold as ice. The wood sprite whispered in her ear: "For seven years you must be as still and quiet as the grave!"

The hunter was still in love with Katie, even though she could not speak. He took her with him in the carriage and traveled back to the castle, where the two lived in prosperity and plenty. The hunter's mother was an evil woman who disliked Katie. She was constantly scolding the young woman and making her life miserable.

When the time came for Katie to deliver a child, she bore a

son, whom the old woman took and choked to death. She took some of the child's blood and smeared it on the mother's mouth. Then she rushed to tell her son: "Take a good look at the woman you married. She has devoured her own child!" Frightened and horrified, he entered his wife's room and found her asleep. The three flowers were still there, untouched. He knew from the wood sprite that the living flowers were proof of her innocence and fidelity.

Katie gave birth to two more sons, each of whom became victims of the bloodthirsty old woman, who had also discovered the truth about the flowers. She tore them to pieces and bewitched her son so that he finally trusted her and agreed to summon the executioner.

Katie went to the place of execution like a walking dead woman. Just a word was all she needed to save her life. Pale as a sheet, she was seated in a chair with her neck exposed. The sword above her head was flashing in the daylight. Suddenly a cloud of dust appeared in the distance, and three riders mounted on three stags shouted as loudly as possible: "Seven years have passed. Now you can finally speak again, dear sister!"

The punishment was visited on the bloodthirsty woman rather than the innocent wife. The castle was bursting with good cheer. Every year the matron of the castle visited the hut of the wood sprite in the woods, and her children decorated the little room inside with flowers. But it was always empty and remained gloomy, with just a cricket chirping beneath the hearthstone.

THE FIGS

There once lived a king who loved figs more than any other food. They did not grow in his country, and so he proclaimed: "Whoever brings me some figs will have my daughter as his wife." A farmer who had a fig tree on his land heard these words. He sent the eldest of his sons to the king with the figs.

On the way to the castle the young man met a dwarf, who asked him what he was carrying. Irritated, the young man replied: "Are you talking to me? I've got a bunch of pigs' snouts." When he arrived at the castle he had snouts instead of figs, and so he had to turn back home empty-handed. Things went the same way for his brother. He replied to the dwarf by shouting: "I'm carrying a bag of horse dung!" And that's what ended up in his sack. Everyone made fun of him, and he, too, had to return home.

The third brother told the dwarf the truth, and the figs stayed figs. On the way to the castle there was an anthill in his path. The ants were swarming all over the hill, and the boy imagined that they must be hungry and gave them some breadcrumbs. The king of the ants came forward to express his gratitude and promised to help out if the boy was ever in trouble.

A little later the young man saw the devil in the midst of a squabble with Death. He settled the quarrel, and the two promised him their help if he should ever need it.

The young man went on his way and saw a little white fish thrashing around on the shore of a pond. He picked it up and helped it back into the water. The little fish was very grateful for the help.

The young man brought the figs to the king. The king was

planning to keep his promise, but the farmer's son was far too humble a fellow for the princess. He would have to pass three tests before he could marry her.

For the first, the princess threw a valuable ring into the sea, and he was supposed to bring it back. He almost gave up and was about to go back home after hearing her demand, for fetching the ring seemed an impossible task. But just then the king of all the fish rose up from the depths of the sea and began to whistle. Every single fish in the sea swam up toward the boy. But not one of them knew where the ring was. The king whistled a second time, and the little white fish swam toward him, ring in its mouth. And that was that.

The second task required him to clean up a huge pile of grain. Once again the young man was daunted by the size of the task, and he turned around and was about to head back home. When he reached the anthill, the ant king said: "Go back. We're going to help you get the job done." And all at once the ants, looking like a black army, appeared and they cleaned up the entire mountain of grain.

As a last demand, the princess asked for the most beautiful flower in heaven. For this task, Death was able to help him out. But the young man was told that although he could borrow the flower, he shouldn't let it leave his hands and would have to return it to Death. The princess was shocked that he had succeeded in acquiring the flower, and she was so infuriated that she made yet another demand, this time asking him to bring her a torch with the tallest flames from hell. The young man took the rose he was carrying down to hell and offered it as a reward to the devil for helping him. The devil hauled a huge glowing beam from hell up to the castle and threatened to burn down the entire place with it. Everyone was terrified, and the princess finally agreed to give her hand to the farmer's son.

THE ENCHANTED MUSKET

There once lived a charcoal burner who had three sons, each of whom had to help him at the kiln. One evening it was the turn of the youngest to keep watch, but he fell asleep, and the kiln burned down. The father was now dirt poor, and he told the boys that they were better off without him and that they should seek their fortunes in the world. He gave the eldest some coins, the middle son a hunk of ham, and Hans, the youngest, was given nothing at all, although his mother gave him some bread and a few pennies for the road.

The three boys found themselves in the woods and reached a crossroads. One took a left turn; the other a right turn. Hans, the youngest, marched straight ahead. He met a dwarf, who asked him for alms, and Hans gave him a penny. In exchange he received a musket that never missed its mark. He tried it out and aimed at some birds perched on the branches of a tree. One shot, and they all fell over dead.

Not much later Hans ran into a second dwarf, and he too asked for alms. In exchange for a second penny, Hans was given a flute that played melodies to which you had to dance. He was invited into a castle, played the flute there for everyone, and the king and queen as well as their daughter danced for so long that they finally pleaded with him to stop playing. The king offered the young man work as a shepherd. When Hans took the sheep out to the meadow, he would play the flute, and all the sheep and lambs would bleat and frolic around him.

Not far from the castle was a meadow with beautiful green grass. No one dared go there, for it belonged to a giant, and he was prepared to kill anyone who crossed his path. Hans decided to confront the giant, and he shot him dead just as the big fellow was about to attack. The sharpshooter took a golden key from around the dead giant's neck and drove his frisky sheep back home.

Everyone was eager to know: "Where were you?"

"I was in the place where green grass grows."

"What did you see?"

"Nothing."

Hans was given plenty to eat and drink, and the next day he went back to the meadow and made himself comfortable. Another giant appeared and came hurtling toward him, shouting: "Why did you murder my brother?" The shepherd reached for his musket and shot this giant dead too. He removed the silver key from around his neck and pocketed it. On the third day he went again to the place that was off-limits. A giant shouted down to him from the mountains: "Why did you kill my two brothers?" The shepherd shot him, too, and pocketed his brass key.

The next day a magnificent castle appeared out of thin air on the meadow. Hans opened the first gate with the key made of brass; the second, with the key made of silver. There were animals everywhere in the gardens, but they all looked as if they had been frozen. The golden key opened the door to the many different rooms in the castle, all filled with gold and silver. A little golden wreath was on a table. Hans took it and put it on his hat, as a decoration. When he returned home, everyone asked: "Where were you?"

"At the village green."

The princess saw the golden wreath on his hat. She asked for it, and he gave it to her.

Hans went to the castle a second time. A woman in white approached him and thanked him for liberating her. In the grand hall there were three enchanted women, all in white. If he freed them as well, the castle would belong to him. "But you have to spend three nights here and stay no matter what happens. You won't be hurt," or so they said.

Terrifying ghosts appeared on the first night. They stretched

Hans out on a cutting board, chopped him into pieces, and left him for dead. But he survived and woke up the next morning as if nothing had happened. On the second night the ghosts put him into a cradle filled with thorns and thistles. He didn't feel a thing. On the third night twelve men came and tortured him, but he got up again and no one had done him any harm. When the twelve men vanished, cheers and songs broke out everywhere in the castle. The women had been freed, and Hans received his reward. He invited the king and the princess to join him on the slope of the meadow. When the king discovered just how wealthy Hans was, he gave him his daughter's hand in marriage.

After a while, the king's new son-in-law decided to visit his parents. He took leave of the princess and said: "In three nights I will send you a message." Traveling through the woods, he discovered a cave where some robbers had been hiding out. Only a parrot was left inside, and it called out: "Be sure you don't go out the way that you came in, or you're a dead man!" Hans forced his way through a crevice, one so narrow that his clothes and some of his skin were left on the stones.

In the course of his travels he stayed at an inn where princes, knights, and monks were all carousing together. He borrowed some clothes from the innkeeper and went to his father's house. But his father and his brothers thought he was the innkeeper, and they welcomed him with curses and blows.

The princess had failed to receive any news at all from her husband. She decided to go and look for him. In the robbers' cave, she found his clothes, and the parrot screeched at her: "Take those with you and then go on to the inn." There she put on a monk's habit and asked someone to guide her to the home of her husband's parents.

"Where is your youngest son?" she asked.

"The moron is sitting over there in a corner of the kitchen."

She recognized him right away as her husband, but she did not say a word. Instead she had him taken to the inn. There the princess revealed that she was his wife. Everyone was elated, and the two celebrated their reunion. They were showered with gifts and the two returned home in high spirits.

THE THREE
ABDUCTED DAUGHTERS

A wealthy merchant learned that the town of Dillenberg housed many treasures. There was a marble fountain right in the center of town. It was said that if you listened carefully, you could hear a clock striking there on the hour, and if you searched around in its works long enough, you would find the key to a magnificent castle. The merchant was haunted by this knowledge, and one day he said to his coachman: "Make sure the horses are fed first thing in the morning. I'm planning to go on the road."

The next day he left, taking his three daughters with him. That night the horses had to pull with all their might to draw the carriage up a steep mountain with a castle at its top. When the merchant climbed out of the carriage, there was nothing in sight but a huge pile of rocks. As he walked around it, he heard awful noises—howling and then banging. The merchant stood still for some time, and then the noise came closer. Suddenly there was nothing but silence.

When the merchant returned to the carriage, he discovered to his horror that his three daughters had vanished. And the coachman was fast asleep. "Where are my daughters?" he shouted. The coachman leaped up from his seat. He had no idea what had happened. He had dreamed about a little old man with a long beard who had taken the girls from the carriage and disappeared with them. The faithful servant had been unable to call for help.

On the return journey, the distraught merchant cried out: "I will bequeath my entire fortune to the person who can bring back my three daughters. And if it takes three to do it, each one will have one of my daughters as his wife."

The news spread like wildfire. Many young men showed up, hoping to help him, but the merchant accepted only the three handsomest suitors. These three left late at night, and they too reached the pile of rocks. Behind it was a magnificent building. They entered it cautiously, and there they found a room filled with precious objects. On a table in the room, there was a sword, and next to it was a note with the words: "This sword will let you cut through anything." The youngest in the trio took the sword, and the three continued walking through the rooms. In the last of them was a golden cradle, with a beautiful child, pale as the moon. One of the three volunteered to keep watch over the child, when suddenly, out of the blue, a dwarf with a long beard appeared and attacked him, scratching his face badly.

The young man wanted to chase him down, but the dwarf had already vanished. The second young man did not fare any better. On the third night, the third suitor kept watch, sword in hand. The dwarf returned, and the fearless young man grabbed him by the beard, wedging it between two doors. "Now you'll get what you deserve!" But the dwarf tore so hard at the beard that it came off, and he raced away.

The young man told his companions about what had happened. "I now know where the dwarf holes up!" he said, and he showed the other two a deep well. Two of them took a rope and let themselves down into the well, but they could not find the bottom. Only the third young man landed, and he discovered a long passageway that led to a lovely garden and a magnificent building. He entered and found a beautiful woman in the first room. She was the eldest daughter of the merchant. At her feet stood a huge lion. As soon as the lion discovered a stranger in the room, it leaped up, opened its jaws wide, and was about to attack. The stranger grabbed his sword and slew the lion.

In the next room was another young woman, and this time there were three young lions. The young man killed all of them with a single blow. In the final room was a golden cradle, this time with the dwarf in it. The youngest of the merchant's three daughters was rocking it. The young man took his sword and chopped off the dwarf's head. And that is how he rescued all three of the merchant's daughters.

The three sisters went back with him, and they returned to the bottom of the well. The young man shouted up to his companions: "Throw the rope down so that the three girls can climb out of here!" And that's how he was going to save the three daughters of the merchant. But the two young men above had their own ideas. "If we leave him down in the well, we can divide the merchant's wealth between the two of us." They tossed down the rope after pulling up the daughters but didn't pull it back up for him. Then off they went.

The young man had been betrayed, and he returned to the underground castle. He looked at the many precious objects in it and walked through a garden that had all kinds of birds flying around, but there seemed to be no way out. Suddenly a snake with jaws wide open slithered toward him. He took his sword and chopped off its head. When the birds discovered that the snake was dead, the most magnificent of them flew over to him and said: "You have slain our worst enemy, a monster that had been taking the young from our nests. Let me carry you away from here and bring you back home. Just hop on my wings."

The young man climbed up on the bird's back, and after flying for some time, the bird landed on a path in the forest. "Just stay on this road and you will reach home." And sure enough, he reached home. He inquired about the health of the merchant's daughters. Everyone told him that two of the daughters were already married. There was no news about the third suitor, not even from the men who had accompanied him on the journey. The fellow had received a ring from the youngest of the three daughters. He went to see the merchant and told him everything, but the merchant refused to believe him. He summoned his youngest daughter to ask if the young man was her rescuer. "If he has my ring," she said, "then he is the man who rescued us." The young man took the ring from his finger, put it on the table, and the girl acknowledged it as her own.

And so the fellow became the husband of the youngest of the merchant's three daughters. His two companions were punished for their crimes.

THE PORTRAIT

There once was a couple, and they worked hard to make ends meet. They lived in a tiny house with their two children. One day, the parents died, and the children were left with no money at all.

A coach drove up to the house, and the children were so sure that some work was coming their way that they almost flew out of the house. The squire in the coach saw the boy right away, but the girl was shy and remained hidden behind the door. The boy asked the squire if he needed a coachman, and he replied: "Yes, of course I could use a coachman. Pack up your belongings, and you can start work right away." The boy was beside himself with joy, even though he felt sad about leaving his sister all alone. But he promised her that he would never abandon her. She gave him a miniature portrait of herself, and they took leave of each other with tears in their eyes. The coach hurtled off and was gone in a flash.

Late in the evening the coach pulled up to the squire's castle. The squire showed the boy his room, and he unpacked the few things he had with him. He hung the picture of his sister on the wall. Every night he prayed that she would not come to any harm.

The squire observed this habit, and one day he asked about the portrait in his room. "It's a likeness of my beloved sister. And every night I pray that she will stay happy and healthy and that no one will harm her." The squire wanted to take a closer look at the image, and the boy gave it to him, but not without some reluctance. The man gazed at the face for a while and then said: "If your sister is really as beautiful as she looks in this portrait, I want her to be my wife. But if the portrait is not a faithful likeness, I'll lock her up in a tower." The boy told him that his sister was even more beautiful than the portrait, and with great excitement he prepared the horses for the journey back home.

The squire's mother had a malicious old chambermaid, who was known to be an evil witch. She slipped into the carriage unbeknownst to anyone and was filled with envy when she witnessed the joy of the reunited siblings. For the return trip the young woman was wearing her most beautiful garments and was seated next to the chambermaid, to whom no one had paid any attention. Her brother said from the driver's seat: "Don't stick your head out the window or you might get scratched by the branches!"

The girl couldn't hear what he was saying and asked: "What did you say?"

"You should stick your head out the window," the old woman said. "There are marvelous birds flying overhead." The girl put her head out the window, and some twigs and branches scratched her beautiful face.

The horses took the carriage past a pond, and the boy said to his sister: "Don't lean out the window or you might fall into the water."

"What did you say?" she asked.

"You should lean out the window," the old witch said. "Some beautiful little fish are swimming in the pond." The girl leaned out the window, and the old woman pushed her so hard that she fell out of the carriage and into the water. The boy never saw a thing.

When the coach pulled up to the castle, the squire was eager to see his bride, but no one was in the carriage except for the witch, who had made herself invisible. The enraged squire threw the boy into a dungeon and hung the portrait by the hearth. At night a guard saw someone come into the room and speak to the mirror on the wall:

"Mirror, mirror, on the wall, the parting was sweet, and now I bring greetings. Tell me where my brother has gone."

"He's lying hidden in the squire's dungeon."

"Where is my portrait?"

"It's by the hearth out in the open."

"Where is the old chambermaid?"

"She's asleep in the squire's bed."

The next morning, the terrified guard reported everything he had heard. The squire had two men stand watch the next evening, and they reported exactly what the first guard had seen. "Tonight and tomorrow night I will keep watch with you," the squire said, and he sat down in front of the mirror, sword in hand, and waited. When the clock struck eleven, a form appeared before the mirror and spoke the same words as during the past two nights.

"Mirror, mirror, on the wall, the parting was sweet, and now I bring greetings. Tell me where my brother has gone."

"He's hidden in the squire's dungeon."

"Where is my portrait?"

"It's by the hearth out in the open."

"Where is the old chambermaid?"

"She's asleep in the squire's bed."

Just then the mirror shattered and the young woman was standing there in all her beauty, with just a little scratch on her face. She told the squire about all the terrible things the chambermaid had done, how she had given her orders and then shoved her into the water.

She finished by saying: "If you had not redeemed me today, I would have been lost forever."

The old witch was burned at the stake. The coachman was freed from the dungeon and treated like a son. The portrait on the hearth was given a place of honor in the finest room of the castle, and the marriage was celebrated in splendor.

And if they have not died, they are living happily today.

ASHFEATHERS

An innkeeper lost his wife. He was afraid that his daughter would feel lonely, and so he decided to remarry. The new wife bore him two children, and the child from the husband's first marriage became a thorn in the woman's flesh. Her name was Ashfeathers, for she had to sort the millet from the ashes, which her stepmother mixed in on purpose. She was never allowed to leave the kitchen. When her father returned from his travels, she received nothing, even though her two sisters were given presents. One day, when her father set out on another journey, she called after him in a forlorn tone: "This time bring back something for me!"

While traveling, the father remembered his daughter's words just as the branch of a hazelnut tree was grazing his hat. There were six nuts on it. He took the branch with him and gave it to his eldest daughter. While she was fetching water from the well for her father, the branch fell into the water. She didn't dare go back home. And in fact when she did return, her stepmother immediately began complaining when she learned about it: "You are just hopeless! I've said it once, and I'll say it again. Go in the kitchen, and stay there!" And then she said to her husband: "If you had spent some real money on her, it would have been wasted. She's just so stupid."

In desperation Ashfeathers returned to the well. A dwarf was sitting near it and said to her: "Don't bother looking for that little branch. You won't find it. But when you go to church, be sure to recite these words:

> Today I'm just a kitchen maid,
> Send me shoes, done in gold braid.
> And give to me the finest gown,
> Papa will sing all night in town."

Before going to church that Sunday, Ashfeathers went down to the well to wash her hands. In a flash she was completely clean, and a beautiful dress, gold shoes, and white silk stockings appeared at the edge of the well. She had turned into the most beautiful princess imaginable, and a little dove was perched on each shoulder.

Ashfeathers walked over to the church. Her stepsisters had no idea who she was. But the two little doves began cooing whenever they looked at their beautiful mistress. Once the service was over, Ashfeathers rushed back to the well, took off her beautiful clothes, and put the patched ones back on. At home everyone was talking about the beautiful maiden. No one knew who she was. One man in particular, a stranger, had taken note of her. "She must become my wife!" he thought to himself, and he asked everyone about her. But no one could say who she was.

The following Sunday she disappeared again, right after church. On the third Sunday, the stranger spread some tar on the stairs. When Ashfeathers walked down the stairs, one of her shoes got stuck. She didn't worry about losing the shoe and raced back to the well to put her tattered clothes back on. The stranger took the shoe home with him. He told his coachman: "Harness the horses! We are going to find that beautiful woman." The carriage stopped at the very inn where Ashfeathers was working in the kitchen.

The stranger said to the innkeeper: "You must have very beautiful daughters. I would like to marry one of them! I will marry the one whose foot fits this shoe." But the shoe did not fit the first girl, for her big toe was too fat. The innkeeper's daughter did not hesitate for a moment; she cut off her toe. Then the shoe fit. The nobleman invited her to join him in the carriage, but the man's dog kept barking: "We have a bride missing a toe!"

"Turn around," the gentleman said. "We have the wrong person." At the inn, the second daughter tried on the shoe. Since it did not fit, she cut off her heel. On the way home, the little dog barked: "That's not the right bride! She has no heel!" The coachman turned around again and went back to the inn. He insisted that there must be another daughter living there. The innkeeper's wife shouted: "There are no others!" When the gentleman refused to take no for an answer, the woman went and fetched Ashfeathers from the filthy hearth. The girl ran back to the well to wash her hands and face. The dwarf was there, and he gave her the beautiful garments as well as the hazelnut branch she had lost. It had turned into solid gold. Ashfeathers wore it on her dress. Back at home the gentleman put the golden shoe on her. Just imagine, it fit perfectly.

The innkeeper's wife could not bear to see how Ashfeathers had turned into such a beautiful young woman. Just then the little dog barked: "At last we have found the true bride!" The gentleman climbed into the carriage with the beautiful maiden, and the carriage drove away to the magnificent castle, where the two lived happily ever after.

The father was invited to the wedding, but the mother and two sisters were not allowed to attend.

TWELVE TORTOISES

There was once a couple so poor that they had to beg in order to feed their children. One day they were at an inn with nothing but a crust of bread to eat. The innkeeper's wife shouted down to them from upstairs: "Sell me your two children. I don't have any of my own!"

The beggars replied: "We can't sell them, but if you want, we will give them to you." The two children were named Elias and Caroline, and the parents took them upstairs and then left. The innkeeper's wife was thrilled to have the children.

One day the children were left on their own, and the innkeeper's wife gave them a card game to play while she was away. They were supposed to go to church when they finished playing. Caroline kept winning at cards, and finally Elias became so angry that he said: "I wish the devil would just come get you!" And the devil appeared right then and there and took her away. Elias was now all alone, and he fainted dead away. When the innkeeper's wife returned home and learned from the cook what had happened, she flew into a rage and kicked the boy out of the house.

Elias traveled down roads day after day. At one point, he learned that a king in the region needed a servant. He lined up for the position and was hired. In the evening he would often take walks by the sea and watch the fish in the waters. One day twelve swans came swimming toward him. The most majestic in the group turned to him and said: "Come back tomorrow and bring a bowl with six roses in it. No one, not even the king, can ask where you are going. In return, we will give you some money for the king. He is in desperate straits."

Elias went back home and said to the king: "When I ride out tomorrow in the coach, don't ask where I am going. And when I return, don't ask how I came by what I will have with me!" The next day he set out on his own and from a distance he could already see the swans in the water, paddling toward him. Each one had a little cask around its neck. The most magnificent among them said: "Put the casks into the carriage and give them to the king. But don't say a word about where they came from."

When Elias returned, the king opened up the first cask. It was full of coins. The king was overjoyed. But when he asked where the money had come from, there was no answer.

Elias went back to spend some time with his friends, the swans. The most magnificent among them asked: "Did anyone question you about us?"

"Yes, but I didn't say a word."

The swan said: "Now you must go deep into the dark forest."

When he returned to the palace, Elias told the king that he would have to travel into the dark forest. The king refused to let him go alone and asked a servant to accompany him. The two left the next day.

While walking awhile in the woods, the two young men met a stranger. He said: "You must have lost your way if you are looking for the dark forest. You'll have to turn around and walk along the path until you reach an inn. Ask for directions there." The stranger vanished.

They found the inn, which was quite beautiful, and they asked about the dark woods. The innkeeper said: "Those woods belong to me!"

The next day the innkeeper's wife handed the servant an apple: "Give this to your master. He will be thirsty." Elias was in fact thirsty when they left for the woods, and he ate the apple. He fell asleep right away, and suddenly the twelve swans appeared and tried to wake him up with their hissing. But they could not. Elias and the servant went back to the inn. The next day the same thing happened. This time the innkeeper's wife gave Elias a pear to quench his thirst. And nothing could rouse him from his sleep.

When the swans still could not wake him up on the third day, the most magnificent among them waited until no one else was around and wrote these words on his hat: "Saddle your horse and prepare to leave. Go back to the inn. Behind the door you will find a stag all trussed up. Chop off its head. Then make your way at once to the glass mountain, and I'll meet you there." Elias did everything as the swan had said, but instead of chopping off the head of the stag, he chopped off the head of the innkeeper's wife. He rode away as fast as he could after sending the servant back home. From now on he was going to be on his own.

When he reached a mill, he asked the owner how to find the glass mountain. "You will have to wait until tomorrow. Every day some giants stop by here for flour, and they take it to the castle on the glass mountain. I'll put you in one of the containers, and the giants can take you up there." And so one of the giants ended up carrying Elias up to the mountain, and the whole time he was wondering why the container was so heavy this time around. Once the giant reached the top of the mountain, he slammed the container to the ground, and it burst into a thousand pieces.

Elias jumped out and ran away as fast as he could. He reached a majestic palace and walked in. No one was around. When night fell, the swans reappeared and told him that he would have to spend the night there. "No matter what happens, you have to stay where you are." At midnight a huge giant appeared out of nowhere and spewed flames at him. Then he threatened to eat him up. That went on for more than an hour. At daybreak the swans returned and said: "Tonight a snake will appear and wrap itself around you." That's exactly what happened, and Elias had to endure the torture for an entire hour. The next day, the swans had another unpleasant task for him. "Tonight," they said, "twelve tortoises will appear. Each one will be as big as a washtub, with eyes the size of windows. You must kiss every single one of them." That night twelve tortoises really did come crawling through the door. He kissed every single one of them, and suddenly they turned into human beings. The first one was the princess who had been living at the palace, the second was his sister, Caroline, and the others were all old friends. He had lifted the curse from them. The princess became his wife.

And if they have not died, they are still living happily today.

THUMBNICKEL

A couple living in the country longed to have a child, but for many years their wish was not granted. One day, they cried out in desperation: "We want a child, even if it's no bigger than a thumb!" And a son was born to them. He was exactly the size of a thumb, and he never grew any bigger than that. He was named Nicholas, but called Thumbnickel.

The farmer carried his son around on the brim of his hat. When he plowed the fields, he would put the little rascal into the ear of one of the oxen, where he could sing and dance to his heart's content.

One day a merchant drove by, and he watched Thumbnickel dancing and singing in the ear of the ox. He turned to the farmer and asked if he could buy the boy. The farmer was not interested in a deal, but the little boy whispered in his father's ear, urging him to accept it. The merchant climbed back into his carriage with the little fellow. The farmer started running behind the carriage. While the merchant was dozing off, the little guy climbed through a keyhole into a chest filled with money in the back of the carriage. He opened the chest and started tossing coins out to his father.

The merchant turned in for the night at an inn. When he was about to pay the bill, he discovered that all his money was gone. He took out a whip and ran after Thumbnickel. But the rascal had already crawled into a barrel of salt, escaping any kind of punishment.

The maid at the inn was about to feed the cows, and she

reached into the barrel of salt. She grabbed Thumbnickel, along with some salt, and threw him into the feeding trough for the cows. One of the cows swallowed Thumbnickel with the salt. When the maid started milking the cow, Thumbnickel began shrieking so loudly that everyone was sure something must be wrong with the cow. The next day Thumbnickel emerged completely intact in a heap of cow dung. The innkeeper took a pitchfork and heaved the dung over a nest of mice.

One of the mice sniffed dinner and sped over to the place where Thumbnickel had landed, mouth wide open. And right behind the mouse was a fox waiting to eat it. Poor Thumbnickel was trembling with fear. But because the mouse had picked up the scent of the fox, and the fox had picked up the scent of the mouse, the two did not move from the spot.

Thumbnickel's father happened to be plowing the field just then. He began plowing right next to the nest and ended up tossing the mouse and Thumbnickel up into the air. The father saw his son and caught him as he was flying through the air, and before long, Thumbnickel was back in the ox's ear, dancing and singing, with his father happily plowing the field.

HANS THE STRONG MAN

 There was once a farmer, and he had two sons. The mother named one of the boys Hans and nursed him for seven years. Then his father sent him out into the woods and told him to uproot a tree. And the boy really did pull a small tree up by its roots, and then he took it home with him. But the tree was not tall enough to satisfy his father, and so the mother had to nurse the boy another seven years. By then Hans was strong enough to bring home a timber tree. The father was impressed, and he harnessed up his two boys so that they could plow the fields. Hans was always way ahead of his brother, who became so annoyed with his strength that he would push him away from the plow. He preferred pulling the plow all by himself.

Around that time a wealthy man stopped at the farm. He had taken note of the strong boy and asked the farmer if he would be willing to make a trade. He wanted to give him the two horses pulling his own carriage, along with a bag of coins, in exchange for Hans. The farmer was willing to make the trade, and so was Hans. The boy was harnessed up to the man's carriage, and he started pulling it.

"What's your name?" the man asked.

"Hans."

"Can you run?"

"A little."

"Then speed up!"

Hans ran faster and faster and didn't listen to the passenger, who was now trying to get him to slow down. One of the wheels on the carriage flew off, then a second, and finally the entire coach fell apart.

"Stop, Hans, stop!"

But Hans would not stop, even though he was now holding nothing but a pole in his hands. The man had to run after him and catch him.

Hans reached the house long before his master. The master's wife made a big fuss about the fine farmhand her husband had hired.

The next day Hans was supposed to take two horses out into the woods. The other farmhands were long gone, and Hans would not get up until a dish of dumplings was set before him. Finally, when he went riding into the woods, the other fellows were already returning, their carts piled high with wood. Hans saw a narrow passageway and went straight to it. There he relieved himself, and when the other farmhands made their way through the passageway, they were soon stuck in the mess he had made. Hans's horses had trouble getting through the passageway too, no matter how hard he whipped them. Enraged, he beat one of the horses until it was dead, threw its corpse on the cart, and harnessed himself up. There were wolves all around, and one of them tried to make off with the dead horse. But Hans killed the wolf, tossed it on the cart, and brought home a load of wood.

The woman was now furious about this stupid farmhand, and her husband finally agreed to get rid of him. He told Hans: "I'm going over to the inn to have a glass of wine. When it gets dark, come over and show me the way home with a bright light." When night fell, Hans set the barn on fire. With the light from it, the farmer could find his way home. When he was raked over the coals for this new prank, Hans said in all innocence: "I was just following the orders of my master. The barn was just a big bright light that made it easy for him to find his way back home."

The farmer's wife was now completely fed up with Hans.

Near the house there was a deep well, which Hans was supposed to clean. "When he gets down there," she said to her servants, "we'll throw stones down after him until he's dead." But Hans shouted cheerfully from below: "There must be some hens up there. They're scratching and scraping, and the pebbles are landing down here." Even a huge millstone did not bother him. He put it around his neck as a ruff, finished his work, and crawled back up unharmed.

Hans's master was baffled, and he decided to send the farmhand to a haunted mill. He was told to grind some grain over there. When the clock struck midnight, there was a knock at the door. Hans shouted: "Come on in!" Twelve fellows marched in and sat down at the table to play cards. Hans watched them carefully and discovered that they were all cheating. Without further ado he grabbed one of them by the shoulders, took him over to the mill, pulled his pants down, and ground his buttocks down with the millstone. Then he carried him back upstairs and sat him down with the others. The horror-struck comrades fled, and Hans returned home with the flour.

Husband and wife now despaired of ever getting rid of Hans. They decided to send him to hell to bring back some money they had loaned the devil. The devil refused to pay back the cash and started a quarrel. Hans came running toward him with the ground-up buttocks of the fellow from the mill and shouted: "You can't get anywhere with this lad!" Hans now had his money and was about to return home.

But one of the more rowdy devils stopped him and said: "I have a bag of coins. Want to make a bet? Whoever can blow the loudest on this horn will get everything that belongs to both of us." Hans found that to be a fine bargain. The devil blew into the horn and the entire world began to shake.

"You moron! Can't you do better than that?" Hans said contemptuously. "Give me that little horn, but let me tie some roots around it so that it doesn't burst into pieces when I blow on it."

The devil began worrying when he heard that. "Stop!" he shouted. "That's no fair! I can't get back to hell without that horn." He dashed off with the horn and left all his money with Hans.

Hans brought the money back to the farmer's wife. She sent him off to his father, along with the money, hoping that he would stay there. And that's how Hans the Strong Man returned home as a rich man.

LOUSEHEAD

One day a little gray lady met a woodcutter in the forest. It was raining, and she was carrying a dirty old sack on her shoulders. "Are you having a hard time too?" she asked.

"I've seen better days," the woodcutter replied.

"I can help you, if you do as I tell you. In fourteen years I want you to bring me something that you do not yet know to exist." And then the old woman vanished. When the woodcutter returned home and told his wife what had happened, she became frightened, for she felt sure she was with child. "Nothing good can come of that!" she said to him.

The woodcutter's wife gave birth to a boy, who grew to be a tall lad. When he turned fourteen, he ran into the woods, and his mother ran right after him. The little gray woman was waiting for him, and when she saw his mother, she threw the sack over her head and turned her into a white mare. The woman caught the boy, and the boy held the horse by the reins. The woman skipped around in front of him and took the boy deep into the woods to her castle. They went to the stables, and she said: "Do as I say. You don't need to give this horse much to eat, but feed the brown one well." The boy had no idea what had happened to his mother, and he did exactly as he was told. After a few days the woman reappeared and praised the boy, for the white horse was thin as a rail, and the brown one well fed and healthy. The woman left, and the mare nearly collapsed.

The boy loosened the sack under the harness. All of a sudden the horse started talking to him: "Give me more food. I am your mother!" The boy didn't have to hear that twice, and as soon as the mare had recovered and was strong enough to trot, he fled with it. They marched into the woods, down to the sea, and then on out into the world.

The two reached a palace, and of course there was a royal stable there too. The boy rode in on horseback. The mare was just fine, but what use did they have for the boy?

It turned out that one of the cooks at the palace had died, and so the boy was asked if he knew how to cook. He hesitated for a moment, ran back to the stable, and asked his mother what he should say. The mare said: "Just say yes to anything they ask." And so the boy became a cook. He would sneak from the kitchen into the stables to get advice from his mother. When the dishes at the table all began to smell and taste better than ever before, the young cook was summoned, and he appeared in the hall with a cap on his head.

The king was annoyed. The princes and princesses laughed and the youngest asked him: "Do you have some kind of problem with your hair?"

The boy blushed and said: "Yes."

And from then on he was known as Lousehead.

The king sent him from the kitchen to the gardens. The royal gardens were a wilderness of weeds and thistles. By following his mother's instructions, the boy was able to turn it into a little paradise, and he grew apples and pears, lettuce, radishes, and garlic. The sons and daughters of the king and the king himself came to see the garden. The children teased him, but the king had nothing but praise for him.

One day, war broke out, and the three princes had to go to battle. The stableboy went with them and rode his mare. During the battle he said to the princes: "Stay close to me." The youngest did as he said, but the others did not, and the enemy captured them. Lousehead raced like a lightning bolt toward a fire-breathing dragon guarding the prisoners, and he rescued them and won the battle.

The king was so pleased that he would have been happy to give Lousehead one of his daughters in marriage, but none of them wanted to marry him. And so he went back to the garden and carried out his many chores there. One day the sun was beating down so hard on his back that he could barely stand it anymore. He tore the cap off his head and dragged himself into the shade. A beautiful pair of eyes was following his every movement.

After a time the king became ill, and the doctors were unable to help him. It was proclaimed that the person who could heal him would receive the hand of one of the princesses. Many suitors appeared but they were unappealing. The young gardener answered the call as well. He wanted to do something to make the king feel better, and he decided to give him some medicinal roots, which just happened to work. The king rose up from his bed, summoned his daughters, and said: "Which one of you wants to marry Lousehead?" The two eldest remained silent, but the youngest smiled, gave him her hand, and then took off his cap. Everyone could now see that he had golden locks rather than an itchy scalp.

SEVEN WITH ONE BLOW!

A tailor went out into the world one day, sword by his side. After a while, he was exhausted and took a nap, falling asleep right on top of his hat. When he woke up, red flies were buzzing all over some cow dung in the road. He found them so annoying that he took out his sword and killed seven of them. Then he pulled out the chalk he used in his trade and wrote on his hat: "Seven with one blow!"

A kitchen boy working for a count happened to be walking in the same direction as the tailor and read the words on his hat. He rushed ahead to let the count know about this fellow. The count was eager to see the brave tailor as soon as possible, and he sent several men out to request an audience.

The count told him: "There are three giants terrorizing my lands. If you can defeat them, you will win my castle, my lands, and the hand of my daughter." The count's huntsmen took the tailor deep into the forest and left him there to fend for himself.

The tailor was terrified and climbed up a tree to take a look around. Just then some giants were gathering right beneath the tree in which he was perched. They made a fire, ate, drank, and went to sleep. The tailor took some stones and let one drop on the chest of the shortest giant, then another on the fellow sleeping next to him, and finally he dropped one on the tallest. The giants started quarreling among themselves, and each one was sure that the other had been trying to disturb his sleep. The tallest of the three rose up and grabbed the two others by the throat, choking them until they dropped dead.

The tailor climbed down the tree, chopped off the heads of

all three, and skewered their tongues with his sword. He took everything to the count and said: "I've now rid the land of those three oafs for you, and it was really no trouble at all."

The lady of the castle was insulted that her beautiful, proud daughter would have to marry a tailor. She persuaded the count to send the good-natured lad into the woods to do battle with a dangerous unicorn. Once again the count's men took the tailor into the woods and left him there completely on his own. Before long the unicorn came galloping through the woods. The tailor quickly hid behind a tall aspen tree. The wild beast charged the tree, and its horn got stuck in the tree trunk. The unicorn was unable to move.

The tailor returned to the count to let him know that he had caught that old "billy goat" out in the woods, and the count's men could bring him back whenever they wanted.

The count's wife still didn't want to have anything to do with the tailor. The count himself had to ask the tailor to fight his enemies, who were making rapid advances on his territory. He told the tailor to choose a horse from the royal stables. The soldiers were already lined up at the castle. But the horses in the stables were all wild stallions. Way in back there was an old nag, and even if you whipped that horse, all it would do was swish its tail. The tailor chose to ride that one, for he knew that old dogs are wiser than young ones.

And so he rode out with the soldiers. Before long they heard music coming from the enemy camp. The old nag started trotting toward the place where the horns were sounding. Right in their way was a field cross. The tailor, who was just about to fall off the old nag, grabbed on to the cross with both arms. But the cross was beginning to fall apart, and he couldn't get a grip. It broke off in his hands. Off he galloped toward the heathen soldiers. They in turn believed that Christ himself was hurtling toward them, and they sped off. When the music died down, the nag turned around and slowly made its way back home, rider on its back.

Now at last the wedding was going to take place, for better or for worse. An honest servant revealed to the brave tailor that his bride was planning to kill him on their wedding night.

When the two entered the bedroom, the groom hung his sword on the bedstead and helped his bride into the bed. Then he pretended to be sleeping, and the minute he heard the door open and saw the assassins walk into his bedroom, he started talking in his sleep, saying: "I have killed seven with one blow, slain three giants, caught a dangerous unicorn, and made infidels flee. I won't have any trouble with these fellows."

The men quickly fell to their knees and begged for mercy. The bride asked him to forgive her for planning his murder. She promised to love him forever.

THE BURNING TROUGH

A farmer had three daughters, and they were all young and beautiful. The three were so determined to build up a good dowry for themselves that they ended up spinning all day long and never took a moment to help out their father. One day the man went into the woods, feeling mildly annoyed already, and then he tripped over a rotting tree stump. Suddenly a dwarf jumped out before him and said: "You will never have to work another day of your life if you just let me spend the night with one of your daughters."

The farmer agreed to the deal. When he returned home, the table was set with the most exquisite dishes. Everyone was thrilled by this stroke of good fortune, and the eldest of the sisters offered to let the dwarf sleep in her bed for one night. When night fell, there was a knock at the door, and the eldest opened it. All she could see was a trough in flames; terrified, she slammed the door.

The next day, there was nothing on the table, and so the farmer went back to the woods. This time, the dwarf was standing on a rock, waiting for him, and he was furious that he had been swindled. The farmer calmed him down and promised him the second daughter for that very night. He returned home and found the table set once again.

But the second daughter also didn't want to have anything to do with that burning trough. Now the dwarf was really angry, and he showed up the next day at the door and demanded that they make amends for humiliating him. Just then, Anna, the youngest, offered to invite the little man into her bed, and she kept her word. When she saw the trough in flames, she jumped into it, hugged and kissed whatever was there, and asked it to come to her room. At that very moment, the monstrous thing turned into a handsome prince, and the girl took a shine to him right away. The next day he gave her a spindle, a bobbin, and a spinning wheel, all made of gold, and they could even be taken apart. He told her that they were a token of his love and that he would come back soon and bring her home as his bride.

But he did not return. Anna soon grew lovesick. She set out with her golden objects, searching for him. When the moon rose, she asked whether it knew where her beloved was tarrying. The moon was sorry to report that it could not see everything going on down below and advised her to ask the sun. She waited until the sun rose and asked it to tell her where her beloved was. The sun was merciful and allowed the girl to put her foot in one of its slippers, so that she could keep up with it. The two moved along swiftly, covering two miles with every step until finally, at the top of a mountain, Anna was able to remove her foot from the slipper. And that was when the mountain exploded and tossed her down into a cave.

There she found an old woman who was waiting on her beloved. Anna asked if she could sleep next to the man who was her master. Every night she gave the woman one of her golden gifts.

On the third morning the spell was broken. The mountain and the cavern had disappeared. In their place was a magnificent castle belonging to the handsome prince. Gratitude and love united the two in marital bliss.

THE KING'S BODYGUARD

A king appointed the most handsome of all his soldiers as his bodyguard. One day he dispatched him to a rich nobleman, who made a point of protecting his wondrously beautiful daughter from soldiers by telling her: "Anna, don't exchange a single word with a soldier!" But this soldier happened to like the beautiful young woman, and Anna happened to like him as well. Before long, they were on intimate terms with each other, and the bodyguard asked the nobleman for his daughter's hand. The girl's father was furious when he heard the request, for Anna was his only daughter, and the bodyguard was sure to be nothing but a fortune hunter.

Some time passed, and Anna gave birth to a sweet little prince. The nobleman said to the guard: "If you reach the top of the mountain made of glass and steal three golden feathers from the tail of the dragon there, I will let you marry my daughter."

The guard began the long march to the mountain. On his way, he passed through a kingdom and had to report the purpose of his visit to the local ruler. When the king learned that the young man was on his way to the dragon, he told him to ask about the golden chain that he had lost some time ago. The soldier would not be able to travel through his kingdom unless he put that question to the dragon.

A year later he was given a task by another king: "I have a fig tree that bears no fruit. Ask the dragon why!"

Another year passed and he met two ferrymen, who wondered how long they would have to keep rowing across the river until the curse on them was lifted.

Finally the guard reached the glass mountain. Since the dragon was not at home, the soldier told his story to the dragon's wife. She fidgeted and squirmed, and then said: "I'm not allowed to let anyone in the house. When my husband returns, you won't be safe." The guard pleaded with her until finally she agreed to let him hide in a corner of the room. She brought him something to eat, and he fell asleep. The dragon came home, ate and drank, and then he fell into a deep sleep. While he was snoring, his wife pulled a golden feather from his tail. He woke up and shouted: "Why did you give me a shove?"

"Oh," she replied, "I was just dreaming about a king who lost a golden chain, and he wanted to know where it was."

"It's at the bottom of a very dark dungeon. If it stays there for one more year, it will belong to me." He went back to sleep. His wife pulled out a second feather. "Why are you pinching me?"

"I was dreaming about a fig tree that bears no fruit."

"A forbidden fruit is buried beneath it." She pulled out a third feather and asked about the two ferrymen who were waiting to be liberated. The dragon was now infuriated, but he told her: "The next time they row someone across, they must shout, 'We're free!'"

The bodyguard traveled back home. When the two rowers saw him, they shouted over to him and asked if he had found a solution. He told them to row him to the other side, and then he repeated what the dragon had said.

Next came the king with the fig tree. The guard told him about the forbidden fruit under the tree and was rewarded with an army and lots of money. A year later he reached the king who was looking for his lost chain. The king started digging in the right place, and there it was. At last the guard could ride back home.

The young man had been away for six years, and in that time the nobleman had gone broke and was now selling dishes. The guard wanted to get revenge, and he rode to the marketplace with his soldiers and ordered them to break all the dishes. The nobleman protested, and the guard threw some money at his feet: "Here you go, old man. Buy yourself some new dishes!" The next day, the guard had the dishes destroyed again. "Have you figured out who I am?" The nobleman did not recognize him until the guard showed him the three feathers taken from the dragon. The nobleman thanked him and expressed his genuine remorse. Now he was finally willing to give the king's bodyguard the hand of his daughter in marriage. He himself received a good position at the court, and so they all lived happily ever after.

THE SCORNED PRINCESS

Three soldiers who had finished their tour of duty were on the way home and decided to spend the night in the woods. To protect themselves from wild animals, they built a bonfire and then took turns keeping watch during the night.

The first to hold watch was a miller's son. While he was standing guard, an old woman came and tiptoed around the fire, pleading with the young man, for God's sake, to let her warm her bones by the fire. He was about to say no when she promised to give him a little hat that had the power to take him wherever he wanted. The soldier tried it out, and the hat really was able to whisk him away and then bring him back again. And so he gave the little old lady what she wanted, and he kept the hat for himself. He also warned the old woman that the next man on watch was a rather gruff chap. "You had better leave as soon as he comes on duty. He might hurt you!" She left without any words of complaint.

The second soldier had just begun standing guard when the old woman reappeared and went over to the fire to warm her bones. He was also annoyed when he saw what she was doing, and he began to threaten her. But she promised him an enchanted horn. "If you blow into the little hole here, then soldiers, exiled and homeless, from all over will come marching out of this larger opening, and they will stand at attention, ready to serve you. If you do the opposite, they will all vanish and go back into the horn." He tried out the power of the magic horn, and it worked just as the old woman had told him. He kept the gift and let the woman warm her bones. Toward morning he told her: "Get ready to leave, for the third watchman is Fortunatus, a shepherd's son, and he has no manners at all. He will not put up with an old woman as company." He went over to Fortunatus, the most ferocious of the trio, and woke him up so that he could take over the shift.

The old woman went right up to Fortunatus, and her voice trembled as she pleaded with him to let her stay by the fire. The new watchman was rude to her, but when she offered him a magic purse filled with gold, one that would be constantly replenished and eventually make him the richest man in the land, the cheeky fellow grabbed the purse, tried out its power, and was delighted with the trade. He let the old woman warm her bones.

The next day the three went back on the road, but they did not swap stories about what had happened that night. They stopped at an inn, where they ate and drank without knowing how they would settle the bill. In the end, the third fellow paid the tab, and after that, the three told each other about the marvelous gifts they had each received from the woman in the woods.

They returned to the road in high spirits, but before long each went his separate way. The fellow with the purse emptied it several times for his pals, and they returned home, married, and were rich and happy. Fortunatus, on the other hand, thought it would be more pleasant and cheery to spend some time indulging in life's pleasures. And so he traveled great distances. His good looks, his wealth, and the lavish feasts he hosted earned him respect wherever he went.

The king, who believed that Fortunatus was a prince from another kingdom, invited him to the castle. The king's daughter fell madly in love with him and was hoping that Fortunatus would ask her father for her hand in marriage. But Fortunatus was unwilling, and that made her all the more lovesick. The princess was sure that he was harboring some kind of dark secret, and she tried to figure out why he was so completely indifferent to her. She brought him the finest foods and set the finest wines before him, and finally he revealed his secret. Then he fell into a deep sleep. While he was asleep, she took his magic purse and had another one made just like it. She filled it up with gold coins and put it in his pocket. When he woke up, she told him again that she wanted to be married, and when he refused, she sent him away.

He was back on the road again. When the purse failed to fill itself back up, Fortunatus knew right away who was responsible. He could no longer pay his servants, and before long, they abandoned him. In order to eat, he had to sell his fine garments. He called on the princess but was turned back at the door and then banned from the city.

Poor as a beggar, he decided to go see his war comrades. After all, since he had made them wealthy, they would never let him starve. He went to visit one of them and was recognized right away. He was given a bed, new clothes, and enough money to live without worrying about the next day. The comrade even presented him with the wishing hat given to him by the old woman, for he no longer needed it. Wearing new clothes, carrying a purse of gold, and sporting a wishing hat on his head, Fortunatus returned to the princess. She was astonished to see him back in his former glory and was sure that he would now agree to what she wanted. But once again she was wrong. Using the same means as before, she got him to tell her everything. Then, when he was asleep, she exchanged his wishing hat for an ordinary hat. He discovered soon enough that he had been fooled again.

He was back on the road, now on foot, and once the money in the purse was used up, he visited the second comrade and told him about his double misfortune. Again he was given a purse filled with gold, and the magic horn to boot. After all, it was just sitting there and never put to use.

Filled with thoughts of revenge, Fortunatus returned to the king's city, the place where so many terrible things had happened to him. At the gates, he blew his horn, and lo and behold, behind him was an entire army of soldiers bearing weapons, some on foot, some on horseback. He surrounded the city and was thinking about blockading it and starving everyone in it. The terrified monarch invited the warlord—who was already atop the city wall—to come in and dine with him. Fortunatus accepted, and the princess had no trouble figuring out who he was. She sat at his side during the banquet, and once again she used her craft to extract from him what she wanted. He succumbed to her seductions, but then he blew into his horn to command his army to retreat. During the night she exchanged the magical horn for an ordinary one, and when the young man refused to propose, he was condemned to death by the king. Fortunatus blew on the horn again, but no one came to his rescue. He was certain that he was lost, but just then, the princess, who had not given up hope, let him escape from the city undetected.

Once again he was on the road, poor and practically starving, when he saw a tree with wondrously beautiful apples hanging from it. He picked one of them and ate it as fast as he could. As soon as he finished the apple, a horn appeared on his forehead. He was beside himself and cursed the tree that had duped him so badly. He went back on the road, hungry as ever, and saw another apple tree. Even though he knew he might sprout a second horn, he ate one of the apples. But lo and behold, as soon as he finished the apple, the horn fell off his forehead. Overjoyed, he took a few of those apples with him and then went back to get some more apples from the first tree.

He returned to the city where the king ruled, disguised as a fruit peddler this time. He had picked the most beautiful apples from the first tree and set them out for display right beneath the princess's chambers. She happened to look out the window and saw those wondrously beautiful apples and was determined to buy some no matter what they cost. The peddler quickly sold his wares and had a nice piece of change in his pocket. Just as quickly he raced off to the city to buy new clothes so that he would not be recognized.

The princess tasted the apples with her chambermaid. As soon as they finished eating just one, each sprouted an ugly horn on her forehead. Sobs and screams could be heard coming from the princess's chambers. None of the doctors, who had been summoned from all over, knew what to do. Proclamations were issued, offering a royal reward for the person who could find a remedy to cure the evil. No one showed up. The news reached Fortunatus at last, and he was overjoyed that his trick had worked. He returned to the city in which the king was living and declared at the castle that he possessed the means to rid the princess of the deformity on her forehead. Disguising himself as a priest practiced in the art of healing, he arrived at the castle. The king went to test the "priest" by asking him to heal the chambermaid first. The "doctor" handed her the apple from the second tree, and the horn fell off.

The king was elated and took the priest to his daughter. When he stood before the princess, he told the kneeling girl, just as if he were a priest, to confess anything that was on her conscience; otherwise he would not have the power to cure her. The princess obeyed and told him about the man who had scorned her love several times now and how she had found revenge. The priest told her to give him everything she had stolen from the man. The unhappy princess gave him the purse, the hat, and the horn, and he in turn gave her the apple. As soon as she finished eating it, a second horn sprouted from her forehead.

Quickly, he put on the hat and wished himself to the top of a mountain near the city. Then he blew on the horn, and before long he had an army as strong as the previous one. He used it to attack the city. Once he had conquered it, he burned it to the ground. The king and his daughter perished in the flames, as did everyone in the court.

The victor ruled over the entire country and for a long time he reigned as king.

PART II

ENCHANTED
ANIMALS

THE TALKING BIRD, THE SINGING TREE, AND THE SPARKLING STREAM

A nobleman had three daughters, each more beautiful than the next. One day the girls were sitting in the royal gardens, chattering away about their wishes and dreams. The eldest wanted to marry the king's counselor, the second hoped to marry his chamberlain, and the third declared that she would be quite satisfied with the king himself. It happened that the king was also in the gardens, and he overheard the entire conversation. He summoned the three sisters to ask them what they had been talking about in the garden. The first two confessed everything; the youngest was less eager to do so. But then all at once the king declared: "Your three wishes will be granted."

Even though his mother was opposed to the wedding, the king decided to marry the youngest of the three daughters of the nobleman. While he was with his troops, the queen gave birth to a beautiful boy.

The king's mother and a wicked confidante put the queen's child into a basket and set it out on the water. They told the king that his wife had given birth to a small dog. The king was so upset that he had his wife locked up in a tower. When he returned, however, he relented and was glad to take her back.

The king's wife gave birth to a second beautiful boy, once again while the king was away. That boy suffered the same fate as his brother. The king was told that his wife had given birth to a cat. Enraged, he ordered his wife imprisoned. But once again, when he returned, he was willing to forgive her right away, for he loved her dearly. The queen gave birth a third time, now to a wondrously beautiful girl, who suffered the same fate at the hands of the evil queen. Yet again the king forgave his wife, and she was back in his good graces.

The three baskets with the children in them washed up, one after another, on the shores, near where a fisherman made his home. The fisherman and his wife were happy to raise the three orphans, for they had no children of their own. When the foster parents died, the three siblings inherited the land and the house on it.

One day an old man came to visit them. He told them that they could make their fortune by going to a distant mountain and fetching a talking bird, a singing tree, and water from a sparkling stream the color of gold. The eldest of the brothers decided to go, and when he arrived at the mountain, the old man was already waiting for him. "Take the bird first, then a branch from the tree, and finally water from the stream. But don't turn around, because if you do, you will be turned into a pillar of stone." The young man was too curious for his own good. He turned around and was changed into stone.

The second brother followed the advice of the man and refused to turn around, no matter how much screaming and shouting he heard behind him. He took the bird, clipped a branch from the tree, and filled a flask with water from the sparkling stream. And that's when the curse was lifted from his brother and all the others who had been turned into stone.

When he returned home he put the bird into a beautiful cage, planted the branch in the garden, and made a little hole in the ground for the water. The branch quickly grew into a tree, and its leaves played melodious tunes that wafted in the breezes. The king and the queen heard the sounds and followed them to the house of the siblings. "Now you can jump for joy; your father and mother are here," the bird sang. When the king heard those words, he went into the garden, saw his beautiful children, and learned everything that had happened from the bird. The king was overjoyed to discover his very own children, and he returned home with them. The queen's confidante was burned at the stake. The old queen herself was already dead, and so she escaped the punishment she deserved.

THE WEASEL

A weasel, white as snow, was frolicking about in a meadow, moving around as quickly and gracefully as a will-o'-the-wisp. Some boys ran by with their dogs and started chasing the little animal, until it collapsed, exhausted and surrounded by the dogs. A little girl was standing nearby, and she felt so sorry for the small creature that she picked it up, held it tight, and made those nasty boys run away. All she had with her was an egg, and she offered it to the weasel, who gobbled up the whole thing, even licking out the shell. As soon as the little animal had finished its meal, it disappeared, perky and happy. The eggshell left behind, as it turned out, was as heavy as the inside of the egg. And it had a dull sheen as if made of silver, and it was.

At home the girl kept a hen, and every day it laid one egg. After the girl's trip to the meadow, the hen started laying two eggs a day, right on a rocky slope where the weasel made its home. When those eggs were cracked, their shells turned into silver in the course of the day. The girl soon became wealthy. She became more and more beautiful and would have had many proposals, but she had no interest in marrying any of the oafish farmhands who came around to see her.

One day the girl brought the little animal an Easter egg that had been blessed by the priest. When the weasel crawled out of its hole and started nibbling on the egg in the girl's hand, the egg burst into flames that shot up as high as a palace. The dazed girl came to her senses and awoke as if from a deep sleep. Suddenly, she was in a grand palace, and next to her was a handsome young prince, holding her in his arms.

Through compassion, and with the help of the consecrated egg, the courageous girl had lifted the curse put on the weasel and turned him back into a prince. Before long she became his wife.

THE KNIGHT'S SASH

A hunter's widow had a son named Hans, and the two were without a home and always on the move. One day they were lost in the woods, but in the distance they could see a castle. It turned out that a giant was living there. He took them in and eventually married the widow. The little boy was quite happy, and when he grew older, he went out every day to hunt deer.

While looking for game one day, Hans discovered a clearing. He saw a tree with no branches at all, and hanging from its tippy-top was a sash, the kind worn by knights. The boy shinnied up the tree and took it back down with him. On it he could read the words: "Whoever puts me on and wears me will have superhuman strength." He put the sash on, shot a deer, and carried it home on his back. His mother and the giant could not believe their eyes. They started worrying about the boy's amazing strength and began to plot to get rid of him.

The two hatched a scheme that started with the giant feigning an illness, for which the only cure was milk from a lion. Not so far away there was a mother lion living in a cave, and she was nursing her cubs. Hans was so obliging that he decided to try to bring back some milk from her for his stepfather, the giant. When he reached the cave, the lion was standing on her back paws, and her front paws were clasped together as if she were pleading for something. Hans threw his weapons aside, and he playfully stroked the cat's fur. The lion followed him to the castle. When the parents saw Hans strolling along with the lion, they decided they would have to send him on a more dangerous mission.

Not far away from where they lived was another castle, belonging to another giant. A tree was growing on his property, and it had special apples on its branches. Hans was supposed to fetch a few of them, because they would cure his stepfather. This time Hans left without the slightest idea about how to bring back those apples. He reached the castle, which was built right by the seaside. It was locked up tightly, for the giant was out with his friends, robbing and looting wherever he could. First Hans grabbed some of the apples from the tree in the garden and then he picked the lock on the castle door, entered the castle, and discovered a woman there. She was stark naked and tied up. She told Hans that she was a princess and that the giants had kidnapped her. Hans started a huge fire and the smoke from it drew the attention of the army in the princess's country, revealing her location. Before long, ships landed, and men from the neighboring country made preparations to bring the princess back home. They asked Hans to come with them, but he explained that he had to bring the special apples back to his father.

Hans was no longer in favor with his own family. His mother began trying to figure out the source of his strength. One day she noticed the sash he was wearing. She prepared a bath for her son and persuaded him to take the sash off and put it where it would stay dry. Then she took the sash to the giant, who wasted no time at all making sure that he was rid of Hans. He poked both his eyes out and threw him out of the castle. The lion was right there at the door and served her blind master as a guide.

Exhausted from his travels, Hans paused to rest for a while. Just when he was about to die of thirst, a wine merchant happened to be traveling down the road. The lion jumped up on his wagon, shoved a barrel down from it, and took it over to Hans. The merchant saw what had happened, and he felt so sorry for the blind man that he offered him a ride. When they entered the city, the princess happened to be looking out her window and recognized the man who had rescued her. She dashed down the stairs, embraced him, and took him to an artist for a pair of artificial eyes. Then she and Hans went to see her father, the king, who was so happy to have the young man as a son-in-law that he named him his successor.

During the festivities after the wedding, someone noticed that Hans was blind. The news about his blindness traveled quickly among the people, and they decided that they did not want a blind man as their king. There was rioting in the streets and, along with the princess, Hans was sent into exile.

The two were forced to lead a nomadic life. The princess loved her husband and took good care of him. They sat down one day, by a brook, to rest from their travels. Out of nowhere two mice appeared, one blind, the other able to see. The one that could see guided the blind one to the brook and sprinkled some water from it on its eyes. The other mouse was suddenly able to see. The princess did not hesitate for a moment to repeat what the mouse had done, and suddenly Hans could see again. And so the two returned to their kingdom, where they received a rousing welcome. They lived together happily for a long time, and when Hans died, the lion lay down on his grave and stayed there until she, too, was dead.

THE GIRL AND THE COW

There was once a rich miller with three daughters. He kept some cows in a stable, and one of them would leave every day at noon and return late at night. No one knew where she had gone or what she had been doing.

The eldest of the three daughters said to the cow one day, just as it was about to leave: "Let me go with you!"

"You can come along," the cow replied. And so the girl followed behind the cow. They reached a small lake. The girl was terrified when she saw the cow wading into the water and preparing to swim across the lake. The cow told her to hold on to its tail and to come across with her. Before long they reached the other side, and the two were standing before a wondrously beautiful castle. The girl was eager to go inside, and the cow called out: "Don't stay too long! I'll shout your name out three times. If you don't return when I call your name the third time, it means that you will have to stay in the castle."

The eldest daughter walked around in the castle and was astonished by the beauty of the rooms and the precious objects housed in them. She was especially taken by some magnificently beautiful clothes spread out in one room, and she feasted her eyes on everything. She stayed inside until the cow called out her name a second time. Then she quickly grabbed a few of the splendid garments and rushed down to where the cow was standing. The cow took her across the water in the same way that they had come, and they returned home.

When the girl showed her sisters her fabulous clothes and told them everything that had happened, the middle sister wanted to swim across the lake with the cow to the castle. The cow agreed, and everything happened just as it had with the first sister. She returned home, laden with beautiful clothes.

On the third day, the youngest and most beautiful of the three girls said: "My dear cow! My sisters went off with you, and each brought home precious things. Now it's my turn!" She followed the cow, and the two crossed the lake and reached the castle. The princess went into the castle without heeding the cow's warning.

Once she was inside the castle, the youngest passed through hallways and rooms, dazzled by the beauty of the place and all the precious things in it. But she was perfectly satisfied with doing nothing but looking at all the wonderful things everywhere she turned. She was so absorbed in contemplating them that she did not hear the cow call her name a second time. The third time she ran downstairs, but the cow had already left and was swimming back across the lake. The youngest of the miller's daughters had to stay right where she was. She consoled herself with the thought that the cow would probably return the next day. And she walked up the staircase into the castle and went to bed.

At midnight, her sleep was interrupted by a ghastly screech. Suddenly the door to her bedroom opened, and a big black cat stepped into the room. It lay down right next to her and ordered her to cut off its tail when the clock struck twelve. The girl didn't want to do that, but the cat threatened to kill her if she would not.

The poor girl had to go down to the basement with the cat. There was a chopping block and an ax down there. When the clock struck midnight, the girl took the ax and used it to chop off the cat's tail. The cat immediately disappeared. The girl went back up to her room, lay down in bed, and was hoping to get back to sleep.

When she woke up the next morning, a handsome man was sleeping next to her. He owned the castle, and a wicked witch had turned him into a cat. He thanked her for lifting the curse, and then he showed her everything in the castle and offered to make it hers. He asked for her hand in marriage. The girl agreed, and the two enjoyed a long and happy life together.

THE CALL OF THE
SHEPHERD'S HORN

A white calf trotted over to a princess one day and settled down to live with her from that day on. The calf played with her every day and slept by her side. The princess grew up to be a beautiful young woman, and many men sought her hand in marriage, but none could separate her from that white cow. Whenever the cow was endangered in any way at all, the princess would let out a scream, as if someone had punched her. One very persistent suitor went so far as to draw his sword and threaten to kill the cow. He scratched a spot on its hide, and the princess began to bleed in the exact same place. The king finally decided to make an announcement: "Whoever can free my daughter from this monster will have her as his wife!"

Not far from the castle there lived a poor woman with her son. She owned a flock of sheep, too. She sent the boy to the king with a horn. As soon as the young shepherd blew on the horn, the cow perked up its ears, leaped into the air, and ran over to him. The king was delighted. He told the boy to return home, and he began making preparations for a royal wedding to a prince. The shepherd felt humiliated and blew on his horn again. At that, the cow returned to the castle and trampled everything within sight of the princess. A second try to get rid of the cow failed, and the king had to make peace with the fact that the cow was there to stay.

One day the king lost his way in the woods while hunting.

He discovered a cottage in ruins. Next to its entrance there was a big rock with a shepherd's horn on it. The king sat down on the rock. He wanted to give the other hunters a signal, and so he blew on the horn.

As soon as the horn sounded, the white cow came racing down toward the king and attacked him with its sharp horns. The king went into the cottage and shut the door tight, but the wood of the door was rotten and split into big chunks that landed on top of the king and knocked him down. He was now on his back, and the cow was bellowing as it pawed the ground and stomped on the wooden door.

Suddenly it was completely quiet. The king freed himself from the cow, stood up, and saw an old woman standing before him. "You probably do not recognize me," she said. "But you will more than likely remember this ring!"

The king looked carefully at her. "Of course!" he cried out. "You are my dear wife from long ago! I stupidly believed that an accusation made against you was true, but someone had deceived me. I decided to spend one last night with you, and this is the ring you took from my finger before I left! But what happened to the stone that was in the ring?"

"I've been asking myself that same question," his wife replied, "ever since our child was turned into a white calf." The king was alarmed when he heard this news. "That must have been the work of the evil magician up on the mountain!" he cried. He drew his sword, cut a few hairs from the white cow, took the ring, and threw everything into the flames at the hearth. Suddenly there was a thunderous noise in the cottage, and the flames leaped up to the ceiling. The fire went out. There on the ground was the ring with its precious stone. And instead of a cow, a beautiful young woman was kneeling on the floor.

The hut had burned to the ground, and suddenly there was a great commotion all around it. The king's subjects arrived with torches, as did the princess, and then finally the young shepherd. "Here is the daughter that I lost," the king said. "And here is her mother, who is a countess. I am going to keep my word, and I will give my daughter's hand to the man who liberated her. He is in reality the son of a countess from an aristocratic house."

The wedding was celebrated in great splendor, and they lived happily and peacefully for many a year.

THE MARK OF THE DOG, PIG, AND CAT

Once there was a good king who was married to an evil woman. The queen poisoned him so that she would be able to rule until the day when her son, the prince, came of age.

When the prince grew up and was crowned king, his mother chose a variety of brides for him, but he rejected all her choices and picked a bride whose dowry was nothing more than virtue and beauty. His mother felt insulted by the choice and began to contemplate revenge. She made an alliance with the royal midwife.

While the king was at war, his wife bore a beautiful son, and the midwife took him and substituted a little dog for the child. The king received a message about the strange birth, but he was not upset and imagined that something had just gone wrong.

Once again the king had to go to battle, and his wife gave birth to a second beautiful boy. The midwife put a pig in place of the child. The king heard the news, and once again he forgave the queen and thought that something must have gone wrong.

Before he left for war a third time, he told his mother that he could not stand the idea of another deformed creature instead of a child. The mother took in his words. And when the queen gave birth to a third child, a kitten was substituted for the child.

The king returned and his wife was nowhere to be found. His mother explained that her daughter-in-law had given birth for a third time to an animal. "That must be a punishment for adultery. I thought I was doing you a favor when I had that guilty woman drowned." The king went into mourning, for he had loved the queen with all his heart.

The mother searched in vain for a new bride. Her son became withdrawn, and he stopped seeing his friends. He spent most of his time in the woods, weeping silently in a quiet place.

Many years later he lost his way in the woods while on a hunt. He followed a babbling brook and reached a mill. Six boys were playing there together, and three of them were especially tall and handsome. He took a closer look and noticed that one of the boys reminded him of his wife; another had his own features.

While they were playing, one of the boys muddied his hands, but he didn't go to the nearby well to wash up. Instead he went down to the brook. When the king asked him why the brook, he replied: "I go down there instead of to the well, because the water in the well rushed away from under my mother's feet." The king asked the boy where his mother was, but the only reply he received was that she was "in the water."

Later that day, one of the other boys tore a hole in his pants. He picked up needle and thread and started to repair them. The thread was too thick for the needle, and he went down to the brook to wet it. The king asked why he was going all the way down there, and he was given the same answer that he received from the other boy.

The third boy wanted to wash the ball that he had used to bowl, and he did exactly what his brothers had done.

The king was lost in thought, and he went over to the mill to ask about the boys. The miller's wife became unnerved and abruptly replied: "All of them are my children, the one as much as the other, and I love them all equally."

The king went down to the brook and stayed there until night fell. Something lit up in the thickets surrounding him, and he followed the light. But before long he gave in to his exhaustion and fell asleep under a tree.

When he awoke in the morning, he could hear water splashing nearby, right where the undergrowth was the thickest. Curious about the source, he bent the branches apart and saw a beautiful woman perched on a branch over the water, splashing her feet. It was his wife. His astonishment was great, but his joy at being reunited with her was even greater. The queen gently said to him: "My mother-in-law brought me here and thought I would end up starving and freezing to death. The wood sprites kept me from starving by giving me food during the day. They braided my hair and brought me fresh garments whenever mine were wet. I moved my legs back and forth to keep the water from freezing over and to keep myself from getting cold. The good little women came to visit me often, and they warmed up my feet. They comforted me by bringing news about my children. And they promised that my reputation would be restored and that I would see my children again."

The wood sprites confirmed what the queen had said. They dressed the poor woman in beautiful clothes and gave her jewels to wear. Then they pointed her in the direction of the mill, where she would be able to find her children.

The three handsome boys were already running toward her. They rushed into the arms of their mother, whom they recognized from a picture given to them by the wood sprites.

The miller's wife came over to them and said: "I'm going to stop calling these boys my children. I have three boys of my own. Every time I gave birth, my husband would discover a container that had washed on shore. And there would be a baby lying in it. The children were so beautiful and they smiled at me in such a charming way that I could not bear to part with them. My husband agreed to keep them and raise them as if they were our own. Take a look at the arms of the boys. They are all tattooed—one with a dog, the second with a pig, and the last with a cat."

The king blew on his horn. His retinue appeared and he introduced his wife and the three princes to them. He asked everyone around to name the punishment for someone who had treated his family so badly. The answer came: "That person deserves to be drawn and quartered." And that's exactly what happened to the evil old woman.

The royal couple lived happily ever after in peace, and they remained grateful all their lives to the miller's wife as well as to the wood sprites.

THE THREE-LEGGED GOATS

Three young men, a tailor, a miller, and a soldier, found themselves lost in the woods one day. It was growing dark, and they still could not find a way out. The tailor decided to climb to the top of a tree, and from there he could see a light in the distance. He started walking in that direction, without saying a word to his companions, until he reached a castle. The first room he entered had nothing in it but three-legged goats and cats. Some of the cats were playing the fiddle on tables and benches; others were dancing to the tunes. The tailor was hungry, so he sat down and ate some food. Once he was done, he stuffed his pockets with good things to eat and went back to give some of the food to his companions. After the tailor returned, the miller also climbed up that same tree, saw the light, found the castle, and discovered everything the tailor had found.

The soldier was eager to go to the castle as well. He found everything his companions had described, but he stayed a little longer. Once a full hour had passed, he was no longer able to leave. The dancing and singing came to a halt. Suddenly a young woman dressed in black appeared and gave him a staff made of iron along with seven candlesticks. He was supposed to use those objects to disenchant her. If he failed, he would die.

The next night the soldier painted a circle on the floor of the dance hall. Then he placed the lit candles around the perimeter and stepped inside the circle. The cats and goats arrived soon enough and blew out all the candles but one, which they just could not put out. They tried to lure the soldier out of the circle and began to attack him. But whenever one of them got close to him, he poked it with the staff, and then it was swallowed up by the earth. At midnight, the spooks all vanished.

The young lady dressed in black reappeared in the morning. Her arms had turned white, and the soldier spent some time with her. On the next night, the exact same things happened, but the attacks became more vicious. The soldier struck his staff on the ground three times and was able to ward off the mysterious animals. By the morning the young woman's dress had turned half-white, and she told him to hit one of the three-legged goats so hard that it would burst into pieces. He should then pick up all of the pieces and put one into each corner of the castle. He finished on the third night, and now the young woman was completely white and the spell was broken. Soldiers were standing watch in every corner of the castle, and the cats and goats had turned into human beings.

The soldier and the princess, released from the spell, were married, and they lived happily together. But before long the soldier began to feel homesick and was longing to see his parents. His wife agreed to let him leave, and she gave him a wishing ring: "If you turn it three times to the right, you will be able to wish yourself anywhere you want. If you turn it three times to the left, I will appear before you."

When the soldier arrived back home, his parents simply could not believe that so many good things had happened to him. He took out the ring, turned it three times to the left, and the princess appeared right there in the shabby hut. She was so dismayed when she saw the circumstances in which her husband had been raised that she took the ring and disappeared with it that very night. Her husband did not want to lose her, and he searched everywhere for her.

At the top of a mountain, he met up with three thieves who were quarreling about how to divide up three valuable stolen objects: a coat that could blow harder than the wind, boots that let you run rapidly, and a sack of gold. The soldier cut an apple up into different-sized pieces and said to the thieves: "I'm going to throw these three pieces down into the valley.

Whoever comes back with the biggest piece will own the valuable coat." That suited the three just fine. But while they were racing to find the pieces of the apple, the soldier put on the boots, threw the coat over his shoulders, and sprinted to the castle with the sack of gold. He decided to conceal his identity there, and so he asked innocently for news at a shoemaker's house. "Tomorrow the princess is getting married!"

"I have to be there for that!" he said, and everyone burst out laughing, because he looked so pathetic.

The next morning he walked over to the church and threw the coat over his shoulders. A terrible gust of wind blasted through the place, picking up all the wedding guests and depositing them in the very same place where they had come from. The princess was at the castle when a stranger came calling. She recognized her husband right away but asked her father: "What should I do? Should I choose a new broom or take back the old one?"

Her father gave her some good advice: "Sometimes old brooms work better than new ones, which just sweep dirt into corners."

She decided to take back the soldier, and he was now in her good graces. From then on, the two lived happily and peacefully.

THE TRAVELING ANIMALS

A man who owned some horses kept a big dog out in the pasture. But instead of herding the horses together when it rained, the dog would just run away. The animal began worrying: "What should I do? If my master sees that the horses have run away, he will beat me to death. It's best for me if I run away." On the road, he met up with an old tomcat and asked: "My dear cat, where are you headed?" The cat told him that his master wanted to have him skinned, because he was now too old to catch mice. And so he had run off into the woods. The dog and the cat went on their way together.

A little later they met a rooster who also seemed to be at loose ends. He started complaining to the two others: "The farmer who kept me went drinking and dancing and gambling every day and returned home late at night. Exhausted from long nights of carousing, he threatened to wring my neck if I woke him up. But I couldn't stop myself, for I just have to crow at a certain time, even if you put a lock on my beak. That's why I ran off." The dog and the cat invited the rooster to join them.

They then met a fox. "Where are you headed?" the rooster asked.

"I go wherever I can find something to eat," he said, leering at the rooster. "But now that I've lost my teeth, I often go hungry." And so the fox joined up with the trio.

Then an ancient ox, with ribs that stuck out from its sides like the teeth of a rake, linked up with them. The ox had

worked like a dog all its life and was given little to eat, and
now his master was planning to sell him to the butcher. And
so he was hoping to run away. He and an old mare complained
to the other animals about their wretched treatment, and they
went off with them.

All six of the animals traveled deeper and deeper into the
woods. Their stomachs began to growl, and the dog told the
cat to climb up a tree and see if there were any signs of life in
the vicinity. The rooster turned out to be a more agile climber
and began crowing to let the others know that he had seen a
light. The other animals were wildly excited, and they ran as
fast as they could through the underbrush until they reached a
little hovel in a clearing. The dog and the fox wanted to figure
out if anyone was living in the hut. They stole up to the house
and looked through the window, and what did they see but a
bunch of thieves sitting at a table!

The animals held a conference and made a plan to create a
ruckus out in the back. The thieves were scared out of their
wits, and they dashed out of the house. Now the new guests
were able to make themselves at home. The rooster did not fail
to find some grain left in a pot on the stove, and it began
downing what was in there. There were plenty of oats in the
stable for the nag, and in the barn there were piles of hay and
straw for the ox. As for the dog, the fox, and the cat, they
found plenty of butter, flour, eggs, and meat in the cabinets.
There was room at the table for everyone.

At midnight, the thieves decided to send the dullard in their
group back to the house to see what was going on. He crept up
to the house from a distance, and since he couldn't hear anything, he went over to the oven and looked up at the ceiling.
Just then the rooster dropped something unspeakable on his
nose. When he reached the stable, the nag kicked up her legs
and hit him on the head. In the barn, the ox used its horns to
pick him up and throw him out. In the kitchen, the cat
scratched his face, and the dog bit him hard on the ankles.

The robber hightailed it out of there and told his companions
about the ferocious fellows who had taken over their house. "I

was treated horribly by them, and they hit me, pushed me, stuck me, scratched me, and bit me. I'd rather face the gallows than go back to that place."

The thieves did not dare to return to the house. And so the animals became good friends and lived a happy life in the den of the thieves. They lived peacefully until the day they died.

THE SNAKE'S TREASURE

 A shepherd was getting on in years, but he still spent a good part of each day in the woods with his flock. Every now and then he would hear a wondrous melody, but he had no idea where it was coming from. One day he discovered a beautiful woman up near the top of a mountain. She beckoned to him and said: "I want you to come back tomorrow and pick me out from among the snakes in this grotto. Then you must give me a kiss. I will have a key in my mouth, and you can take it out. Don't be afraid, even if I leap into the air. It will only be out of pure joy. If you think you are not up to the task, you can just leave now, but, better yet, bring three men with you tomorrow. There will be plenty for all four of you." The shepherd decided against asking others to join him, for he wanted the treasure all to himself.

The next day he went to the grotto and found the snake there, with the key right in her mouth. She leaped into the air for joy. The shepherd became frightened. He tried to take the key out of her mouth three times, but each time she recoiled. Discouraged, he went back home. While he was tending his sheep the next day, he could hear a woman weeping in the distance. Once again he saw her high up on the mountain, and she beckoned to him. "Your greed kept you from bringing along a few other men," she said. "You would have all received more than enough. And now I will continue to suffer. Seeds will be sown in the forest, then a tree will grow, and someone will saw boards from the timber and make a crib from it. The first child who sleeps in that crib will be able to lift the curse on me." She disappeared, all sobs and tears. When the shepherd turned around, he saw the snake slither into a crevice in the rocks.

THE SNAKE SISTER

A merchant had two children. One was named Hans; the other, Annie. The merchant's wife had died some time ago, leaving him alone. Annie had a friend whose mother was said to be a witch. She made Annie so ill with her sorcery that neither doctors nor baths could cure her. "Tell your father that you won't get better until he marries me." The father went ahead with the marriage for the sake of his child. After the wedding, he disappeared without a trace.

Hans lived in one of the two houses the merchant had abandoned, and beautiful Annie lived in the other one with her stepmother and her ugly daughter. Annie had to wait on both of them, and her life was hard, with little to eat. Whenever her brother came over for a visit, the best foods were served so that he would think his sister was in good hands. One day he discovered the truth, and he decided to go away and seek his fortune as quickly as possible. He gave his sister a shiny knife, thrust it into the trunk of a tree, and said to her: "If this knife ever gets rusty, it means that I have taken a bad turn. But if it stays shiny, that's a sign that I will be back." He left for the wide, wide world after saying those words, and then he was gone.

The old witch pretended to be ill and sent Annie to the zoo to fetch some water from the well of healing that was over there. The water was supposed to cure her, but the witch knew that the well was guarded by all kinds of wild animals. She was hoping that they would tear the girl to pieces and then she would inherit her husband's entire fortune.

The girl walked over to the zoo. A dwarf was guarding the

entrance and asked: "Why are you here?" Because she gave an honest answer, the dwarf gave her a crust of bread, which she was then supposed to toss to the wild animals. That meant she could scoop out as much water as she wanted, without risking her life. That's what happened, and when the girl left with the water from the well, she heard a voice:

> "Stop!
> Scrub me clean, wash me fresh,
> Heaven may greet me in the flesh."

She saw a skull, washed it clean with the water she had, and was about to go back for more when a second skull made the same request, and then a third one too. She took care of all three of them, and just as she was about to return home, the first skull called out to her:

"May you become even more beautiful than you already are!"

And the second called out:

"May you succeed in everything you decide to do!"

And the third called out:

"May you become a queen, even if it means that you are first turned into a snake!"

And so Annie returned home, looking radiantly beautiful.

The old woman was wildly jealous, and she sent her own daughter to the well so that she would become just as beautiful. The girl encountered the three skulls and washed them all, but then she threw them back in the mud. When she turned to go home, the first skull cried out to her:

"May you return home even uglier than you already are!"

And the second cried out:

"May you fail at everything that you decide to do!"

And the third:

"May you be burned at the stake after you become queen of the land."

In the meantime, Hans ran out of money while he was on the road. He arrived penniless in a city ruled by a king. The king's grooms let him sleep in the stables. They noticed that every morning and every evening, the young man would remove from his pocket the picture of a wondrously beautiful young woman. He would kiss the picture and begin to weep. They told the king about it, and he ordered Hans to let him see the picture of the young woman. When he learned that she was the sister of Hans, he was beside himself with joy and declared that he was determined to make her his wife. Without delay he asked Hans to bring his sister, his stepmother, and his stepsister to the castle.

The king's castle was surrounded by a lake, which Hans had to cross with all three of the women. During the boat ride, the old woman pushed the beautiful girl into the water and turned her into a huge snake. The king was enraged when he saw the mother and her daughter, and he felt betrayed. But he had to keep the promise he had once made and marry the ugly girl. He threw Hans into a dungeon.

The old woman told her daughter to beg for mercy for Hans. The king told him that he would spare Hans's life if he built a bridge across the water, but he would be sentenced to death if he failed.

In the evening Hans sat down by the edge of the lake and began to weep. Suddenly a huge water snake appeared and said: "Don't worry. I'm going to help you. Just go to sleep and in the morning everything will be done as commanded." The bridge was there when the sun rose, but Hans was not released from the dungeon. At least now, though, he was given something to eat on a daily basis.

The old woman could find no peace, and she asked her daughter again to beg for mercy for Hans. All he had to do was build a small castle opposite the palace, so that each could be seen from the other. Hans went down to the lake again and began to weep. The water snake appeared again, comforted him, and helped him. When the sun rose, the castle had been built, and it was even more beautiful than the palace. Now Hans was given food twice a day and was allowed to walk on the grounds.

The old woman could not stop fretting as long as Hans was alive. The daughter had to beg for mercy one more time. This time Hans was ordered to bring the water snake into the court-yard. Otherwise he was a dead man. Hans walked down to the lake again, full of sorrow, and the water snake said: "Just go to sleep until sunrise. I will put my head on your shoulder, and you can carry me into the courtyard. They will chop me into bits. Don't let my right eye out of your sight. Take it, and bury it under the threshold at the entrance to the new castle, the one in which the old woman is now living."

That's exactly what happened, and now Hans was given food three times a day. One day the king was looking out the window of his palace and saw a beautiful young woman emerge from the threshold at the entrance of the new castle, but he saw her only from the waist up. It was the woman whose picture Hans had shown him. Hans was summoned at once. He recognized his sister, ran over to the castle, and dug her out using his fingers, which began to bleed. He was overjoyed and took his sister to the king.

As punishment, the old woman was torn to pieces by four horses. The false queen was burned at the stake. And beautiful Annie became the king's wife.

"FOLLOW ME, JODEL!"

 An elderly farmer had two sons, one named Michael and the other Jodel. The father was especially fond of Jodel, who had a good heart even though he was not as bright as his brother. The father was hoping to leave his farm and all his possessions to Jodel, but Michael insisted that he, as the older of the two, should inherit everything. A quarrel broke out until finally the father declared: "Whoever brings home the most beautiful silk cloth will inherit all my property." Michael headed off right away to seek the prize, but Jodel, who had never been away from home, sat down on a bench and began to brood over his misfortune.

A toad hopped over to him and asked: "Why are you so sad?" At first Jodel was reluctant to confide in the less-than-beautiful animal, but when she insisted on knowing more, he told her why he was so miserable. "Follow me, Jodel, and then you will have the most beautiful silk cloth imaginable." Jodel didn't want to crawl on the ground and get his clothes dirty. But the toad insisted and so the younger brother crawled after her until the two reached a beautiful house in the woods. The door to the house opened right away. The toad hopped up the steps and entered a hall. She sat down on the sofa and called out: "Where are you, Mouse?"

A little mouse came running in and asked, "How may I help you?"

"Bring me the trunk with the beautiful silk fabrics!" The little mouse brought the trunk in, and the toad picked out the most beautiful fabric in it. She gave it to Jodel, who ran home with a spring in his step.

The brothers compared the two cloths back at home. It was not hard to tell that Jodel had the finer one. Michael insisted on a new bet and asked their father to propose another task. This time they were supposed to bring back new jackets instead of just fabric. Michael tore off like an arrow, but Jodel sat down on the bench and began brooding again. The toad reappeared. "Jodel, come follow me!" she said, and he was given the most beautiful jacket imaginable.

Michael was really angry now, because Jodel had come home with a jacket that was more beautiful than his. He insisted on a third task, and his father said, "All right, whoever brings back the loveliest bride will have my entire estate." Unsure of what to do, Jodel sat down near the door. The toad appeared again, but Jodel didn't want to listen to her because he was sure she could not help him with this particular task. The toad did not give up on him, and she said, "Jodel, follow me!"

When they were back in the same house, the toad told Jodel, "Listen carefully and do everything that I tell you! Wash me, put me in bed, and then lie down next to me!" Jodel had to follow her orders, whether he wanted to or not. He washed her, put her under the covers, and lay down next to her. Sleeping next to that ugly animal gave him the creeps, but he soon grew tired and nodded off.

When Jodel awoke in the morning, a lovely maiden was next to him in bed. He looked around in the room, and it had turned into a radiantly splendid hall. Then he went to the window and realized that the house had been turned into a castle, with extraordinary grounds surrounding it. He rang a bell, and servants came rushing in, included the little mouse, which had been turned back into a chambermaid. The lovely maiden woke up and thanked Jodel for lifting the terrible curse put on her. She offered him her hand in gratitude, along with her entire estate. Jodel was at a loss for words at first and didn't know what to do. The maiden gave him signs of encouragement, and so he was happy to accept her offer.

A carriage drew up to the entrance, and Jodel climbed in

with his bride and rode off to his father's house. Poor Michael had returned home with a pretty young girl. But his tears of sorrow turned to joy when Jodel told him that he could keep the farm, for he now had plenty of money and did not need anything from his brother. The father of the two young men was overjoyed that Jodel was now so well situated and that Michael was content as well. He went to live with the son he liked best, and they dwelled in harmony. If they have not yet died, then they are still living happily today.

THE TOAD BRIDE

There was once a man with three sons; two were clever and the third was foolish. He gave some flax to each of them and said: "Whoever spins the finest thread will inherit my house." The two clever ones found spindles and a spinning wheel and set to work, spinning day and night. The foolish one took the flax and ran with the wind, back and forth and everywhere imaginable, through forests and swamps, until at last he found himself sinking into the mud.

Some toads started hopping toward him and one of them said: "Give me your flax, and we will set you free. But be sure to come back!" After returning home, the fellow came back. The toad gave him this order: "Take the thread with you. Then let everyone know that you are planning to marry. Be sure to put a bridal veil and dress on the altar."

The thread brought home by the third son was much finer than what his brothers had produced, and the father gave him the house. Everyone was planning to come to his wedding, but there was no bride in sight when they arrived. The church bells were ringing, and the groom was standing at the altar when a toad appeared and slipped into the wedding dress. All at once she turned into the most beautiful woman ever seen. "You set me free!" she exclaimed. "I was put under a spell by an evil witch and the curse could only be lifted when a young man needed my help. After I finished spinning the thread for you, the spell was broken." The young man married the beautiful woman, and they lived in harmony for many years.

PRINCE DUNG BEETLE

There was once a poor girl named Barbara, whose mother was ill. She had to run over to the doctor and druggist for help. On the way, she jumped across a paving stone and slipped, almost flattening a dung beetle. When she realized that she had sprained her ankle, she felt terrible and cried out: "Now who is going to bring back the doctor? My mother is going to die!"

The beetle muttered: "Climb up on my back." Startled by the strange voice, the girl began to sob uncontrollably. The beetle slid right under her, spread its wings, and lifted her up in the air, carrying her to the doctor and druggist in a flash and then back home to her mother.

"You must be sure to feed your little horse," the mother said to her daughter while they were eating bread and sipping water.

"Yes, of course, but my little horse seems to have wandered away," Barbara said. She searched every corner of the house and looked out all the windows. Suddenly one of the king's horsemen appeared on the horizon, riding toward them.

"Oh, that must be the Blue Prince," the mother called out, as if he were an old friend. The door flew open, and the prince marched right in, looking radiantly young and handsome. He greeted the mother warmly, and then he looked at the young woman, took her by the hand, and said: "You lifted the curse on me, and I want to thank you by giving you everything I own." Barbara did not know what to do, and she looked first at the prince, then at her mother. She was afraid of the stranger.

But he explained what had happened to him: "For many years, more years than there are trees in the woods, I have been living as a beetle, crawling around in dust and refuse, beaten down, crushed, tortured, and in pain, all because I did the same things to animals when I was a boy. My punishment was to turn into a beast and to suffer as they do. You took pity on me, miserable beetle that I was, and that's how you lifted the curse. I want to ask your mother for the hand of the angel who saved me!"

The girl turned pale, and both mother and daughter were deeply moved.

The prince threw open the shutters and blew on his horn. The mountains wafted the melody over the forests, and everything there awakened and came alive. Barbara and her mother began to realize that the many people who had suddenly appeared with horses and carts were the prince's subjects, and they, too, had been rescued by the love of a simple young woman. The mother was soon healed, and her beautiful, rosy-cheeked daughter joyfully accepted the prince's proposal.

At the wedding, the fleas played the fiddle, the birds whistled tunes, and all creatures with feet, large and small, danced and leaped through the air.

PART III

OTHERWORLDLY CREATURES

THE THREE SPINDLES

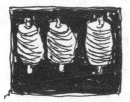 A young farmer's daughter got herself in trouble, and her parents threw her out of the house. She wandered around aimlessly until finally, in desperation, she sat down on a tree stump with three crosses carved into it. She began to weep. Suddenly a wood sprite raced toward her, pursued by a group of frenzied hunters. The girl jumped to her feet to make room for the sprite, for she knew that it would find safety there from what were known as the devil's hunters, hordes of demons that rode in with the winter storms.

The girl herself was knocked down so hard that she fainted. When she came to, the wood sprite was still sitting on the stump and asked her why she had been crying. When the sprite learned what had happened, she said: "In exchange for helping me escape those hunters, you may come with me, and all will be well."

Together they walked to a boulder with a door carved into it. When they entered, they found themselves in a clean, bright room with a little bed that looked mossy, but only a bit so. Two young wood sprites were sitting and spinning moss onto spindles. Every day one of the little women would spin a spindle full, and the older sprite would exchange the yarn for food. The farmer's daughter was supposed to do some spinning as well, but the yarn she spun was never quite as fine.

At last the day arrived when the young woman gave birth to a little boy, much to the joy of the wood sprites. They took good care of mother and child. Their only wish was that the child could stay with them forever, and the young woman decided to grant them that wish. The wood sprites gave the young mother cakes that looked as if they were made of moss but tasted like honey, along with water that tasted like wine.

After some time had passed, the wood sprite took the young mother back to the tree, right to the stump where they had first met. She took leave of her and gave her three spindles of yarn. She warned her to take good care of the spindles, for as long as they were in her home, she would want for nothing. "But if you are ever in real need, unspool some yarn—as much as you need—and you will still have as much as you started with. After that, put the spindles behind the beams of the hut, and don't let anyone see you." The wood sprite disappeared and was never seen again.

When the young woman returned home, her parents hardly recognized her, for she was covered all over with moss. Once their daughter was back home, fortune began to favor them. The daughter married and became a wealthy farmer's wife. But she never forgot her promise, and every Saturday she would bake a cake made with flour, milk, and eggs and put it down with great care on the stump in the woods.

THE LITTLE FLAX FLOWER

 There were once two young women, one pretty, the other plain, and they spent their days in the fields sowing flaxseeds. The pretty one worked in the hills; the plain one, in the valley. One day, while they were walking behind a plow, the pretty one began to sing:

"I'm searching for a love so true,
  As pure as linen through and through,
  With bright red cheeks so very dear,
  Glowing like violet and gold so clear,
  With beautiful eyes ever so blue,
  Like little flax blossoms in their hue.
  Whoever chooses me to wed,
  Will win as well both cloth and thread."

The other girl didn't sing but kept quiet. Every once in a while she would distract herself by playfully tossing a few seeds aside for the Lady of the Woods. She looked timidly up at the pretty, tall farm girl, who was as graceful as a doe and who managed to land only a small number of seeds in the furrows.

When the harvest had matured into a velvety yield, the two girls reappeared in the fields and began weeding. The pretty girl was like a purple rose. She spent much of her time standing up and gazing into the distance to see if her looks had succeeded in attracting a suitor. The bad-looking one worked hard, and she was so quick about her work that before long she had cleared the whole area of thistles and weeds. She did

not forget to take a few stalks of flax for a little hut that she
had built at the edge of the field. She called out:

> "Lady of the Woods, the Woods, the Woods,
> Here I've placed your share of the goods!
> Give the flax a nice good start,
> And let's dress up so we look smart."

The two girls went about their work in different ways, one
up in the hills looking for suitors, the other with her eyes
trained on the flax and the field. Hot weather and weeds killed
off the flax in the higher regions, while the flax in the valley
flourished and grew tall.

In the spring, after the young women had spun and woven
the flax, they both took the linen out to the fields to bleach it
in the sun. You could see right away that the pretty girl's
linen—and there was little of it—was rough, coarse, and un-
even, while the plain girl had plenty of exquisite fabric, fine as
silk. The pretty girl was upset, and she scolded the other one,
saying: "I know just how you did this, you little night owl!
You're a witch and you were in cahoots with the Lady of the
Woods. You're just as plain as she is, and just like that forest
spinster, you'll never marry."

Just then a golden carriage with four horses flew like the
wind across a path in the woods. A handsome young man was
riding in it, dressed like a prince. He stopped to greet the girls
and took the hand of the pretty one and said: "I would like to
marry you, but first I'd like to take a look at your handiwork.
Is your linen bright?"

"No, it's not!" a voice called out from the woods.

The prince let go of her hand and turned to the plain one. "I
would like to marry you. Is this your work here?"

The voice in the woods called out: "Yes, it is!"

The prince hugged her and kissed her and told her he wanted
to marry her. And just then the aroma of flowers enveloped the
two of them, and the young woman became pretty and charming. And all at once she was wearing a dress with jewels, and

the enthralled prince knelt before her. Voices whispered in the woods and carried the news up hill and down dale.

The pretty girl was overcome with envy, and she was suddenly as hideous and as unsightly as a toad.

A shining horse and carriage dashed off with the couple. The girl who had once been pretty returned to her village, weighed down by her own grief as well as by the scorn and contempt of the villagers.

Since then the young women who work in the fields no longer sing songs. And not a one forgets to bind together some of the flax stalks from the fields and make a little hut for the Lady of the Woods. They remain faithful to the customs from times past.

WOODPECKER

After a successful hunting expedition, a wealthy young count found an angelic-looking boy on his way back home. He was glad to have rescued the lost boy and decided to raise him at home, where he was put to work as a servant.

The boy grew up to be tall and strong, but he was also lazy, with no interest in doing any work at all. While the other servants were plowing, mowing, and threshing, he would be strolling in the woods or fields, singing and whistling like a bird. And that's why everyone called him Woodpecker or, just for laughs, Prince Woodpecker.

The count was well disposed toward the boy, and one day he asked him what he hoped to do later in life. The answer was:

> Woodpecker is my given name,
> I chew things up, tasty and tame;
> The hard stuff's not at all my game.
> I whistle like a little bird,
> The hardest work you've ever heard!

The nobleman replied: "I'd like to have some proof of that hard work. See that pile of wood over there in the courtyard? Chop it up into small pieces before the month is over. If you don't finish by then, I'm going to chase you off my land!" The Woodpecker was in a panic. He was a master in the art of laziness, and he was also just like the lilies of the field when it came to work. Those flowers just grew and grew, even though they could not spin or weave. It didn't take him long to figure out that he would never be able to chop up all that wood in so short a time. And the count was not about to go back on his promise to kick him off his property. And so he sat for days on end by the mountain of wood, the ax at his feet. His head was hanging like a bird in a cage. He planned and plotted, but he could not figure out how to get out of this fix.

All at once a window in the castle opened, and there was the beautiful child of the count. She had been quietly observing the tall handsome servant and was impressed by how calm he was. She called down to him to tell him that he should start working; otherwise he wouldn't be around for long. He jumped up, grabbed the ax, and began chopping the wood eagerly. But by the time he took a second swing at the wood, the ax had swung out of his hands and cut into his leg. The girl was alarmed, and she took her maid with her down to the courtyard and bandaged up the wound, using a salve. She asked: "Why were you so intent on defying the orders and doing nothing? The count will be here soon and he'll be so upset that he'll make good on his threat to banish you. And how in the world are you going to be able to walk around with that injured leg?"

"Well," he replied, "your hands have a healing power. But who is going to bring me all the beautiful flowers and birds and pieces of gold from the crevasses that are too treacherous even for birds?"

"He's too far gone for my help," the girl decided, and she walked away with a mournful look on her face, for she had always enjoyed spending time with the strange boy when the two were young.

It soon dawned on the young man that the count's daughter was in love with him. He was so distraught about failing to carry out the task assigned to him and, on top of that, losing the girl forever that he began rubbing together two sticks of wood to light the wood on fire. He was planning to die in the flames.

Just as the first sparks began flying from the smoking wood, a tiny little woman crawled out of the woodpile and began giggling and chirping like a cricket. She said: "Now that you have summoned me, tell me what you want." He liked the mysterious little person so much that he tried to grab her and catch

her. She would make a perfect gift for the princess, just like a
dormouse in a cage. But the creature was like a will-o'-the-
wisp, and just about as easy to catch as a shadow. The little
woman cried out: "Just stop it, Ralf, my boy, and tell me what
you need!"

He laughed and said: "I need to chop all the wood in this
pile."

"I will take care of that, Ralf, my boy," the little woman
said. "But under one condition: You must build a little fire
using twigs on that stone over there, and then just stand there
and wait." Since it was already late in the evening, the young
man was overcome by fatigue and fell asleep.

That evening everyone in the castle heard a lot of noise
down in the courtyard. In the morning, they told the count
that the woodpile had disappeared and in its place was a huge
stack of chopped wood. The count went down to the courtyard with his entire entourage and found Woodpecker sleeping
peacefully next to the pile of wood, which had been chopped
up into fine little pieces. He decided to wake up the sleeping
Woodpecker, for he was beginning to suspect that there was
more to the young man than had at first seemed. Woodpecker
asked if he could start a little fire over by the stone and burn
his ax. He rubbed two sticks of wood together, and they began
to make a flame. Just then the little woman reappeared and leaped
into the fire on the stone.

And that was the moment when a beautiful young woman
appeared before the eyes of the count. It was the Lady of the
Woods, whom he had married long ago. "Count Hermann!
Do you recognize me and my son Ralf? Woodpecker is our
son!" she cried out, to the astonishment of everyone gathered
round. And then she disappeared.

"That was Hilda's voice," the count said. "Yes, dear Woodpecker, you are our son. The veil has been lifted, and now I
know who you are." And he embraced Ralf, the Woodpecker,
and there was a great celebration at the castle. Ralf sat sorrow-
fully by the side of the young woman who was now something
of a sister, and for whom the lavish feast was also not a happy
occasion.

Count Hermann had his son trained as a knight, and when he returned home victorious after perilous battles—he was wearing a golden locket given to him by the emperor—there was another, even more festive celebration, this time the wedding of Ralf, outfitted in gleaming silver armor, and the charming young woman who was the count's foster child, as it turned out.

THE RED SILK RIBBON

Schönwerth's note: *Mermaids are highly evolved female creatures that dwell in the water but are not restricted to living there. They are able to take on human form partially or entirely and to become radiantly beautiful women. They long for the love of handsome men and lure them down to the watery depths, or they go on land and spend time with them there. Mermaids seek youth, beauty, and a long life through the love of mortals.*

 A fisherman was working for a count, a man who paid him well, for he was good at bringing in a nice haul. But one day his luck ran out, and the count was so dissatisfied with him that he let him go. For a time, the fisherman lived from his savings, but soon he had nothing left. He tried his luck a few more times, but to no avail, and he sat in his boat, weeping bitter tears.

Suddenly a beautiful mermaid emerged from the water. "Why are you weeping?" she asked, and he explained why he was so distraught. "I'll help you out, but only if you promise to give me what you do not know is in your house. I was the one who sent fish to you in the first place, and I'm also the one who kept them away from you." The fisherman made the promise, and right away he had another huge haul of fish. He returned home cheerfully. When he told his wife the price he had paid for the catch, her face fell. She was carrying a child, which he did not yet know about. But the two consoled themselves with the thought that they would baptize the child. The fisherman's luck was back, and once again he caught the best fish in his nets. He brought them to the count, who took him back in his service.

At the appointed time, a son was born, and he was called Lucas. He was strong in body and spirit, and it was decided that he would take holy orders. But once he had finished with his training, he could not hold his first mass, for he belonged to the mermaid. And so he gave up his studies to become a cooper and went on the road. There he encountered some animals quarreling over the carcass of a horse. They couldn't decide how to divide it up. There was a bear there, a fox, a falcon, and an ant. They asked him to figure out how to divide things up. Lucas threw the hindquarters and front legs to the bear, who had no reason to complain, and he gave the back to the fox, the innards to the falcon, and the head to the ant. Then off he went.

The bear thought it was not fair to let Lucas leave without showing some gratitude, and he ordered the fox to call him back. The grateful animals granted him the power to turn into their shapes whenever he wanted. Lucas burst out laughing and then went on his way. While he was walking he noticed a bunch of partridges picking at some grain. To test the gift he had been given, he decided to turn himself into a fox. He became one in an instant and caught as many partridges as he could carry. He took them with him to the next city and had them roasted at the inn.

Around the same time, four men came into the inn, sat down, and began playing cards and betting. Lucas was lying on a bed of straw behind the oven, and he noticed that one of the men already had a big pile of cash in front of him. He turned himself into an ant and crawled under the table. Then he turned himself into a bear, stood up, and knocked the table over with all the coins still on it. He scared the men so badly that they hightailed it out of there. He returned to his human form, gathered up the coins, lay down on the straw, and went to sleep. In the morning he paid his bill and left.

Lucas reached a town where everyone was in mourning. A black flag with a skull on it was waving from a tower. He started looking for a place to stay and asked the innkeeper what had happened. It turned out that the king had three daughters who were ready to be married. They were all beautiful and looked so much alike that people couldn't tell them apart. But the king had decided that the middle child would be his heir. "'Whoever wants to inherit my kingdom has to guess which one she is.' That's what he is demanding. And if you don't guess the right one, you will be executed. So many men have already died that we are all in mourning," the innkeeper explained.

Lucas went over to the castle and looked in the garden, which was surrounded by a deep moat, and saw the princesses taking a walk. He turned himself into a falcon and flew from one tree to the next. He caught the attention of the princesses, and let himself be captured by one of them. He landed on her hand, and she took him up to her bedroom, where he was given a golden perch. While she was sleeping, Lucas turned back to his human shape, but now he was wearing beautiful, costly garments. He took the princess's hand, and she woke up. He explained that he had been the bird and that he loved her. Frightened to death at first by the strange man and his words, the princess soon took a liking to him and admitted that she was the middle sister. She gave him her ring and showed him a red silk ribbon that she was going to wrap around the middle finger of her right hand. That was how he would recognize her when the time came to identify the middle princess.

The princess opened her window and the falcon flew away. The stranger came the next morning to see the king and to win the hand of the middle daughter. The king and his entire retinue felt pity for the young man. He was so handsome and charming that they were hoping to discourage him from the perilous undertaking. But Lucas was determined, and he was summoned to step into the hall where the three daughters were waiting. The executioner was already there, sharp sword in hand. Lucas was taken to the three sisters. One of them stepped forward just a tiny bit, and she was wearing the red ribbon around her finger. He declared her to be the middle princess, and he was right.

Everyone at the court and in town was delighted. The king had been regretting his vow for a long time and was distressed by the bloody end taken by innocent suitors. He was happy to give the hand of his daughter to a successful suitor.

The two lived happily for many years. One day Lucas went out hunting. His wife tried to keep him from going, for she had felt some kind of dark premonition. But he paid no attention. It was a hot day, and he was thirsty after trying to hunt down a deer. He forgot all about his mother's warnings to stay away from water. He rode ahead of the others and discovered a spring. Just as he was bending over and reaching into the water with his hand, a mermaid grabbed him and pulled him down with her. "I paid a high price for you," she said.

The princess learned the sad news. She did not hesitate to rush over to the stream to try to find her husband. She sat down by the riverbank and began weeping. The mermaid emerged from the water and comforted her by telling her that her husband was living comfortably down below. The princess said she would feel better if she could just take a look at her husband, and she offered the golden comb in her hair in exchange. The mermaid obliged and lifted Lucas's head out of the water, just high enough so that his wife could see his eyes. The princess then offered her ring in addition, and her husband was lifted out of the water up to his torso. Then she offered the golden slipper on her foot. The mermaid let Lucas stand on his wife's hand—and, just imagine, he turned into a falcon and was there right next to his wife.

The mermaid dove deep down, and the waters began to seethe and boil. She emerged and threw a handful of blue sand into the princess's face, and the princess turned instantly into a dragon.

The kingdom was in trouble once again. The king offered half his wealth to anyone who could come to his aid. An ancient magician appeared and promised to help as long as the princess could endure the procedure. He had three ovens built and heated them up until each was hotter than the next. He pushed the dragon into one and took it out again. Its skin was soft, and he cooled it down with water. When he put the dragon into the second oven, its skin split open, and when he pushed it into the third oven, Lucas had to hide because the weeping and wailing was so heart-wrenching.

The princess emerged naked from the oven, and Lucas threw his cape around her and led her home triumphantly. They lived happily together, and they were carefree now that the mermaid no longer had any claim to them.

TWELVE BRIDES

A knight and his wife had many worldly goods but only one child. When the boy turned twelve, his father died, and his mother moved to a castle that was in the middle of a lake. She wanted to mourn her husband in a place cut off from the rest of the world. As the boy grew older, he became more handsome and wise. But he was always pale and somewhat withdrawn. He liked being alone and had chosen a remote bedroom for himself, one that had the most beautiful view of the lake.

He loved to look out at the lake and daydream. When he turned twenty-four, his mother tried to persuade him to choose a bride. Life at the castle had become too lonely for her. But he didn't want to marry. One evening, when his mother tried to convince him to change his mind, he leaned mournfully against the window and looked out to see the image of the moon brightly reflected on the water. He imagined the features of the woman he hoped to wed one day. Finally he grew tired and went to bed. He forgot to close the window.

Suddenly he saw a bright light at the window. He looked up but couldn't make anything out. He was about to go back to sleep when the curtains rustled, and a woman with silky hair and a transparent gown lay down beside him. The dull light from the moon enabled him to see an indescribably beautiful woman with a pale face beside him. She nestled up next to him, and the night passed with playful games and loving chatter. In the morning the beautiful woman had vanished. But before she left, she told him that she would return. She had watched him looking out at the lake in the moonlight, and she would have come earlier if he had just left the window open.

From then on the beautiful woman slept by his side every night, and he was completely in love with her. But he had an odd feeling that it was not always the same woman who was sharing the bed with him. He began to press her to show herself by day, for his mother was pleading with him to find a wife. Even if she was poor, he was prepared to marry her. She would always say: "That's just not possible, my dearest. I can't get married in the way you are imagining. Let me be your wife by sharing your bed."

In the meantime, the young man's mother had been searching for a bride for her stubborn son. But the young woman she found left him cold, and when he fell asleep that night, he could hear the woman sharing his bed sigh. The mother went ahead and set a date for the marriage.

The wedding day arrived. On the first day everyone danced until dawn. On the second day there was a huge banquet. On the third day the women all escorted the bride to her husband's bedroom. When they walked in, the curtains at the bed flew around in all directions. The bride was frightened. She was supposed to climb into bed first, and she had the feeling that the bed was already occupied. The groom was amused by her nervousness, and he climbed into bed. A mermaid was lying between them. The bride felt a cold breath on her cheeks and moved to the very edge of the bed. This happened every night. The knight thought he was holding his bride in his arms. But the poor woman wasted away and died a virgin before the year was over.

The same thing happened to ten other women whom the mother had chosen for her son. All of them died before a year passed. The twelfth bride was clever, and she sought out a witch for advice. From her she learned that mermaids were responsible for what had happened to the wives before her. She could protect herself by refusing to follow her husband to the bedroom on that third night of the wedding celebrations and waiting until after the witching hour. She should follow those instructions to save not just herself but him as well. At midnight, he would tell her that he felt as if someone were pushing him into the bedroom, but she would have to be firm and unyielding. At the same time she must remember to shut tightly the window that looked out onto the lake so that the spirits would not be able to come in. Her husband would feel drawn by mournful sounds and be driven to jump into the water. But he would be protected against that with a charm and with herbs that she should put under the bed. She was also told not to draw the curtains of the bed or to get into bed first—her husband should do that. She must also keep everything that she had learned secret. Otherwise her husband would surely fall back under the spell of the mermaids.

The third day of the wedding celebrations had arrived. It was midnight, and the groom was more restless than ever. He had an odd premonition. He kept wanting to leave but his bride held him back until midnight had long passed. Once they were in the bedroom, he opened the curtains. Twelve sighs could be heard.

The bride spoke magical words and prayed with her husband. For twelve years he had not thought about God. Suddenly they both heard waves roaring and strange tunes. The waters in the lake rose and waves hit the window. But victory was theirs, and peace reigned forever afterward.

THE HOWLING OF
THE WIND

A woodsman had a son. After he died, the son was out of work, and the boy went out in the world to seek his fortune. He got lost in the woods. All he had left was a crust of bread, which he ate. Overcome by thirst, he looked around for a stream and discovered a footpath. By following it, he reached a well and saw a wondrously beautiful woman drawing water from it. She offered him some water, and he drank it. She asked where he was heading. He replied: "Out into the world to find work."

"You can work for me, if you want," she said. She was beautiful, and there was no reason not to follow her to her house near the well.

The two fell in love before long and celebrated their engagement. But there was one condition placed on their marriage, namely, that he must never ask about her on a Thursday. They lived happily together for fourteen years, and they had seven boys together. The husband started to become curious about his wife's secret. The fourteenth year had not yet come to an end when he peeked through a keyhole into her room, saw her sitting in a tub, and noticed that she had a fish tail.

The next day the woodsman shoved his wife away when she came over to whisper in his ear. He didn't want to live with a dragon. She began weeping bitter tears. If he had just been able to wait seven years times two, the curse placed on her by her own mother would have been lifted. Now she was going to have to fly around until Judgment Day. "The howling of the wind will be my voice; swirls of dust will be my food, and I will drink my tears," she lamented. Her husband wanted to prevent her from leaving, but she escaped and began flying around the outside of the house. A boy was seated at each of the seven windows in the house. She wept as she flew toward them to bid each one farewell. They all began sobbing for their mother and were drawn out the window to her. The fine, melancholy sounds of the wind are their voices.

HANS DUDELDEE

There once lived a fisherman who had three sons. He sent them out into the world to seek their fortunes, and he was curious to learn which one would return as the wealthiest.

The sons had learned about an enchanted castle not far from where they lived, and they were hoping to recover all kinds of treasures from it. On the way they passed a forest, and there the two elder brothers separated from the youngest. He was supposed to go into the woods, which were not quite safe, while they marched on to the castle.

The brothers were standing at the entrance to the castle, and they heard the song of a little bird hopping around on the branch of a tree: "Happy as you go in, sad when you leave!" The two fellows paid no attention to the words and went into the castle. Its walls were lined with figures of iron and stone. All the doors were shut tight, but one suddenly opened, as if on its own. The brothers walked in and saw an old man standing before them. His long white beard was wrapped around his arm three times. He asked what they wanted.

"We are the sons of a fisherman who sent us out to seek our fortunes. We came here in search of the treasures in the castle."

"My dear fellows, I am the custodian of the treasures, but I can only give them to the person who can answer three questions. The treasures belong to a princess who lives in a castle high in the mountains surrounded by a lake. There is no chance of finding a way in. She alone has the answers, and without her help you won't be able to answer the questions."

The two brothers asked to hear the questions. Perhaps they would be able to answer them on their own. "I advise you to leave now," the man said, "for if you fail to answer the third question, you will be turned into stone or iron, just like the statues you see here. You won't be able to leave once I have asked the second question."

And then he began posing the questions:

"How many fish are in the lake?"
"How many birds in the land?"
"How long has my beard been white?"
"You have until sundown, not much time."

The younger of the two fellows didn't think he would know the answers, and he had already left. But the elder stayed and wanted to answer the questions. He was not able to give the right answers and was turned into an iron statue.

In the meantime, Hans, the youngest of the three, was trudging through the woods. He had helped his father catch fish, and that was the only skill he had. Near a lake he discovered a palace. He sat down and began worrying about what the future would hold for him. His stomach began growling and so he decided to try to catch some fish in the lake. Before long he caught a glittering fish with golden scales. When he unhooked it from his fishing pole, it began speaking and begged for its life. The good-natured lad threw the fish back in the water. After a little while, it put its head back up above the surface and said: "My dear boy, if you ever need anything, just call me and I will come help you."

Hans was astonished, but he continued fishing and managed to catch a few fish and roast them up for supper. Finally, he decided to return home, but he couldn't find the way back. The lake was straight ahead and behind him the dark woods. He called out:

"Little fish, little fish, down in the waters!"

The fish came swimming up to the surface. "What do you want of me, Hans Dudeldee?"

Hans explained that he was lost and needed to find a place to sleep for the night.

"Climb up on my back; I'll take you to her!"

"To whom?"

"Just wait and see; come and follow me!"

Hans climbed up on the back of the golden fish, which grew in size under him and carried him to a dazzling palace, splendidly furnished. A toad was soaking in an aromatic bath and said: "Oh, my dear Dudeldee, I've waited nearly a thousand years for you, and now you are finally here! I am a princess who was enchanted, and no one has been able to set me free. When they have the courage to try, they end up drowning. I know just how many people have been turned to stone in my castle, only because they tried to answer the questions that the castle guard posed. I alone have the magic mirror in which the answers appear. But the evil fairy that cursed me locked the mirror in a cabinet and then threw the key into the lake. If you can fetch the key, the spell will be broken, and I can give you the mirror that will help you answer the questions and earn the riches in the castle."

Hans had no idea how to find the key. Feeling down on his luck, he went over to the lake and began fishing. He threw all the little fish back into the water as soon as they asked him to. Then he remembered his little golden fish and called out: "Little fish, little fish, in the sea!"

And back came the call: "What do you want of me, Hans Dudeldee?"

The fish appeared, and Hans explained what he needed. The fish leaped out of the water three times and suddenly all the fish whose lives Hans had spared appeared. They deliberated for a few moments and then one after another disappeared. Hans was becoming concerned about how this would all end. But not much later he saw a bright shining object on the horizon coming closer and closer to him. The little fish were swimming together, carrying a gold chain on their backs, and hanging from it was the key.

Hans brought the key to the toad, who opened the cabinet and took out the mirror. The toad said: "Keep the mirror with you. Don't show it to anyone and don't let anyone steal it from you or you will die, and we will all remain enchanted. Go over to the castle, and when the guard asks you the questions, say to the mirror:

> 'Mirror, mirror, bright and clear,
> Give me all the numbers here!
> I'm a stranger from far away,
> Here to plan my wedding day.'"

And so he reached the castle. He heard the little bird singing and marched right in, finding everything as his brother had reported. The gray man told him exactly what he had said to the brothers and warned him. Then he asked the first question:

"How many fish are in the lake?" The mirror showed him only a single fish. At that the old man's beard unwound once from around his arm.

"How many birds are in the kingdom?" The mirror showed him only a single bird. At that the old man's beard unwound a second time.

"How long has my beard been white?" The mirror showed him the number one thousand. And then the beard disappeared.

The old man was suddenly youthful, and the statues of iron and stone were liberated and returned to life. The castle was transformed. The princess was no longer a toad, and the little golden fish was her page, while the other little fish were her servants. They all told Hans how grateful they were to him for rescuing them.

Hans rode to the lake with the princess in a carriage, and a beautiful ship carried them to the castle, where they celebrated their marriage. The lucky pair visited Hans's father and his brothers, and the couple lived happily and harmoniously together with them for many years.

THE BELT AND
THE NECKLACE

There was once a king with a daughter named Barbara. She was so ugly that everyone made fun of her. She lived a lonely life.

One day she was up in her room feeling sad about her bad luck. Suddenly a gnome appeared before her and gave her three plums. He said to her: "March straight down to the sea and throw one of the plums into it. Two mermaids will rise up out of the water, bright as the sun. Throw the second plum into the sea and one of the two mermaids will come on land. She will be wearing a magical belt, and you should take it off her. When you throw the third plum into the water, the other mermaid will come on land. She will be wearing a necklace that can be yours as well. As soon as you put on the belt and necklace, you will become the most beautiful woman of all, as dazzling as the sun. If you wear the necklace as a belt and vice versa, you will become invisible. Make sure you don't take off the belt and necklace, and above all else, don't lose them. But come what may, I will still be there to help you."

The princess did as she was told. She went over to the sea and threw a plum into the water. Two mermaids emerged from below. They were so dazzlingly beautiful that it hurt her eyes. She threw the second plum into the water, and one of the two women came out of the water and gave her the belt she was wearing. It would turn her into a queen. But she set one condition: Barbara would have to turn over her third child, when it turned three. Barbara threw the third plum into the water. The second mermaid came on land and gave her the necklace in exchange for the most beautiful of her children. Barbara put on the belt and necklace and was declared to be the most beautiful in the land. She became queen. Whenever she walked on the grounds, she was as radiant as the sun, and the gardens around her looked like paradise.

Barbara gave birth to her third child, and it was a little boy, just as beautiful as the first two. When the boy turned three, the nursemaid took a walk with him near the sea. Suddenly one of the mermaids rose up from the water and grabbed the child. More children were born to the queen, and the sixth was a boy, the most beautiful of them all. The king loved him more than life itself. The queen put out an order that no one was to allow the child near water. One evening an old woman appeared, and she asked for shelter. A white veil hid her face. The stranger was given a place to sleep and stayed in the corner she had been given. When everyone was asleep, she took the boy and fled with him.

The king's messengers were sent out to search for the boy, but they returned without any news. The queen had to confess how everything had come to pass. The king was furious and had the queen thrown in the water, into the very sea where she had acquired the belt and necklace. But the water could do nothing to her, and she did not even get damp. She sank down until she reached the splendid palace in which the mermaids lived, and there she found her two boys.

When the two mermaids decided to spend some time up on the surface of the water, the mother wore the necklace as a belt and vice versa. She became invisible and fled with the two boys, who had already started to grow webbed feet. The mermaids began to create a disturbance in the waves. They stirred up such powerful storms that it seemed as if everything would perish and go under. But at the king and queen's palace there was nothing but joy.

DRUNK WITH LOVE

A castellan was once asked why he had never married, and his reply was simple: "Once a young woman appeared to me in my dreams. She was so lovely and charming that I never found her equal on earth. Her image is in my heart. I remember everything perfectly, even the details about the place where I saw her in my dreams."

One day he was sent on a journey by his master. He found lodging in a small garden house near a castle. The night was crisp and clear, with a bright moon. He had trouble falling asleep and decided to walk around in the garden. He went down a path, at the end of which was a well. He looked down into the well for a long time, and all at once he saw on the surface of the water the young woman of his dreams.

He walked back lost in thought, and he felt as if the young woman was walking right in front of him. When he opened the door to the garden house, he was astonished to see the beautiful woman standing before him. It did not take long for the two of them to move closer, and the castellan, madly in love with her, asked for her hand. She stayed with him, almost as if she had been his wife forever. The next morning, the castellan was upset that he had kept her with him all night. She just smiled and comforted him with the words: "Don't worry. It was all going to happen sooner or later. Your kind is not like mine, but I will stay with you. Just don't ask me where I come from!" And then she reached into the folds of her robe and, to his surprise, handed him some pearls and jewels.

They lived happily together. The children she bore made him even happier. When she was with child for the seventh time, she became anxious. A boy was born and she took care of him with more than the usual tenderness and affection.

When the boy turned twenty-five, the woman told her husband a secret that had been burdening her for some time now. "It's time to reveal that I am a mermaid," she said. "I have given birth to seven children. Six of them belong to you, but I promised to return the seventh to the waters after twenty-five years passed by. It was the only way to save the other children. Now I have to take leave of a child that I love more than anything else."

The couple talked things over and decided to send their son away, warning him to stay away from the water. And so the young man went out into the world, and he was always careful to avoid being near water. But one day he decided to set sail on a ship. He was so eager to please a beautiful young girl he had met that he failed to heed his mother's warning. The skies were bright blue, and the lake was completely placid, like a mirror. Suddenly the water began to churn, making big waves. The little ship began rocking violently back and forth, making everyone feel as if they were done for. The young man could no longer control the ship, and he jumped into the water. Right away he was embraced by a beautiful woman and taken down into the depths.

He found himself in the arms of a beautiful mermaid, and no one had to talk him into staying, for he had fallen under the spell of her beauty. But he felt sad when he thought of his mother at home. "You can show your face once a month by lifting your head above water," the mermaid said tenderly. "Your mother will be invited to come see you, even though we should not let her, considering that she broke all her promises."

Before long the young man forgot about his mother, despite what the mermaid had told him. He remembered his responsibilities only after a boy was born to his wife. He was planning to go up to the surface to see his mother, but it was no longer allowed.

Over time he had many children, and a seventh was born to

him. He could no longer restrain himself, and he rose up to the surface and could see a little ship passing by above him. A young woman had just married, and she looked just like his sister. When he put his ear up to the ship, he learned that the bride was his sister's daughter. Overwhelmed by the desire to see his loved ones again and to return to land, he let his head emerge from the water. The bride recognized him. He began to howl and then quickly disappeared. At the spot where he had been there was now a pool of blood.

One day his mother, who was still grieving over her lost son, was strolling through the garden when she saw his corpse at the fountain. She knew exactly what had happened, and her time was over as well. She took the precious body and jumped down the well with it. They were never seen again.

The mermaid had had seven children in all, and after the seventh was drowned, she was allowed to remain young and beautiful for another three hundred years.

ANNA MAYALA

A handsome young man named Veri lived in a village, and his beloved was the most beautiful girl imaginable. She was named Anna Mayala, and she was poor. The many suitors who wooed her were a source of grief for both young people, but in the end persistence paid off for Veri and the wedding day was set. Veri had a wild side to him. He was a daydreamer, withdrawn at times, and occasionally he sang shocking songs about the underworld. That's why he was called Crazy Veri.

On the day before the wedding, he went down into the forest to catch some game for the celebrations. He returned with a magnificent roebuck on his back and was walking toward the village. His thoughts were not on his bride; instead his mind was wandering in the strangest places. While he was immersed in mysterious dreams, he reached a footbridge. The moon had already risen and was shining. He became annoyed with himself for being so late and for missing the chance to spend the evening before his wedding with his bride.

The bridge led him over a sparkling stream, and the moon was reflected in its waters. What he saw slowed him down, and he grew melancholy. He kneeled down and put his ear to the surface of the water, hoping to hear something. He began to hear some sweet melodies. The longer they were, the more beautiful they sounded; the more beautiful they were, the more enchanting they sounded. His ear came closer and closer to the source of the wondrous sounds, and he began to think that it would be lovely to sink down into the waters.

He looked down into the depths of the stream. It seemed as if the most beautiful legs he had ever seen were dancing around down there. Veri raised his eyes and saw some beautiful, charming young girls form a circle and dance gracefully to the music. They were all lovely, but one was more lovely than the rest. He asked her what it was like down there. She reached up to him, put her pale face on his shoulder, and said mournfully: "Oh, it's so lovely where we live, so peaceful. And there's more air and more life where we dwell. Will you come with me?"

He agreed to go. She added: "Well, I once lived above-ground as well. You have a bride. Will you be able to forget her? If you come with me, you won't be able to think about her any longer. Your desire for the earthly bride would draw harsh punishments." She looked him in the eye in a manner so charming that he embraced her. The ground gave way under his feet, and he sank down with her into unknown regions. Back at the village his bride waited in vain for her beloved. He did not return. People looked everywhere, and they found nothing but his musket and the roebuck on the bridge.

Many years passed. One Tuesday there was a wedding procession making its way to the church. The bride was beautiful and as delightful as a rose. Her name was Anna Mayala, and her father and mother were walking behind her. The mother looked pale, and it seemed as if she was ailing, although she was not yet that old and retained traces of great beauty.

The procession made its way over a bridge. The mother breathed a deep sigh, and the father tried to comfort her. "Isn't the present," he said to her, "better than the past? Isn't it true that we've lived in peace and remained true to each other? And doesn't your daughter, who has your name, look just like you?" The mother nestled closer to him.

All of a sudden a man appeared, his long hair fluttering wildly in the breeze, and he raced down the mountain right up to the bride. Like a madman he began beating his forehead and then grabbed hold of the girl, claiming that she was his bride. It's true he had abandoned her, he said, but that was just yesterday, and she must go to the altar with him. The bridegroom pushed him aside with his strong arms. The mother was trembling and near collapse, but the procession kept moving.

Two days later the young woman went to the stream to fetch some water. The wild man reappeared, embraced her, and did not want to leave. The woman's husband saw what was happening and chased the madman away. There were reports that he was walking around the village asking about folks who had been dead for years. He was seen at the pastor's house, and after that he was not seen again and no one heard a thing about him.

A Franciscan monk began to appear in the village every year. He was a pale, handsome man who seemed to be ailing, and he liked staying at Anna Mayala's more than at any other house. Whenever he showed up, Anna had a bad feeling, one that she could not explain.

It came to pass that Anna's husband died. The monk appeared and he comforted the mourning widow. He spoke the following words: "My dear lady. Life is hard. Look at me and at all I have suffered and then you will not feel as much pain as you do now."

The woman in mourning looked at him carefully, and she searched his features, paused for a moment, and then became frightened. She recognized Veri, who had long ago recognized Anna Mayala. And now it was his turn to be upset. But he took a deep breath and said: "I lived down there, way down below, in the domain of sprites. I lived with a beautiful, enchanting mermaid as if she were my wife. She was always with me, except on Fridays, when she became invisible to me. I might have been completely happy with her love, but there was always an empty feeling in my heart that could find no satisfaction. For a while the feelings of emptiness tortured me, and I could not find a way to make things better. My wife was simply not a normal woman. Her feet were always bound with ribbons, and she never took them off. She gave birth to six children, and their feet were bound as well. The children grew up quickly. Whenever she gave birth to a child, the one before it was no longer an infant.

"The mystery of the feet tortured me again and again. One evening, while my wife was sleeping, I undid the binding and discovered that she had feet like a goose, webbed with little claws at the end of each toe. I flew into a rage, cursing and hoping that the seventh child would be a human being and would be born with human feet. And my wish came true.

"When the mermaid set eyes on the child for the first time, she let out a scream of horror that she had become the mother of a crippled being, and she bombarded me with insults. Before long other mermaids came to celebrate the birth of the child. As soon as they saw the child's feet, they became enraged. They took the child and tore it to pieces, greedily devouring its little limbs, for human flesh endows mermaids with beauty and youth for three hundred years and makes men fall passionately in love with them.

"I could do nothing but watch in silence. My wife touched me with a staff, and I fell asleep. When I awoke, I was on the exact spot at which I had slid into the water many years before. I watched the wedding procession of your daughter. When I saw her, I thought she was you, for everything was like a dream. You know the rest. The pastor was the one who explained everything to me, and he told me that twenty years had gone by, when I thought that only a single day had passed. When I was at the monastery, I repented my sins. I have brought along some pearls and jewels for your grandchildren."

Anna was on her deathbed sometime later. The monk reappeared. He kneeled down before the dying woman and put her hands in his. His head sank down. Both turned into corpses. Two white doves were seen flying out the window. The larger one had seven black flakes caught on its feet, which fell off at the windowsill when the smaller dove came in contact with it. They turned out to be scraps of paper on which were written the names of the mermaid's seven children. Their father's pious ways had earned them salvation, and they, too, were able to enter heaven.

One of the grandchildren went to the stream to fetch some water to wash the two corpses. Prayers had been said already for the evening, when she reached the bridge and met a friend who asked her why she had come for water at such an odd time. "Oh," she replied, "my grandmother just died, and her beloved Veri as well." She heard a soft whisper in the air, asking, "Who died?" And the waters in the stream began stirring, huge waves rose into the air and moved toward the house, and water began to flood the room where the two bodies were lying at rest. The corpses tumbled around in the room. Everyone was terrified, and once some holy water was sprinkled on the corpses, the waters withdrew. But six additional corpses were left behind, handsome boys and beautiful girls between the ages of ten and seventeen, with their feet bound, and holding in their hands scraps of paper with the words: "We have been redeemed." Among the corpses were the feet of a boy whose body was outlined on the floor as if it were a shadow. Next to it was a piece of paper with this explanation: "The body has been consumed; the soul endures." It was the mermaid's seventh child, and the feet were all that was left of it.

On every anniversary of Crazy Veri's death, the stream begins stirring, and the next day waves ripple toward its banks. Since Veri's death, the moon no longer appears reflected in its waters.

IN THE JAWS OF
THE MERMAN

There was once a village near a large body of water, and many beautiful girls lived there. The more often they swam in the lake, the more lovely they became. Everyone adored them. Girls living in other places heard about them. They came in from many different regions to swim there. But since many were ugly and couldn't stay underwater as long as the girls in the village, they did not become prettier. In fact, many of them drowned.

Girls stopped traveling there, but suitors from all four points of the compass came courting. All the girls in the village were married on one day. The morning after, there was an enormous uproar. Everyone was running, and the grooms had grabbed their wives by the hair and were pushing and shoving them to the point of exhaustion, and then they raced away.

It turned out that there was something not quite right with the girls—they had fish scales. A judge appeared on the scene with his officials, took a look at the brides, and ordered all of them to be burned at the stake at once. As the flames were licking the stake, tall waves rose up and washed into the village, and a huge head emerged from the waters. It spewed water like a whale and put out the fire. The brides all walked across an arc of water as if it were a bridge leading from the woodpile back to the water and then into the gatelike jaws of the merman. Since that time girls no longer swim in that lake.

THE KING'S RING

 A man made a vow to travel to the Holy Land before he died. He was unable to keep this vow, and his wife and three sons—the boys were all hunters—decided to embark on the journey for his sake. The travelers entered the thicket of a dark forest. After they made a meal for themselves, they prepared a bed made from leaves and greenery. One of the brothers had to keep watch at all times, for they did not feel safe in those woods.

The eldest made a fire and kept watch. A bear appeared, raised his paws in the air, and began to lunge at the sleepers. One of the brothers pulled out his hunting knife and cut off the bear's paws. The bear let out a growl and fled. The hunter took the paws, dried them out by the fire, and put them in his hunting pouch for safekeeping. When the second brother held watch, a wolf came slinking by, and he suffered the same fate as the bear.

Night was falling just when the youngest woke up to keep vigil. He looked around, climbed up a tall tree, and saw a bright fire burning in the distance. He took his musket and aimed it toward the fire. Three giants had gathered around it and were feasting on a deer. One of them raised a joint of meat to his lips, and—*bang*—the tasty morsel flew away from his mouth. The second one was about to take a drink, and—*bang*—it flew away from his mouth. The third giant said: "There is a mighty good marksman around here. Let's go look for him."

They soon found the bold huntsman. "You must be a sharp-shooter!" they shouted.

"I'll say," the young man replied. "The genuine article."

"Listen to us," the giants said. "We'd like to hire someone like you, and you could do us a big favor."

"Let's hear," the huntsman replied.

"Not far from here there is a castle built into the mountains, and a princess lies in it. She has been enchanted, along with all her treasures and retinue, men and horses. She is fast asleep, and everyone around her is also slumbering. But you can't get near the castle, because as soon as you move close to it, a little black rooster lands on the embattlements and starts screeching and squawking and racing around in the castle, fast as the wind, so that everyone in the castle wakes up. We've tried to throw stones at the thing, but it never works. Maybe you can land it with a bullet. You won't regret the chance to enter the castle."

"So you're planning to free the princess?" the huntsman asked. The giants nodded and growled: "From her wealth, anyhow." As they started walking toward the castle, the little rooster was already up on the embattlements, tiny as a mouse and as speedy as a weasel. It crowed, but only one time, for the huntsman hit it. When he picked it up, a key to the gates of the castle fell out of the animal's mouth. "Let me go in first," the huntsman said, and he crawled in. A sword was hanging on the wall, and just as the giant was squeezing his way in, the huntsman chopped off his head and dragged his body in. He did the same thing with the second and third giants and then pushed their corpses aside.

Everyone in the castle was asleep. The huntsman threaded his way through a labyrinth of passageways and halls, on past the finery and splendor of the rooms in which people were sleeping. Finally he reached a staircase in a tower, where the princess was fast asleep. Under the spell of her beauty, he gazed at her for a long time. Finally he touched her with his finger, and she woke up. She turned pale and was frightened by the stranger. But once he told her who he was and what had happened, she became less shy. And before long, she leaped to her feet, embraced the huntsman, and kissed him. She thanked him with sweet words for having broken the magic spell and liberated her from the evil giant. She was so elated that she offered to give him the ring she was wearing. She was hoping to become his wife and wanted him to stay and rule the kingdom with her. He remained in her arms for only a short time, but promised to return once he had finished the pilgrimage to the Holy Land. He put the ring in a safe place.

When he returned to his family in the woods, they were all still asleep by the campfire. They woke up with the sun, and without saying a word about the adventures that had taken place that night, he silently began the journey with them to the Holy Land. After enduring many perils, they all returned to the place in the woods where they had once slept. On the street was a sign with the words: FREE FOR THE POOR, BUT THE RICH MUST PAY.

The pilgrims were poor, and they stayed at the inn, where they were given generous portions of tasty dishes. After dining, they entered the garden at the inn, a beautiful spot with all kinds of lovely flowers and greenery. They met the lady innkeeper there, and she was even more beautiful than the flowers in the garden. The young huntsman blushed when he looked at her, for he seemed to see his beloved princess in the eyes of the woman. She came over to speak with the group and asked them who they were, where they had come from, and how they had fared on their travels.

The eldest son described his fight with the bear, and when the others were skeptical, he pulled the paws out of his pouch and showed them to everyone. The second son showed them the wolf paws, whereupon the youngest began to tell about his adventures with the giants and the princess. Everyone started laughing and calling him a liar, but he opened his jacket and took out the ring that was hanging from a string around his neck. He displayed it to prove that everything had really happened as he said it had.

The lady innkeeper stood up and left, but she came back right away and said: "I built this inn for your sake. I heard about your travels and was waiting here for you. In fact I made up the words for the sign to make sure you would stay here. What the huntsman has said about the giants and the princess is all true. I didn't recognize him right away, but he has my ring, and I am the princess, and he is my husband. Just take a look; my nursemaid is bringing our son right over here."

The three huntsmen and their mother were overcome with joy. And if they have not died, they are still living in happiness today.

THE THREE
GOLDEN CROWNS

 Once there was a king who had three exquisitely beautiful daughters. But the trio had been kidnapped by three royal giants. One day three fellows came to the castle to beg. They were told curtly that they would have to bring back the three princesses before they were given anything at all.

The three lads made up their minds to find the princesses, and they scattered in different directions. The first one discovered an empty house in the woods. He walked in and found no one there, just a roast goose on the spit. Famished, he took the meat from the spit and started eating it. While he was feasting, a little gray man with a long beard appeared and asked the fellow to give him a small bite. Just as the kind boy was leaning down to give him a taste, the rascal jumped on his back and began choking him so hard that the lad took to his heels as soon as he got away.

The same thing happened to the second fellow. The third was a little more clever, and when the gnome asked him for a bite to eat, he said: "Chop some wood for me, and then you will have your reward!" The little one went out and chopped some wood. The tip of his beard got stuck in the crack of a log he had split, and he was caught. He shouted for help, but the fellow refused to come to his aid unless he told him where the princesses were. The little man said: "If you get this piece of wood off me, I will help you out." The boy did not trust him at all, and so he carried the gnome with his beard still stuck in the log.

The two reached a hill with an opening that led way down. A basket was hanging there from a string. The boy climbed in and lowered himself while the gnome stayed up at the top with his two companions, who had met up with him again. The basket came to a stop on the ground, and the boy found himself in a spacious house, a beautiful place with a red floor. He looked around and found a sword dangling from the wall in one room. It swayed back and forth. He found a whistle in the drawer of a table, and began to blow on it. Suddenly the sword fell right down into his hands.

He made his way through a long wide passage to a glass door, and when he looked through it he saw one of the princesses, the youngest. She was sitting by one of the giants, and he had three heads. The young man cleared his throat, and the giant stuck his three heads out the door. With his mighty sword the fellow chopped the giant's heads off in one stroke. Now the princess was free. He took her to the basket and pulled on the cord to have her taken back up.

Later he discovered a second room with the second princess and a third room with the third princess. Each one was sitting next to her giant husband, and the second one had six heads; the third, nine in all. The young man did to these two what he had done to the first. Then he put the princesses in the basket and sent them back up aboveground. And so he was the last person left underground. He didn't quite trust his companions up there and decided to test just how well disposed they were to him. And so he put the eighteen giant heads in the basket.

When the basket was halfway up, his comrades let go of the rope, and all the heads fell down and lay in pieces at his feet. Since he was at a loss as to what to do, he took out his whistle and used it. Suddenly a horde of little gray men appeared, all wanting to know what he desired, for he was their master. When they learned that he wished to reach the top again, they gave him a staff of iron. "If you want to make an opening anywhere, just tap the wall with this staff. And in case you need us, all you have to do is stamp your foot."

The young man emerged from the mountain and returned to town. He took an apprenticeship with a goldsmith. The goldsmith had received a commission from the king to make a crown for his eldest daughter. He was delighted to have a capable apprentice, and he turned the work over to him.

That night the lad asked for a roasted calf and as much wine as he could drink. When he was alone he stamped his foot on the ground. The gnomes appeared and brought him the crown of one of the princesses in the giant's chambers. They stayed all night, and they ate their fill and drank until they were tipsy. In the morning the young man placed the exquisite crown on the master goldsmith's table, and he proudly took it to the king, who commissioned a second one, just like it, for his other daughter. The apprentice agreed to do the additional work for his master, in exchange for food and drink. The gnomes appeared again as soon as he stamped his foot, and they ate and drank their fill. In the morning, a second crown was ready.

Exactly the same thing happened with the crown for the youngest princess. She recognized who had written her name, which was also inscribed on her ring, and told the king. He summoned the master and asked about the origin of the crowns. The master revealed that it was the work of his apprentice, and now everyone knew who had really rescued the princesses.

The king gave him the hand of his youngest daughter, as well as the kingdom as his reward. The two companions, who married the sisters, had to serve as his vassals.

NINE BAGS OF GOLD

There once lived a miller with two sons named Hans and Michael. He owned two mills. When he grew older, he arranged for his sons to marry, divided the mills between them, lay down to rest, and died.

Hans's wife was with child before long, and Hans began to think that it would be a good idea if his sister-in-law were also pregnant. Then the two children would grow up together, and the mills would stay in the family, with the children as owners.

Michael learned that his own wife was ill and could never have children. He went to his brother's house and said: "My wife will never be able to have children. How about this? If you have a son, I will adopt him, and he can be my heir." Hans was all too happy to hear those words, and he waited impatiently for his wife to deliver their child. To Hans's disappointment, his wife gave birth to a girl, named Marie. Michael said: "I'm not about to give the mill to a girl. I want a boy with my name!"

The girl was adorable and flourished as she grew older. Her mother was delighted to have a girl who was so pleasant and happy even when she was helping out with chores. The little girl felt sad from time to time. "Everyone I know has a brother or sister, but not me," she complained.

One day when she was playing alone in the parlor, she grumbled about that again, and elves came in through the floorboards. They were hoping to be her brothers and sisters and wanted to play with her and teach her things, without her parents knowing about it. The child kept their secret, and the little elves kept her company when she was by herself. They taught her how to read and write, and they also taught her the art of knitting. The girl's mother could not figure out why her daughter liked to be home alone so much, but she began leaving the house for even longer periods of time. She decided to send the girl to an aunt living in another place so that she would get an education. How astonished she was when she learned from her daughter that she could do everything already. The girl showed her the pretty things she had knit. The mother was thrilled.

When the girl, who had a lovely face and a fine figure, turned sixteen, her father wanted her to marry a wealthy man in a nearby town. The girl didn't want to, for the elves had told her that she would be unhappy with the man. He would squander everything they owned and then abandon her.

Marie had a second reason for turning down her father's proposal. There was a handsome, hardworking young man at the mill, and she was devoted to him. She told her father about him. He replied in a sober manner: "You aren't interested in my proposal? So be it. But you can't marry the apprentice until he hangs nine bags filled with gold on the spokes of the wheels in the mill." The elves burst out laughing when they heard that, and they comforted the unhappy girl by telling her that they would help her out.

Around that time, news came that the prince of the kingdom was on his deathbed, and that the doctors had exhausted every possibility of healing him. The elves rushed over to Marie and said: "We made the prince ill, but he won't come to any harm. You are going to save his life. Tomorrow your father will be leaving on a trip, and you can go into town and give the prince a small dose of this medicine. He will recover from his illness right away."

Marie went over to the palace and let the queen know that she would be able to heal her son. The queen somehow had faith in this visitor, who had an honest face. She was taken to the patient, and she gave him a dose of the medicine she had with her. All at once he was healthy again. Marie was given a bag full of money. She took it home, but she was not entirely happy. How would she manage to find eight more bags? The elves were shrewd and said to her: "Let's see just how much money is in that bag." It turned out to be nine hundred talers. The elves found nine bags, filled each with a hundred talers, and tied them up with little red ribbons. Then they said: "Marie, your father may be a little ill-mannered at times, but he is a man of his word. Tomorrow is Sunday, and he won't be operating the mill. While he is at church, go hang the little bags on the spokes of the wheel. You can show him the bags when he returns home. And then ask him if you can marry the apprentice. Your father may make a face and scratch himself behind his ears. But he won't break his promise." And so Marie married the man she loved, and her father was more cheerful and contented than ever before.

Marie did not forget what the elves had done for her, and she brought them all kinds of tasty morsels. They thanked her and said: "Don't forget us, Marie, and in a year there will be another joyful event in your life." After the usual time had passed, Marie gave birth to a boy. Her father was beside himself with joy. Michael, who had abandoned the mill after his wife's death, came to see them. He said to Hans: "Give me the boy, and you and your wife can come live with me. You can manage the business. I have enough to live on."

And so Marie was given her father's mill and lived happily ever after with her husband.

TWO BROTHERS

 Once there was a king who had two handsome
sons. They looked so much alike that it was im-
possible to tell them apart.

The elder of the two decided to go on a journey. He took leave of his father and his brother.
He was very fond of his brother, and as he was
leaving, he handed him a small vial filled with
water, saying: "If the water turns cloudy, it means that I'm ill.
If it turns red, it means that I'm dead." And with those words,
off he went, on the road until he reached a city where a young
woman was ruling as queen of the land.

The prince was handsome and well mannered. It did not
take him long to win the affection of the royal lady, and before
much time passed she offered him her hand in marriage and
her throne. He became king of the country and lived happily
with his wife.

In the autumn months, the royal couple would move to a
smaller castle at the edge of the forest. One evening the king
and his wife were looking out the window and noticed the bat-
tlements of a castle nearby. The king asked the queen about
the mysterious castle.

"It's an enchanted place," she replied. "Don't ever go in there,
because no one who goes in ever returns."

The king's curiosity was aroused. He arranged a hunt for
the next day, taking his servants with him into the woods,
along with his faithful companions—a tame lion, a bear, and
a wolf. As he was leaving, the queen begged him not to go near
the enchanted castle. She asked the servants to make sure that

they would always keep an eye on her husband and especially that he would not go near the enchanted castle.

The king was excited by the idea of an adventure, and he devised a scheme to rid himself of his entourage. All he needed was some nice strong wine to put them all to sleep at the inn, and once they were slumbering, he could slip away to the castle, accompanied by his faithful animals.

On his way he crossed a bridge over the moat around the castle. There he saw a little old lady dressed in rags, who was holding her hands behind her back in such a way that he could not see her arms. She asked the king for alms. He felt sorry for the poor woman and gave her a gold coin. The old woman told him that she had no hands and asked him to put the coin on the ground. The well-meaning king leaned over and was about to put the gold coin at her feet when she struck him with a whip hidden under her clothing. He turned into stone. The lion, bear, and wolf also became statues.

In the meantime, the king's entourage had woken up at the inn, and it soon dawned on them that the king was gone. After searching for him everywhere, the servants returned to the queen with heavy hearts. She wept day and night, grieving for her lost husband. She put on a mourning dress, and no one could console her for the loss of her husband and his terrible end.

Some time passed and the king's younger brother decided one day to look at the bottle given to him by his brother. The water in it was turning red. Fearing the worst, he traveled in disguise from one kingdom to the next, from one city to the next, until finally he reached the place where his brother's wife was living. While she was telling him her tale of sorrow, he realized that her husband must be his brother. He had fallen in love with the queen and decided to take advantage of the resemblance to his brother. He had clothes made up in the same style and color that the king wore, put them on, and went to the castle. The servants were sure that he was their master, and they threw themselves at his feet, so elated that they kissed the hem of his clothing.

The queen was half-dazed when she heard the joyful news.

She took her "husband" into the bedroom and tenderly re-proached him for failing to send news for an entire year. The new king was very cautious about what he said and avoided answering her questions as much as possible.

The two lived happily for some time, until the queen moved back to the palace at the end of the woods. She was standing at the window looking at the mysterious castle, when her husband asked about it. When the queen became suspicious, he changed the subject. After all, his brother had already asked about it, but he vowed to figure out what was going on in the castle.

The new king arranged a hunt, put the servants to sleep with wine, crossed the bridge to the castle, and found the statues of stone at the gate. The poor old woman without hands asked once again for alms.

The king raised his sword and threatened to kill the old woman if she did not tell him right away what had happened to his brother. He insisted on seeing her hands, but she re-fused, telling him that they were repulsive to look at. At last, the old woman had had enough of his questions and pulled out her whip. She was about to strike the king, but he was pre-pared for her tricks, and let his sword land. The hand holding the whip fell to the ground. He picked up the whip quickly and held it tight. She refused to tell him anything, until he started swinging his sword over her head, and at that point she gave him a second whip, which she told him he could use to disen-chant the stone figures. She pointed out exactly where his brother and the three animals were.

The false king touched every single stone with his magic whip, and then finally he lifted the curse on his brother and the animals, who were shocked to see him standing there. The brothers embraced, and everyone thanked their rescuer warmly for breaking the spell. There were celebrations in the castle.

The joyful feelings did not last long. When the king learned that his brother had betrayed him with the queen, he flew into a rage and could not restrain himself. Drawing his sword, he plunged it into his brother's chest. Everyone fled the castle, horrified by this terrible deed. The true king began searching for his wife, and she was looking for him, too. Their joy was boundless when they found each other, although tarnished by the feelings of pain about the brother who had betrayed them and his violent death. A messenger brought the news that the brother was in fact not dead and that he was still alive and had returned home. His little pet dog had stayed by his side, licked his wounds, and stopped the flow of blood. The two brothers realized that the old woman had most likely blinded the brother and provoked him to carry out the violent deed. They reconciled and returned home.

The reunited couple lived happily for many years and passed on their peaceful and calm kingdom to their children.

TRICKING THE WITCH

An evil witch kidnapped three princesses and would not set them free. While they were in captivity, the girls learned a few magic tricks from the witch.

One day a young prince lost his way in the woods, and the two-faced witch welcomed him warmly, but she was actually plotting to kill him that night.

Although the princesses were not allowed to speak, the youngest of the three, Reinhilda, alerted the prince to the perils facing him. She had taken a liking to him, and she whispered in his ear: "When the old woman takes you to your room, don't step on the threshold but jump over it! When she gives you something to drink for the night, don't touch it because it will be a sleeping potion. Don't sleep *in* the bed but *under* it. Leave everything else to me!"

After dinner the witch took the stranger up the stairs to his bedroom, and the youngest of the three sisters lit the way with her candle. The young man jumped over the threshold, and when the witch handed him something to drink, the candle went out, as if by accident. The prince poured the brew into his boot and settled down to sleep under the bed. Later that night the princess woke the prince up and fled with him using the magic she had learned while in captivity.

The two were able to soar through the air, but just as the day was dawning, Reinhilda realized that they were being followed. And indeed the witch, as soon as she had woken up, had known exactly what had happened with the prince and the youngest of the three princesses. She had sent one of the two other princesses out to catch her and bring her back.

It looked as if the two were about to be caught, when the princess said: "I'm going to change into a rosebush, and I'll turn you into a rose. My sister is chasing us, and she won't be able to do a thing because she can't stand the smell of roses." Just when the girl was closing in on them, a fragrant rosebush sprang up right in her path with a magnificent rose in bloom. The girl had been tricked, and she had to turn back. The witch scolded her no end. "You stupid girl," she grumbled angrily. "If you had just plucked the rose, the bush would have followed." And then she sent the eldest of the three to find the two fugitives.

In the meantime the couple returned to their human shapes, and they continued on their way. Reinhilda turned around at one point, and she saw that they were still being pursued. She decided to take advantage of her magic powers again, and she said to the prince: "I'm going to turn myself into a church, and you are going to climb up into the pulpit and hold a stern sermon about witches and their sinister magic."

When the third sister caught up with the pair and was just about to overtake them, she suddenly found herself near a church, and right there in the pulpit was a preacher raging against witches and their black magic. The sister returned, and when the old woman asked her what she had seen, she said: "I could see her from a distance, but when I reached the spot where she had been, there was nothing but a church there with a preacher denouncing witches."

"Oh, you foolish thing!" the old woman said. "If only you had just shoved the preacher out of the pulpit, the church would have come back with you. Now I have to go after them. Well, they don't stand a chance against me."

The princess resumed her natural form, but now the old woman was chasing the two of them, and she was hot on their trail. "My magic is not as powerful as a witch's," Reinhilda said to her beloved. "Give me your sword. I'm going to turn myself into a pond and you will become a duck. Just stay in the middle of the pond, no matter how much the old woman tries to lure you to come on shore. Otherwise we will be lost."

The old woman did what she could to bring the duck on land, using terms of endearment and throwing tasty morsels

on the water, all in vain. The duck stayed in the middle of the
pond and would not paddle any closer. Then the old woman
climbed to the top of a dam in the pond and drank every drop
of water in sight. The princess was now in the belly of the
witch. She turned back into a human and cut the witch open
from inside with the sword the prince had given to her. The
witch was now as dead as a doornail.

The loving couple was reunited and in safety. The princess
gave her hand to the prince at the altar, and the two lived happily together with the sisters, who had been freed from the
spell.

THE ENCHANTED FIDDLE

 A woman had a son named Jacob, and he was the source of much pain and sorrow. Her irritation with him grew until one day she cried out: "I've had it! It's time for you to leave home and find a master, even if it's the devil himself!"

Jacob heard these words and felt so bad that he left home and decided to find an apprenticeship. As he was walking along, he met a man who asked him where he was heading. The boy replied: "My mother ordered me to find work, even if it's with the devil himself."

"Well, then you are quite welcome to come with me," the stranger said, and the two started walking together.

Their path took them through a mountain canyon, on to an underground cave. The boy was ordered to tend fires under many different cauldrons. His master warned him that he must never lift up any of the lids or look inside.

Once, when the devil was visiting the world aboveground, Jacob was overwhelmed with curiosity and lifted one of the lids, despite the warning. A humming noise rose up as if flies were swarming around him, but as it turned out, it was the noise of souls who had been damned, then boiled up in the pot, and were now simmering on the fire. After giving in to his curiosity, Jacob suddenly realized with horror that his grandmother was among the wretched in the cauldron. She recognized her grandson and asked how he had traveled down to where she was. Jacob told her everything that had happened. His grandmother said: "You won't be able to stay here much longer. As soon as Satan returns home, he is going to give you your wages and let you go. But don't take more than three coins from him. If you do, he'll break your neck."

When he returned from his visit aboveground, the evil one knew exactly what had happened. He summoned the boy and told him that he would have to leave. And he gave him his wages, but the boy took no more than three coins, and Satan let him off the hook and allowed him to depart.

When the boy was back from below, he met a woman who asked him for alms: "I was in service for three years and all I have left are two kreuzers." Jacob gave her one of his three coins. A second beggar woman asked him for a kreuzer, and he gave her another of the three coins he had received and kept going. Then an old man saw him and said: "I was in service for three long years, and I have nothing to my name." Jacob took the last kreuzer out of his pocket and gave it to the beggar. The man said: "You have been so generous in dividing up your wages among us that I am going to grant you three wishes, all of which are guaranteed to come true."

The boy said: "First of all I am going to wish to end up in heaven. Then I would like a musket that always hits its target and a fiddle that makes everyone dance to its tune." He was granted all three wishes.

Jacob decided to try out his enchanted musket at a shooting contest. And just imagine, he won all the prizes, much to the chagrin of the other sharpshooters. They accused the boy of using black magic, and after a short trial he was sentenced to death. His execution was to be carried out in public.

On the day set for the execution, Jacob was allowed one last wish. He climbed the ladder and asked to hold his beloved fiddle one last time before a rope was put around his neck. Once he was up there, he started playing like a wild man. The executioners began dancing on the ladder and plunged to the ground. The priests and all the men and women in the crowd began whirling around madly, bumping up against each other, but Jacob kept playing more and more wildly, until everyone fell to the ground, exhausted from the frenzied movement. He quickly climbed down the ladder and slipped away while everything was still quiet.

Ever since that day Jacob has appeared from time to time when people are dancing, and every once in a while someone will drop dead while he is fiddling.

THE DEVIL AND
THE FISHERMAN

 A man hired a fisherman, but the fellow had no luck at all catching fish, and so he was about to lose his job. On the way home, the unhappy fisherman met a little man wearing a green jacket and a red hat on his head. "Sir fisherman! Where are you heading?"

"May God have pity on me, a poor fisherman."

"Why in the world?" asked the little man. The fisherman explained that he was unhappy because he had no luck at all catching fish and was about to be let go. The little old man was sure that he could help him out. In exchange all he would have to do is turn over something that he did not know was in his home. Then he would have to make a cut on his arm, and write his name with blood in a book.

The fisherman thought: "That's fine with me, for whatever I know is at home, my wife also knows is there." He signed. Then he returned to his fishing spot, and now he was wildly successful, catching more fish than ever before. At home his wife asked how he had managed to catch so many fish. He told her the story of his encounter, and she suddenly made a long face. She revealed to her husband that she was expecting a child.

The fisherman's wife gave birth to a boy, who was called Zacharias. The devil showed up and said that he would come fetch the boy when he turned seven. When the boy was old enough to go to school, his father explained the painful fix he was in to a priest. The priest gave him a prayer that the boy was supposed to recite on a daily basis so that the evil one would not be able to touch him. The boy dutifully recited the prayer every day. One evening he forgot to say it. That night the devil appeared and took him away. While the devil was flying through the skies with him, Zacharias woke up and said the prayer, and the evil one had to drop him. The young man fell down and landed between two rocks.

The next day Zacharias realized that he was up on a mountain in the woods. From his perch he could see a grand palace on top of another mountain. He took a path that led over hill and down dale to the palace and walked right in, discovering one splendid room after another. In each one there was a three-legged giant with a lion's tail. Next to the castle was a beautiful garden, vast in size. Three-legged cattle, with what looked like antlers, were roaming around in it.

A little man was seated in the middle of the garden, and he beckoned to the young man. Zacharias went over to him, and the man asked whether he was interested in staying. When he said he was, the man added: "There will be a price for staying here. But I'm going to give you my staff, and you can use it to master all the perils in this place. Don't breathe a word about its power; otherwise you will be lost. Two giants are going to come by here, one tonight, another tomorrow night, and the night after that a giantess will appear. When the first giant appears, strike him with the staff, and he will collapse. On the second night, do the same thing with the other giant. Then chop them both up into little pieces and put one piece into every corner of the castle. On the third night, hit the giantess with the staff, then turn the staff toward the setting sun and throw it to the ground. The earth will open up and swallow the giantess. Then take the staff and turn it toward the rising sun and stamp your foot. A beautiful young woman will appear. As soon as she becomes visible, all the animals here will be rescued, and the castle and young woman will belong to you."

Zacharias did exactly what the little man told him to do. That night a powerful giant appeared and stormed up and down in the room. He roared: "What's going on? We've been here over two thousand years, and now we're supposed to leave? If your name were not Zacharias, you would be dead, like all the men before you." The enraged giant was about to stampede and kill Zacharias. But Zacharias used the staff and hit the giant with such force that he collapsed. The next night the same thing happened, and Zacharias conquered the second giant as well. As ordered, he chopped the two giants into little pieces and left the pieces in the corners of the castle.

The next night a monstrous giantess showed up, ready to tear him to pieces. He didn't blink an eye and knocked her to the ground with the staff. Then he pointed the staff toward the setting sun and threw it to the ground. He heard a loud rumbling and the ground opened up, swallowing up the dead giantess.

Zacharias then turned the magic staff toward the rising sun and stamped his foot. A chasm opened up, and an enchanting young woman rose up from it. She walked toward him and embraced him for being so courageous. Life in the castle was transformed with her arrival: The entire court, all the servants, and the animals, too, came to life and cheered for Zacharias, the man who had rescued them. The young woman gave Zacharias her hand, and her heart, too. And the palace with its inhabitants was his to rule.

The two celebrated their marriage and lived happily together for a long time.

THE EXPERT HUNTER

A hunter had three sons. On his deathbed, he asked them to hold a vigil, one at a time, at his grave and to tend a fire while they were there.

After his death, the eldest of the three was the first to keep watch. At midnight, a man dressed in black appeared with a pick and shovel, and he started digging around the grave. The son shot an arrow at his head and then threw him over the wall of the cemetery. The next morning he buried him but did not say a word about it.

The following evening the second son had the same adventure. And he, too, did not say a word about it at home.

When the youngest son took over the vigil on the third night, three dark men appeared at the grave site and were planning to dig up the body. But the boy shot down all three of them and, just as his brothers had done, he tossed the bodies over the wall. In the meantime the fire had gone out. The boy climbed up a tree and saw a small fire in the woods. On his way over to it, he met a little man who seemed in a big hurry. Hans asked why he was running so fast and when he heard him say, "I am Night and behind me you will see Day, and I can't let him catch up with me," he tied the little man to a tree.

A little while later he met a second man, who was running just as fast, and it was Day. He tied him to a tree as well, walked a little farther down, and found the fire. Five giants were gathered around it and were roasting an ox. Hans amused himself by shooting away each piece of the ox just as it was about to go down the gullet of one of the giants. When he tired of this little activity, which was deeply annoying to the giants, he emerged from the darkness and sat down to have a meal with them.

The giants were quite happy to play host to a sharpshooter. They told him about a princess who lived nearby and how she was guarded by a dog with huge, gaping jaws. They were hoping that Hans would kill it and clear the way for them. The giants left the campfire and escorted him to an underground passage leading to the castle. The young man walked down it and found the dog right at the end of it. After he killed it, he became curious about the princess. He was determined to find her, and he passed by various sleeping sentries and then entered her chamber. She was lost in dreams, and she looked beautiful lying on her bed fast asleep.

A sword was hanging from the wall but he could not reach it. Right below it was a bottle with the words: "Whoever drinks me can wield the sword."

The hunter drank the potion, and the sword dropped right down into his hands. He then took one of the slippers under the bed, along with half of a silk kerchief, and returned the way he had come, tiptoeing past the sleeping sentries up to the entrance. There he called the giants by name, and when each of the fellows, curious to see what was happening, poked his head out, he chopped it off. After that, he slipped back into the forest, released Day and Night (for it had been dark the entire time), and returned home to his mother. He left the sword behind.

The lead sentry discovered the heads of the giants the next morning and declared himself to be the great rescuer who had earned the hand of the princess. But the princess was suspicious and demanded to have her slipper and kerchief. Next she asked to have seven years to think it over.

During that time she ran a tavern in the woods with a sign: THE RICH CAN PAY WITH COINS, THE POOR PAY NOTHING. She ran the tavern herself as a way of finding out who had rescued her.

The brave sharpshooter was so poor that he had to give up

his house. He and his mother were without a home and had to move from place to place. The old woman was exhausted and could hardly put one foot in front of the other. When she read the sign on the tavern door, she walked right in. The princess, whom the son recognized immediately, asked about the young man's adventures. She quickly recognized him as well, and he showed her the two mementos he had taken with him as proof that he had been there. She was thrilled, and she took the hunter to her father and presented him as the true rescuer. Her father agreed to give him her hand in marriage.

A POT OF GOLD IN
THE OVEN

A soldier who had once moved as fast as lightning was aging and decided to give up the military life. He tossed away his lance and traveled across the country back to his home. When he returned home, he found that he did not know a soul. During the war, his village had been destroyed, along with the old castle that had once stood there. Only a few houses were left standing.

Things went well for him as long as his leather money belt, which he had fed like a proper little hamster while looting and pillaging, remained full. He even found himself a wife. He discovered a hideout in the corner of the castle ruins, right near an old oven, which was still standing. It took almost no effort to put a roof over his head and settle in.

His wife told him again and again that he would be better off taking on a trade or working in some kind of business. Then she would no longer be called a soldier's wife, something that irritated her no end. But the soldier had no interest in work or in haggling. He preferred to nap on his bed of straw near the hearth. When he would make faces at the wall, the roughly chiseled face of a little man in the charred stones would grin back at him and thumb his nose at him.

Pretty soon the soldier's leather money belt turned into a flabby pouch, and the soldier exchanged it for a loaf of bread. Hunger settled down on his house, and his wife began to bicker and nag like a spiny hedgehog. When it was suppertime, she would bang on the cold oven, run off, and leave the soldier alone in the freezing kitchen. He began to notice that

the little man in the wall would twitch and twist, as if someone were beating him, whenever his wife banged on the oven.
The soldier tried to get to the bottom of things.

One day his wife was away longer than usual. The afternoon
passed and before long it was evening. Time was on the soldier's hands, and he began poking at the crumbling concrete
until the stones were free of it. The little man started to stretch
and bend like a bunny in clover. Suddenly blue smoke poured
out of the stove, and it threw a light as strong as a lantern.

The soldier jumped up, for he knew that some kind of treasure must be buried around there. The little man on the wall
was protecting it and pointing him to it. In a flash he took the
entire stove apart and discovered a copper pot, larger than a
helmet, filled right up to the top with big gold coins. Skilled in
the art of looting, he put his hand above it and chanted:

> "The cock crows and the spell breaks,
> I'll speak my piece whatever it takes.
> First I'll saddle the dragon of gold,
> Then spit at the devil until he's out cold."

Just then the soldier's wife screeched: "Turn around! Turn
around!" In a fright he turned around, went over to the door,
and looked out, but no one was there. A ruckus broke out in
the ruins, and strange beaks began poking their way out of the
rocks and crowing and screeching. When he ran over to the
stove, he saw that the little round opening where the pot had
been was still there, but the pot was gone and the stony little
man on the wall had vanished, never to return.

CONTESTS WITH THE DEVIL

One evening the devil came to see a charcoal burner who was keeping watch at his kiln. "Come join me," the devil said. "Let's try to find some work together." The man went with him, and before long the two reached an inn. "Go on in," the devil said, "and ask if there is any work for us!"

The innkeeper told the charcoal burner: "I could use someone to help with the threshing, but I really need six men, not two."

"We can thresh as much grain as six men," the devil replied. And the innkeeper went ahead and hired the two men.

The two worked hard and soon finished the job. But the innkeeper was not completely satisfied because the grain was not as clean as it could have been. "I'm not going to pay you until it's completely clean!" he said. The devil began to blow on the grain, and it was soon clean as a whistle.

"How much are you going to pay us?" The innkeeper hesitated for a moment. "Give us as much grain as we can carry on our backs!" the devil proposed. The innkeeper thought that was fine, but when he saw that the two were carrying off the entire pile of grain, he was outraged.

The innkeeper told a farmhand to let one of the bulls out of the stable, and it chased after the two fellows in a fury. The devil grabbed the bull by the tail and threw it over his shoulder, and the two arrived safely back at the charcoal burner's hut.

The devil took his leave and said: "Tomorrow I'll return with a horn. Whoever can blow the loudest on it will have everything in sight." The next day he arrived with the horn and blew so hard on it that the trees all around began shaking. The charcoal burner took some roots and wrapped them around the horn so that it would not explode when he started to blow on it. The devil let out a loud shriek: "Give it back. If the horn isn't in one piece, I won't be able to return to hell. I'm going to go get a stone instead and throw it so far that it will disappear." And he took a stone and actually did throw it so far that they could no longer see it.

The charcoal burner was supposed to fetch the stone, but he said: "Anyone who can throw that far has to fetch the stone himself!" And so the stupid devil was the one who had to run that errand. The charcoal burner picked up the stone and said: "I'm going to throw it at the sun."

"No!" the devil shrieked. "I need that stone to get back to hell. I can't just let you throw it away. I'll come back tomorrow, and we'll see who has the longest claws."

That was just fine with the charcoal burner. He said to his wife: "When the devil returns, tell him that I went to the blacksmith's to have my claws sharpened."

When the devil returned the next day, he saw that he had been beaten at his own game again, and said: "I'm done with that fellow. No wonder they say that you should never tangle with a charcoal burner."

WOUD AND FREID

A powerful man and his wife once ruled over the land, and they were both adepts in the magical arts. Even the elements obeyed their commands. He was named Woud, and she was called Freid.

The king was a powerful man with a long, flowing beard. His eyes flashed with fires that could blind you if you looked into them too long. He usually wore only a loincloth to cover his nakedness. The cloth was fastened with a belt of infinite length, and the king's power was dependent on that belt. As long as he kept the belt on, he would remain the sole ruler. It was impossible to remove the belt because his hips and shoulders were so broad that it could never be lifted over them. Sometimes he wore a cape that covered it completely.

His wife was the most beautiful woman imaginable. She wore a sarong around her hips, like her husband, and her hair was so thick and long that she was completely covered by it. She drank water from a single stream, and her husband drank only a certain type of wine. If Freid leaned over to scoop water into her hand from the stream, her hair would sparkle in the sunlight, and her arm looked like pure snow.

This beauty was also a very jealous woman, for she was always afraid that she would not be enough for her fiery husband. To find out how to ease her pain, she once consulted dwarfs who practiced magic. They fashioned for her a necklace that had the power to win the heart of anyone who set eyes on her and that would also keep her beloved from ever wavering in his devotion. The dwarfs demanded her love in exchange for the necklace.

Freid wore the jewels, and her husband was enthralled. But when Woud discovered the price she had paid for the jewels, he abandoned her. Freid woke up in the morning and reached across the bed to touch her husband. He was gone. She touched her hand to her neck and found that the necklace was missing. She was already overwhelmed with despair, and the loss of the jewels only deepened her passion for Woud. She did her best to catch up with her husband, pursuing him across continents, year after year. In the evening, exhausted by her travels, she would sit down, put her head in her lap, and weep. Each tear transformed itself into a precious pearl.

Finally, when time had run its course, she found Woud and told him about her anguish. She showed him the pearls she had wept for his sake. Woud counted each pearl. There were exactly as many pearls as there were precious stones on the necklace. He was willing to forgive her, and he gave her back the jewels as a peace offering. He had traveled all over the world, but in all that time he had never found anyone as beautiful. He had remained faithful to her.

PART IV

LEGENDS

THE MOUSE CATCHER, OR
THE BOY AND THE BEETLE

Once there was a village so badly infested with mice that no one knew what to do. A stranger arrived in town and told the farmers that he would be able to get rid of the mice. They promised him a generous reward in return. The stranger pulled out a little whistle and blew into it. All the mice in the village ran after the man, who took them to a big pond, where they all drowned. The stranger returned to the village and asked for his reward. But the farmers refused to give him the full amount. The man blew into another little whistle, and this time all the children in the village came running after him.

There was a young boy living there at the time whose mother had died. His stepmother was very mean to him. One day she sent him into the woods to pick an entire basket of strawberries. After a while he grew tired and decided to lie down for a short time and take a nap. A little man appeared and picked enough berries to fill up the basket. He gave the boy a small box and told him not to open it unless he was desperate.

Just when the boy was getting ready to return home, the stranger with the whistle passed by, and the boy ran after him with all the other children. The man took them to a huge mountain, and the children had to go through a door into the dark mountain. They were terrified.

The boy remembered the little box. He opened it up and an old beetle flew out of it. The beetle gave him a key. The boy opened the door in the mountain, and the children were all able to get out. But they had no idea where they were, for they had traveled a great distance from home.

The boy reached a huge cliff that turned out to be an enchanted castle. He thought: "I'd better make sure that the beetle is all right." The beetle came flying by at once, scraped around in the ground a bit, found the key to the castle, and opened its doors. The boy saw all kinds of precious objects there. Before long a king arrived with a princess and many servants. The king said: "You have lifted the curse on us. I was the old beetle." And he gave the princess to the boy in marriage.

All that happened in our homeland, the Oberpfalz.

PEARL TEARS

A young knight decided to marry the beautiful daughter of a servant, and he had to endure the resentment of the nobility in the region, especially the mothers. They refused to appear at the wedding and shunned the young couple, who lived alone in their castle.

The two lived happily together, with no complaints about their peaceful isolation. When the time came for the wife to give birth, she turned to her husband, who was deeply worried about finding a godfather for the child, and said: "Go out through the garden into the streets and just ask the first person you meet to do you this favor, even if it happens to be a servant."

Before the knight had even left the garden, he met an elegantly beautiful woman, who told him: "I understand your concerns. But stop worrying. I will be the child's godmother, and you won't regret it." And so he escorted the noble lady, who was wearing a blue veil—it was the Madonna—up to the castle, and she helped out with the birth, comforting the young woman as she delivered a girl. When the child was baptized, she was given the name Maria. The mysterious godmother parted with the words: "I am not going to give the child a gift now. The child will need me later, and then I'll help her."

The child Maria grew up, and when she reached the age of seven, her mother died. Her father, who felt abandoned, married a young woman living nearby. She was beautiful and proud, and she loved giving orders. It was a difficult time for Maria. Her stepmother was arrogant and despised her, and she had to take on all kinds of menial labor. Her father was not happy about that, but he didn't dare oppose his wife.

The stepmother was becoming more and more abusive with each passing day. One day Maria burst into tears and curled up in a corner. All at once Our Lady of the Angels appeared before her and said: "My dear child, I am your godmother, and I made a vow to your mother that I would appear before you if you needed help. Come with me, and I'll make sure that you are safe." The girl took her hand eagerly, and the two went out into the woods.

They reached a mountain and Our Lady of the Angels knocked on a sheer surface three times. A door suddenly opened onto a beautiful palace with twelve rooms. In each of them, strands of the most precious pearls were hanging from the walls. At the windows and on the tables were beautiful roses. Maria was supposed to take care of them and make sure they did not wilt. In exchange, she was allowed to dine with our dear lady at a table where food magically appeared at appointed times.

One day the fair lady had to leave on a journey. Maria was supposed to manage everything in the palace, but she was told not to enter the thirteenth chamber. On the evening of the third day, she was so overcome by curiosity that she opened the door to the mysterious room. Bookcases lined the wall, and on them were massive books. The Lord was sitting at a desk with his Son, and they were composing the destinies of those who had been born and endowing them with gifts to guide them in their paths through life. Sometimes they noted how gifts were squandered or used in ways that were not part of their master plan.

When Our Lady of the Angels returned home, she said: "You have disobeyed my order. I am not going to punish you, but you can no longer stay here. Go back home to your father. You will find the way easily, and I will make sure you have everything you need." She gave Maria a white dress, and after placing a wreath of roses on her head, she sent the girl away.

At home, Maria discovered that her father was living in miserable circumstances, for his wife had spent the entire fortune. The man was overjoyed to see his daughter, who appeared to be flourishing, especially since he feared that she had died long ago. The stepmother was not at all thrilled when the girl she hated reappeared. She was hoping to get rid of her by hiring her out as a kitchen maid.

Maria wanted to live with her father no matter what, even if it meant carrying out the most menial tasks in the kitchen. As far as the stepmother was concerned, Maria could do nothing right. And her new stepbrothers teased her and made fun of the filthy maid in the kitchen. The stepmother joined in the laughter.

One day the brothers took things too far, and they beat the girl until she began bleeding. She retreated to the kitchen and, leaning over a washbasin, she began weeping. Her blood trickled into the basin, and each teardrop that fell into the basin made a ringing sound. The girl's stepmother scolded the children for fighting all the time. She noticed something shiny in the basin and discovered some of the most beautiful pearls she had ever seen.

There was great joy at the castle, for now they could return to festive times, and even Maria was invited to one of the dazzling balls. She was so thrilled that she began to laugh, and one rose after another dropped from her mouth.

Before long the profits from the pearls were exhausted. The stepmother and her sons began to torture Maria in order to raise more money, and she wept more pearls and laughed more roses.

An old servant was living in the castle, and she was distressed that Maria had to suffer so much. She comforted her with the words: "Just be patient, my child. I was once your nursemaid, and I'm happy to go wherever you wish. The next time you weep, give me the basin and we'll collect the pearls in it!" The two left to search for a place where they could live peacefully.

The girl had become so beautiful in the meantime that many a young man fell in love with her. Maria had no feelings for any of them. One day Our Lady of the Angels appeared before her and offered these words of comfort: "My dear child! Stop worrying. I have given you the gift of being indifferent to the stirrings of love. Follow me to my palace, which I am going to turn over to you. My time in this region is over, and I am moving on. From now on you will have the chance to give shelter to the ill and to the impoverished until the day when I call you to me." She knocked three times on the wall of the mountain cavern, and a magnificent palace appeared before them.

Maria moved in, and she invited all those who were poor and ailing to the castle, where she took care of them. Whenever she had a problem, she went back into the forbidden chamber, where she had once seen God the Father with his Son. She was always given help. The noble woman remained young and beautiful for her entire life. When she died, no one could believe that she was really gone, but Our Lady of the Angels had come for her soul. Maria was lying on a bed, a pale virgin in a white dress, with red roses in her hair.

FLOUR FOR SNOW

There once lived a fellow who was tired of slaving away to make a living. He spent a lot of time complaining to the Lord about how hard he worked, especially when it was snowing. Snow made his work all the harder, and what good was snow, after all? It had not fallen in Paradise, and it was also not on Noah's ark. It could not possibly be a part of God's creation.

One day this fellow was in the forest chopping wood, when thick flakes of snow began to fall from the sky. Cursing his fate, he crawled into a nearby hollow. Just as he was settling into a place where he could stretch out, an angel appeared to ask why he called so often on the devil, but so rarely on God. "The Lord doesn't pay much attention to me, and so I can't really pretend that I'm friends with him." The angel asked what he needed from God to change his mind. And the foolish fellow said that he wanted to see flour falling from the sky instead of snow.

Just then, flour began falling down from the sky in thick clouds. People came running to collect it, and suddenly they had enough bread and didn't have to work anymore. But the next time a house burned down or a wall collapsed, the people who had once worked as carpenters and masons would not lift a finger. And so it happened that everyone started making their homes in caves, just as they had when the world was first created. They lived on plants and roots and walked around naked, just like Adam and Eve. The number of wild animals multiplied, and thorny hedges, shrubs, and trees took over where there had once been cozy homes and pathways lined with flowers.

The worker realized the foolishness of his ways and understood just how stupid he had been to question the divine order
of the world. Filled with remorse, he rose up from his resting
place to find the angel, and then—he woke up. When he
emerged from the hollow, there was snow at his feet. He fell to
his knees to thank the Lord for teaching him a lesson through
his dreams. From then on, he was at peace with the world.

HOYDEL

There was once a carpenter named Hoydel, and over time, he turned into a thief and hard-hearted killer. He kept track of his murders by putting a notch on his walking stick for each one. Before long, there were so many notches on it that he had room left for only three more.

One day he ran into a priest. Hoydel was such a scoundrel that he actually asked him to hear his confession. When the pious man learned about all the grisly murders, he was in a state of shock and wanted to get away as fast as possible. Hoydel beat the man until he was dead and cut another notch on his stick. Then he murdered another person. All that was left on the staff was room for one more notch. Hoydel met a priest living as a hermit, and he asked him to hear his confession. If the fellow refused to absolve him, he was going to kill him, too, then cut another notch on his stick and kill himself.

The hermit asked the miserable sinner whether he still had the staff that he had used to murder his first victim. Hoydel told him that he did. The priest told him to put the thing in the ground and to kneel down before it and pray. "If the staff begins to grow leaves, blossoms, and then bears fruit, you will find salvation," he told him and went on his way.

Years later the hermit passed the spot, and Hoydel was still kneeling by the staff, which, in the meantime, had grown to be a tall tree bearing beautiful red apples. The priest touched the kneeling man, and he turned to dust. A white dove emerged from his remains and flew up to the heavens.

PART V

TALL TALES AND ANECDOTES

THE TALKER

There once lived a couple, and they were both stupid is as stupid does. The wife ruled the roost, and one day she sent her husband to the market-place to sell their cow. "Whatever you do, don't sell it to a talker," she shouted as he was going out the door. "Did you hear me? Don't sell it to a talker." Her husband promised to do as she had said.

Many buyers showed interest in the hale and hearty cow, but the farmer decided to follow his wife's advice and declared each time: "I'm not going to sell you my cow. You are way too chatty."

The market day was drawing to a close, and the farmer had not yet sold the cow. Out of sorts, he set out for home. On the way he had to cross a bridge, on which there was a life-size image of John of Nepomuk. It was carved from wood and painted. When the farmer saw it, he said: "Why don't you buy my cow so that I won't have to bother bringing it back home?" He waited a long time for an answer, but the man on the bridge remained silent. The farmer thought: "Well, he is certainly not a talker, and I can sell the cow to him." He tied the cow to the railing on the bridge and said: "Time to pay up!" The saint did not say a word. "All right," the man said, for he wanted to close the deal. "I'll give you some time to pay up. I'll be back in a couple of weeks for my money." And he returned home.

Back at home his wife asked if he had sold the cow.

"Of course!"

"But you didn't sell it to a talker, did you?"

"Of course not! The man who bought the cow hardly said a word."

"What did you sell the cow for?"

"He bought the cow at the price I demanded, but he has not yet paid up. I told him that I would come and get the money in two weeks."

"Do you know who he is?"

"How could I not? You know him too! I meet up with him every time I go across the bridge."

"What does he do?"

"I didn't ask. He was wearing a black hood, just like the priest, and he had five stars on his forehead."

"Oh, you stupid idiot. You are right that he can't talk. That is Saint John. Go back and find the cow; otherwise someone will steal it."

The silly fellow had to return, but the cow was no longer there. He asked Saint John what he had done with the cow and told him that he was back to collect his money. When the holy man refused to speak, the farmer grew angry, took his walking stick, and began beating the statue so hard that its head broke off at the neck. A hundred guilders fell to the ground with it. Someone who knew that the head was hollow had hidden the money there.

The farmer picked up the money and said: "Well, why not? Now that you had your beating, you can pay me!" Elated, he returned home and reported to his wife how he had told off the buyer and then received in return even more than he had demanded.

THE CLEVER TAILOR

A group of hardworking farmers settled down in a certain region to work the land. They had plenty of money and never needed to beg for anything. They were also never idle. One day a young woman came to visit the farmers with her son, a handsome fellow who was almost fully grown. He didn't like to work, for his father was a powerful man who provided generous support, enough for him and his mother to live in comfort. The farmers in that area were not keen to have the two living with them, and they were secretly hoping that they would settle elsewhere.

But kindness did not go far toward dislodging the unwelcome guests. And so the farmers decided to kill the boy in the dark of night. But the boy uncovered the plan and traded places with his mother. The bloodthirsty group murdered her instead. The boy dragged her corpse out of bed, took it to the house of the priest, and leaned it up against the door. When the priest opened the door that morning as he was about to go to church, the corpse fell at his feet. The boy was nearby, and he began hollering, accusing the priest of killing his mother. The priest was terrified and paid the boy a tidy sum to keep his mouth shut.

The mother was buried, and the son lived a carefree life with the money he had been given.

The farmers were at a loss about what to do. Finally, they decided to put the young man into a barrel. "Even if he survives, he won't have any idea where he is and won't ever come back here," they figured. They carried out their plan. The barrel was rolled up onto a clearing, where there was a chapel.

The farmers left it there and then went into the chapel to thank the Lord for ridding them of that scoundrel.

The farmers departed. The fellow was still in the barrel and began shouting: "I won't, and I can't!"

A shepherd was tending some pigs nearby, and he went over to ask: "What's going on and why are you shouting, 'I won't, and I can't'?"

"Well," a voice said from within, "I'm supposed to marry a princess, and I don't want to."

"Here's a thought," the shepherd said. "Let me take your place, and I'll be happy to marry her." He opened up the barrel and climbed in. The young man locked the barrel back up and shoved it into a pond nearby. Then he took the pigs back home and sold them to the farmers.

The farmers were up in arms. Indignant and angry, they wanted to know how he had managed to round up all those pigs.

"Just go over to where I was, and you will find as many animals there as I did. Be sure to take all your pigs with you," he added. He led the animals over to a nearby dam. The farmers looked into the water and saw the pigs reflected in it. Eager to take possession of the creatures, they asked how to round them up. "It's not hard," the young man replied. "All you have to do is jump into the water. The waters will part, and you will be standing on ground. Watch how I do it. Once I'm in the water, jump in after me, and you'll have your pigs." The fellow was a good swimmer, and he jumped right in. The farmers jumped in after him, and they all drowned, for not one of them could swim. The young man swam over to the dam and drove the pigs back home. The womenfolk asked after their husbands. "Too bad," he answered. "They all drowned." And the women broke into tears and lamentations.

The young man was worried about staying on, for he had a hunch that the women would take their revenge. He was heating up an iron to press his clothes (he had since become a tailor) when he realized that the women in the village were outside, getting ready to storm his house. Since there was no way of escaping, he decided to lie down on a bench near the oven, cover himself up with a white cloth, and play dead. He took the iron, which was still hot, in one hand. The women stormed the house and discovered him. They fell for his trick, and one of them said: "Lucky for you that you're already dead or else we would have beaten you to death."

They left, but one of them returned with the idea of honoring the fellow one last time. She walked over to him, took the cloth off his face, hiked up her skirts, and was about to moon the dead man. The young man was not at all slow to respond, and he took the iron and applied it to her behind. The woman shrieked like a child who has been burned and ran to catch up with her neighbors. She was in pain, but she managed to tell them that the scoundrel must be in hell, for he was already wielding a fiery poker.

Once the women had left, the young man decided that it was time to move on. He packed his worldly belongings and left the region to seek his fortune as a tailor elsewhere.

LEARNING HOW TO STEAL

A farmer had a son named Klaus, who refused to learn how to do anything at all. And so he sent him on the road, hoping that he would learn, at the very least, how to steal. That trick didn't require knowing how to read or write. When Klaus finished his apprenticeship, he returned home. But his father was still angry with him, and so Klaus went back on the road. But first he had to renew his traveling papers, and he was asked what he did for a living. He declared to the authorities that he had mastered theft. The officials there mocked him, and the judge was sure that he had not developed theft into a fine art. "You won't be able to move my horse from the stable, even if I give you permission." Klaus took up the challenge, and he could barely contain himself as he was leaving. The judge ordered two men to guard his horse, each using one side of the harness to keep the horse's legs from moving.

That night an old man appeared and asked for shelter. "I would be perfectly happy with a little corner in the stable." He had a bottle of the finest wine with him. It turned out to have a sleeping potion in it, and he used it to put the guards to sleep. The old man cut the harness, mounted the horse, and trotted off. Who else was it but Klaus the thief?

The next day Klaus returned, and the judge gave him a second task: The lad was now supposed to remove his wife's wedding ring without her noticing it and to take the sheet out from under her while she was sleeping. That evening someone put a ladder up against the house right by the judge's bedroom window. The judge, who was keeping watch, took a shot, and the figure fell to the ground. In a panic, the judge raced out of the bedroom to hide the corpse. Just then the thief walked into the bedroom and, mimicking the judge's voice, told the wife he needed the sheet to wrap up the dead body. While taking the sheet, he removed the woman's wedding ring. The next morning the thief appeared with both sheet and ring. The "corpse" turned out to be a skeleton wearing clothes.

The judge had a third task for the thief. "Bring me the schoolteacher wrapped up in a bedsheet!" That night the thief let some crabs loose in the church. He fastened candles on their backs. Then he called the teacher to tell him that some poor souls were wandering around in the church. The teacher was cautious, but he was also curious. That's how the thief persuaded him to wrap himself up in a sheet before coming to the church. The schoolteacher put the sheet on himself, fastened it at the top, and then made his way to the courthouse and the judge.

Once the master thief had carried out all three tasks, he was given his papers and went on his way.

"DON'T GET MAD!"

A farmer had three sons. The eldest said to him: "Father, I'd like to have my inheritance now so that I can travel." The farmer gave his son the inheritance, one hundred guilders in all, and the son left home. A priest gave him a job as a farmhand. When the priest noticed that the boy had money on him, he said: "Let's have a contest, and I'll stake as much money as you now have. Whoever loses his temper first also loses the bet." The boy agreed to the wager.

The next day the boy was supposed to go out and plow. The priest gave him two oxen, and they were so stupid and useless that he wasn't able to plow a single straight furrow. The boy began to swear a blue streak. The priest came running up and asked: "Have you lost your temper?"

"Yes, of course I have," the boy said. "Who wouldn't be furious?"

"Well done," the priest said. "Hand me your money."

The boy was down in the dumps, and not much later he put down the plow and returned home to his father empty-handed. He told his father how it had come to pass that he lost his entire inheritance.

The second son also wanted to have his inheritance in advance. And his father gave him a hundred guilders. The boy went to work for the very same priest, and he fell into the exact same trap. He turned his money over to the crafty priest and returned home.

The youngest of the three sons, whose name was Hans, now

also wanted his inheritance. His father told him: "If your brothers, who have more brains than you do, could not succeed, how can you possibly make something of yourself? Just stay here at home!" Hans would not stop pleading with his father, and finally he, too, had his inheritance.

The boy went to the same priest and was hired as a farmhand. The priest then made him the offer he had made the other two. Hans asked if the priest was interested in quadrupling the wager. After all, he had to win back what his brothers had lost. And so the two agreed to a contest with higher stakes.

The next day Hans was given the same stupid oxen, but he let them do as they pleased and just whistled cheerfully as he walked behind the plow. When the priest went outside and saw what was going on, he said: "Well, my boy, how do you feel about your team?"

"The oxen have no idea what they are doing, and so I'm just letting them go wherever they want. Does that make you mad?"

"Not at all," the priest lied. "You can take their harnesses off now!"

The next day Hans had to tend the cows. It was hot outdoors, and the animals were running in circles to avoid beestings. A cattle dealer came along. Hans sold him all the cows except for the very weakest one, which he herded between two trees right next to each other in the woods. The weak cow got caught between the trees and couldn't move. Hans decided to lie down in the grass, and he began whistling a tune. The priest came by and asked about his cows. "They're all lost," Hans answered, "except for that skinny one over there, which is stuck between the trees." The priest made a face when he heard this tale. The farmhand asked coyly: "Any chance that you are annoyed?"

"Not at all; I can always buy others." The priest was sure that cows were not worth four hundred guilders.

On the third day, Hans was supposed to tend the pigs. He herded them over to a swampy spot. A hog dealer happened to be passing by, and Hans told him that the pigs were for sale, and a deal was struck. All he wanted was the tail of one of the animals. He stuck it into a spot on the meadow and took a little nap.

When the priest came by to see how the pigs were faring, he found the farmhand fast asleep and the pigs had vanished. He demanded to know what had happened to his livestock. Rubbing the sleep from his eyes, Hans told him that the pigs had sunk down into the meadow and all that was left was the one tail sticking up in the air. He went over to the tail as if he were going to pull the pig up by it, but the tail stayed in his hand. "Look," he said, "the tail has already come off. The pigs must all be dead. Are you by any chance angry?"

"Not at all," the priest replied, and he scratched himself behind the ears. He had no idea what to do with Hans, who was doing his best to make him lose all his worldly goods.

In the evening the priest called the farmhand over: "Hans! I'm going to have to put a watchman in the garden because some thieves have been sneaking into it at night. Can you stay in there tonight and make sure that nothing is taken? Here's a nice, heavy stick. If the intruder doesn't speak up after three warnings, you can go ahead and beat him as hard as you can. If anything is stolen, you lose our contest."

The clever priest sent his cook into the garden to fetch something for him. She tiptoed in, but Hans heard her anyway. He shouted, "Who's there?" three times in a row, so quickly that the cook didn't have a chance to answer. The boy jumped up and beat her up so badly that she couldn't move an inch. The priest heard the screaming and asked what was going on. "I was just following your orders," Hans said. "The cook was about to steal something, and I beat her up so badly that she's half-dead. Are you upset with me?" The priest did not reply and just walked the cook back to the house.

The next day was a holiday, and many guests were expected at the priest's home. The cook was in bed, recovering from her injuries, and a new cook was not so easy to find. The priest told Hans to make a fire at the hearth and to cook up some kind of stew. And he mustn't forget to include potatoes and to throw parsley on top. Hans followed every order to the letter, and while the meat was cooking up in the pot, he took the priest's dog, whose name was Potatoes, and his cat, whose name was Parsley, and put them both in the concoction.

The priest returned from church, looked around in the kitchen, and then asked Hans whether he had been sure to include potatoes and parsley. Hans replied: "Oh, yes, for sure, but I had trouble catching Parsley." The priest nearly fainted. He lifted the lid of the pot, and his faithful cat was right in there, baring its teeth at him. All that remained of his dog was a bushy tail.

The priest could no longer keep quiet, and he called Hans an idiot.

"Are you angry, by any chance?" Hans asked calmly.

"How could I not be angry? I have nothing to serve my guests!" the priest shouted.

Hans won his bet. He took the priest's money and left him high and dry—no livestock, no money, no supper, and no cook. He raced back home and told everyone the story of his cleverness.

OFERLA

Once there was a pastor who was living on a farm with his mother. Her name was Oferla. They had a servant who prepared their meals. There was also a schoolteacher named Fink, and he had a hard time of it, for he had too many children and too little money to take care of them.

Fink learned that the pastor had slaughtered two pigs and that their meat was hanging on hooks by the chimney. The teacher stole into the pastor's house and went into the kitchen while everyone was asleep. Then he took every bit of the meat in the kitchen and returned home.

The next morning the cook discovered the theft and reported it to the pastor and to Oferla. "Who could have done that?" they asked.

"The only person around yesterday was Fink. He must have stolen the pork."

"That can't possibly be true," the pastor said. "Our schoolteacher is an honest man."

But the cook was sure that the teacher was the culprit.

"I have an idea," Oferla said. "We'll let the teacher know that the pork was stolen." She turned to the pastor and added: "Then you can tell him that you're planning a trip and are worried about leaving your valuables at home. After all, they might be stolen, like the pork. And so you're hoping to leave some things with him. Then I'll climb into the big trunk over there. We'll put some bread in there so that I won't get hungry, and then you can take the locked trunk, with me in it, over to the teacher. That's how I'll find out whether they're cooking pork. You can pick me up in the evening—just tell him that you didn't manage to get away."

The pastor found the idea appealing. He took out the trunk, and Oferla climbed into it, taking a couple of loaves of bread with her. The pastor then carried the trunk over to the teacher named Fink and asked if he would hold on to the chest full of valuable items. The teacher was happy to help out, and they put the trunk, with Oferla and her two loaves of bread in it, into a corner.

At noon, the teacher's children shouted: "Father, give us some of the pastor's pork. We want more of it!"

When Oferla heard those words, she could not keep quiet and shouted: "You're the pork thief after all! Now that we know, we'll have you locked up!"

Everyone was terrified when they heard Oferla's words. The teacher lifted the lid of the trunk and saw her in there. He was in such a panic that he strangled her to death and stuck some bread in her mouth. Then he shut the lid of the trunk. That evening the pastor returned and said that he wanted to bring the trunk back home. He had decided not to take the trip after all. The teacher helped him carry it home and went back to his house.

When the pastor lifted the lid, what do you think he saw? The corpse of his mother! The cook shouted: "God has punished us! We were wrong to suspect the teacher, and now she's suffocated. What are we going to do? People will think that we killed her for her money. We have to get her out of here! Run over to the teacher, and he can help us figure out what to do!" The teacher happened to be strolling by, just as if by chance. The pastor confessed everything and begged him to get rid of Oferla's body so that no one would suspect him of anything. He gave him a reward of two hundred kreuzers.

Fink took the money as well as the corpse, along with a pitcher that Oferla had used for beer. He went over to the inn, climbed the stairs, and leaned the corpse against the door-frame. Then he put the pitcher in Oferla's hand, rang the bell, and hid.

Every Sunday Oferla would go to the inn to buy beer. When the bell rang, the girl who worked at the inn opened the door and took the pitcher from Oferla as usual and went to fill it. When she turned around, the woman had fallen down the stairs. The girl wanted to help her get up, but then she realized that Oferla was dead and thought it was all her fault. "Run over to the teacher's house," the innkeeper said, "and confess everything to him! Let's hope that he can come over and help us find a way out of this fix. If not, we'll end up in jail. Tell him we'll pay him three hundred kreuzers to help us out."

The girl went over to the teacher's house and told him the whole story. He went over to the inn, collected his three hundred kreuzers, and told the innkeeper not to worry and that he should not say a word about what happened. The teacher would keep quiet too.

A grumpy old farmer, whose harvest had been stolen more than once, lived in the neighborhood. The teacher carried Oferla's corpse, along with her basket, to his field and put them down near a furrow, with Oferla bending down over the plants. When the farmer went out to work in the morning, he saw Oferla right there in his field next to her basket. He picked up a big stick, made his way over to the thief, and hit her as hard as she could until she fell over. "Oh my dear God," he said. "What have I done? That's just Oferla. She would never have stolen from me. She was probably just picking a few leaves for her pet rabbit. What should I do? If anyone finds out, I will end up in jail."

The farmer went over to talk with the teacher, spilled the beans, and promised to give him one hundred kreuzers if he could remove Oferla from his property. Then no one would suspect anything. The teacher took the hundred kreuzers, put the corpse into a sack, and carried it out into the woods that evening.

Now it was completely dark, and the teacher heard some noise. It turned out that three brothers were there, all robbers, and they were returning from a job with three sacks of smoked meat. The teacher hid behind a tree, and when they passed by, he shouted: "Stop right there, you scoundrels!" The thieves were terrified, dropped their sacks, and ran off. The teacher replaced one of the sacks with the one containing the dead woman and returned home. He now had six hundred kreuzers and a sack filled with meat and could live high on the hog.

When the thieves returned, they found their sacks, picked them up, and returned home. Their mother emptied the sacks and took out the meat. When she opened the third one and pulled out Oferla's hair, she said: "Looks like you brought home some flax."

"Oh, no," they said. "It's just meat." She turned the sack inside out, and to her surprise the corpse of an old woman fell to the ground. They buried her as quickly as possible and no one was the wiser. Then they devoured with gusto the meat they had stolen.

PART VI

TALES ABOUT NATURE

SIR WIND AND HIS WIFE

The wind and his wife were both present at the creation of the world. The two were overweight, and on top of that, Sir Wind had a long beard that wrapped around his body three times. Still, both were able to pass easily through a mere crack in a wall, or any opening at all, for that matter.

There once lived a count who detested the wind and was forever speaking ill of it. One day he was passing through the forest on his lands when he met a woman of some heft. The count asked: "Who are you, where are you from, where are you heading, and why are you so fat?"

The woman replied: "I am known as Madame Wind, and I know that you don't like me."

"Where is your husband?" the nobleman asked.

"You will see him in a moment!" she replied. And Madame Wind began to blow and carried the count to a glass mountain, where she set him down to wait. Then she slipped into a crack in the mountain. Before long a man of huge girth appeared. His beard was wrapped three times around his gigantic body. "You may have guessed that I'm Sir Wind, the man you've scorned for so long." And he beat the count with a whip. All at once the count turned to stone, and although he had become a statue, he could still see and hear everything that was going on in the glass mountain. Every day more people were turned to stone, and he learned, to his dismay, that in ten years all the nobles would be roasted and the common folk would be boiled.

Two years went by, and the count was aching to see his faithful wife. He was sure that she would be able to free him.

Before long, a strange bird appeared, one he had never before seen. It landed on his head and dropped a ring—his wife's wedding ring—along with a little note, to the ground. Just then, the count returned to his human form. He read the note, and it instructed him to follow the bird wherever it might fly.

The bird flew straight ahead, and the count followed it. He reached a castle that was in flames. The bird flew right into the fire, but the count did not dare follow and stayed outside. After a while a prince in full regalia came out of the castle, took the count by the hand, and led him through the flames into a splendid hall filled with statues. The bird said: "I lifted the curse that had you under the spell of the wind. Otherwise you would have suffered the fate of all those statues made of stone, still waiting at the glass mountain. I was also turned to stone, but the flames liberated me. Take a look at this figure made of stone." And the bird pointed to a statue. "He was once a king, and now the bird that is the spirit of water will free him." As soon as he spoke those words, another bird flew into the hall with a little note in its beak and landed on the statue's head. Suddenly the statue came to life: It was the king. On the note were written words declaring that each of the three—the count, the prince, and the king—could make a wish that would correspond to the size of the pieces in which they tore the note. The count wanted to be as fat as possible, the prince as wide as possible, and the king as tall as possible, so tall that he would be able to touch the stars.

The prince, who had the sharpest vision, led the trio out of the castle by way of an underground tunnel. Scores of armed figures were lined up at the glass castle, with Sir Wind right up front, and his wife holding up the rear. When the prince looked up, he saw legions of armed birds in the sky. The king made himself as tall as he could, and as soon as he pulled the birds down to earth, the other two slew them.

Sir Wind left the glass mountain with his army and began menacing his three adversaries. Once the clock struck eleven, he would have power over them. The count made himself as fat as possible, opened his mouth wide, and Sir Wind and Madame Wind moved in. "Close your mouth!" the prince shouted, and the count swallowed them both up. They landed in his stomach, which began to ache painfully. The count spit the heavy weight of the two into the sea, and Sir Wind and Madame Wind sank deep down into the waters.

Ever since then the seas have been restless, and the wind blows from the direction of the ocean.

THE ICE GIANTS

Once there was a woman with three daughters, and they had nothing to eat. The woman left home and was planning to end her misery by drowning herself. But a voice called out to her: "Stop what you're doing and go over to the mountains. Your luck will turn!" The message was repeated twice, and so the good woman walked toward the mountains.

Once she had made her way across the mountains, she saw a man standing at the door of his house. She asked for alms and received them, along with the promise that her misery would be at an end once she returned home. As she made her way back, night fell, and she lost her way. In the morning, she discovered that she was near a body of water that had frozen, a sea of ice. Three giants were gathered there, wearing hats made of gold and playing with golden apples. All at once a blast of cold air sent the protective hats in the direction of the woman, and all three hats landed at her feet. The giants offered her their golden apples in return for the hats, for they were not able to leave the frozen expanse and go on land. The woman was more than happy to oblige, and she returned home with three golden apples. She sold the apples along with the silver leaves on their stems, but she kept the stems themselves. If she wanted to make a wish, all she had to do was knock three times with the stem, and any wish would be granted.

The woman grew rich and lived in peace, until her daughters came of age and were ready to marry. She left home in search of the man who had given her the alms. She offered him her eldest daughter in marriage, along with one of the stems from the apples as a dowry. One stem was not enough for the man, and so she returned home to fetch a second one. Once again she passed the sea of ice. The three giants were waiting for her. They wanted her daughters to become their wives, and they offered seven golden apples in the bargain. The woman found this offer much more appealing than the exchange with the man. She traveled with her daughters to the giants. The giants welcomed them into their underground palaces, and they all lived happily together. The children all became, like their fathers, ice giants.

WHY SNOW IS WHITE

After God had finished creating the meadows and giving plants and flowers all their beautiful colors, he turned to the snow on the ground and said: "You can choose whatever color you want. You end up covering everything up anyway."

The snow looked at the grass and said: "Give me your green color!" It went to the roses, to the violets, and to the sunflowers, for it was vain and wanted to have a beautiful skirt. But the grass and the flowers made fun of the snow and gave it the cold shoulder.

The snow turned to the flowers known as snowdrops and said in despair: "If no one is willing to give me a color, then I will be like the moon—always upset that no one can see it."

The little flower replied: "If you like my shabby little coat, you can have it." The snow took it, and from then on it was always white, and it became the enemy of all other flowers.

THE SUN TAKES AN OATH

The Sun and the Moon are man and wife. When they married, the Moon, who had a reputation for being cold and dull, was not passionate enough for his ardent wife. He liked to take naps.

The exasperated Sun proposed a wager: "Whoever wakes up first will have the right to shine during the day, and the lazy one will have the night. If we both wake up at the same time, we can shine next to each other in the skies." The naive Moon had a good laugh. He agreed to the deal because he was convinced that he could not possibly lose. With a smile on his face, he fell asleep. And from that day on, he kept his smile.

The Sun was so upset that she could not sleep for long. By two in the morning she was already awake and lighting up the world, and then she woke up the frosty Moon. She boasted about her victory and reminded him that, as his punishment, the two would never be able to spend a night together again. That's why she had proposed the wager, and she strengthened the result with a vow that she was bound to the terms and would not back down. Since then the Moon shines at night, and the Sun by day.

After a while, the Sun began to regret the vow she had taken in anger, for she was in love with the Moon. And the Moon likewise felt drawn to his wife and had imagined the entire wager a mere joke. His iciness had been playful rather than serious. Now the two were hoping to reunite. They started moving closer to each other, and from time to time, they met, at moments that we call solar eclipses. But then they began to quarrel again, each blaming the other for their separation. They were unable to smooth over their differences.

The time remaining for a reconciliation began to run out, and soon the Sun had to begin her journey, as she had sworn she would do. She was red-hot with rage as she went her way. If they had not fought again, they would be together now. A long time passed before her anger died down. During one period of complete darkness, they must have met again.

And so the Sun always appears in a state of heated, passionate resentment. But sometimes, when she is moving along, she sees how wrong she was and weeps bloody tears and goes down in fiery flames.

The Moon is equally sad and distressed that he cannot meet the Sun. For that reason he keeps shrinking until all that is left of him is a small crescent. He then begins to grow with the hope of meeting the Sun again, but once he is restored to full size, he realizes that he must be wrong and begins to wane once again. He has become melancholy from his unhappiness in love. And that's why his light is so dim and soft. It's also why unhappy lovers send their laments up to the Moon.

THE SUN'S SHADOW

After the Sun and the Moon were created, Death ruled the world. Once the two celestial bodies grew up, they drove Death underground and into a corner, and it, in turn, killed off everything created by the Sun and Moon.

The three began quarreling so violently that all things created nearly perished in a flood.

The Titans decided to hold a meeting and sat down on some stone benches they had gathered together in the mountains. They were unable to come to any decisions, until a white weasel crawled out from a crevice and began licking their eyes. They decided to take the side of Death. Death refused to give them the final word on the matter, for as a man he was able to rule over the Sun in any case, since she was a woman. Quarrels broke out again, but with such passion that the Titans tore all of Death's clothes from his stout body. The Sun took pity on Death and threw a dark cape over him so that he could cover himself and hide from the Titans.

Since that day, Death wears a cape from the Sun, and the Sun throws dark shadows.

WHAT THE MOON
TRIED TO WEAR

One evening the Moon was traveling alongside a tailor on a cold winter night. Every once in a while the Moon chatted with the tailor and said: "I'm so cold that my heart is about to break into pieces."

The tailor laughed and said: "I don't feel a thing, because my fur coat is protecting me. Have one made up for you!"

"I've been dying to do just that," the Moon replied. "And I'll give you a huge reward if you can manage to have one made for me."

A few days went by, and the tailor appeared with a coat for the Moon to try on. It was just a bit too small and the Moon said: "I can't wear it unless you let it out." The tailor left and returned a week later, but this time the Moon could not even manage to slip on the coat. The tailor was furious and said: "I've never seen anyone as fat as you are." The tailor took the coat back, and he let it out even more. He returned to the Moon and said: "Here's your coat, and it is going to fit you perfectly!" The Moon put on the coat, but now it was way too large. The tailor threw a fit, took the coat, and tossed it to the ground, right at the Moon's feet. "Go find yourself a tailor up in heaven!" he said, and then he disappeared.

THE SINGING TREE

A carefree young tailor was making his way through the woods one day when he heard a sweet melody in the air. He had to search for a long time before he tracked the sound to a tree growing on a patch of green grass. Fascinated and unable to stop himself, he took a needle from his pocket and poked it into the trunk of the tree. He was determined to figure out how music could come from that tree. Presto! The needle turned into a key lodged right in the bark. The tree opened up like a door, swallowed the tailor, and pushed him right down its gullet.

The tailor was out cold for a while. When he came to his senses, he was lying in a room filled with thousands of sharp needles glittering like frost and crystal. He rolled himself into a ball to keep from getting scratched or stabbed. He was about to burst into tears when it suddenly occurred to him to take his scissors and make a hole in the wall. He slipped through the wall and reached another opening in the tree, and there he found thousands of scissors, making a din, dancing up and down.

The tailor feared for his life. The needles had turned his body into one big sponge, and the scissors had torn his garments to shreds. He suddenly remembered that he had a heavy iron with him, and he used it to force his way through the onslaught and pass through the wall. He crawled out and fell straight down, this time into a thicket of thorny shrubs. Worse yet, a storm was on the way, and suddenly it began pouring—but not in raindrops. Big, heavy irons were falling down all over the place.

The tailor was black and blue from the irons that had hit him. He pulled himself out of the thorny underbrush and crawled into a hollow tree, where he was hoping to recover from the barrage.

All at once thousands of tiny red ants started marching in his direction, and they bit and stung the miserable young man. He groaned and moaned, sneezed and wheezed, and he would have hightailed it out of there, but outside the irons were still falling from the sky. They would have killed him. And so the tailor hopped around, scratching and scraping the bites. He swore to high heaven that he would never again do anything to harm a leaf on a tree, let alone the entire tree, as long as he survived this time around.

Suddenly the rain came to a stop. The tailor tore off and got out of those woods as fast as he could.

Commentary

THE TURNIP PRINCESS (p. 3)

Combining the ordinary with the extraordinary even in its title, this tale works magic with rusty nails and turnips, turning metals and plants into fairy-tale gold. The prince faces numerous mysterious ordeals, and even when he follows instructions, he finds himself in trouble. Pulling a rusty nail from the wall of a cave seems an odd, somewhat surreal means of lifting a curse, but that is the action that leads to the final disenchantment of the old woman and the bear.

THE ENCHANTED QUILL (p. 6)

"Pull one of my feathers out, and if you use it to write down a wish, the wish will come true," a crow tells the youngest of three sisters in Schönwerth's "The Enchanted Quill." The girl reluctantly plucks the feather, uses it as a pen, and what does she do first but write down the names of the very finest dishes. The food promptly appears in bowls that sparkle and glow. This microdrama packs wisdom about fairy tales into a small golden nugget. Wish fulfillment often takes the form of enough food to eat, and in this case it means that the heroine, who lacks culinary skills and burns all the dishes she tries to prepare, will no longer be the target of ridicule. In fairy tales, the highest good, whatever it may be, is always bathed in an aura of golden light, luminous and radiant, yet also contained and framed with metallic substantiality. And finally, in a self-reflexive gesture, the crow's magical writing instrument reveals the power of words to build fairy-tale worlds, sites that remove us from reality and enable us to feel the power of what-if in a way that is palpably real. You can almost see and smell the dishes, even if you can't necessarily touch and taste them.

The German title can be translated as "The Enchanted Feather" or as "The Enchanted Quill." The crow's feather turns out to operate as a writing instrument, and this tale gives us a rare instance of wishes written down in order to make them come true, reminding us that there is magic in language, in the dramatic shorthand of curses, spells, and charms. With the magic quill, an instrument that signals the power of the pen over the sword, the youngest of the three sisters succeeds in duping the trio of would-be suitors and inflicting bodily punishments on them and the monarchs in the tale.

Closely related to "Cupid and Psyche," as well as to "East o' the Sun and West o' the Moon," in addition to Beauty and the Beast tales, this story gives us a beast less ferocious and slimy than most. Although crows and ravens are part of the same family of birds, the crow is smaller than the raven. In Norse mythology, Odin was often represented as accompanied by two black birds, Huginn and Muninn, thought and memory. The bird in this tale may be regal in some instances, but he seems less divine emissary than understated symbol for an ordinary man awaiting transformation back into human shape.

THE IRON SHOES (p. 9)

"The Search for the Lost Husband" (ATU 425) is a familiar tale in Western culture, and it includes such classic stories as "Beauty and the Beast" and "East o' the Sun and West o' the Moon." Less well known is "The Man on a Quest for His Lost Wife" (ATU 400), in which a boy leaves home, liberates a bewitched princess, loses her by boasting about her beauty, and sets out in search of his wife, enduring a series of tests to win her back. Note that folklorists describe the wife's efforts as a mere search, while the husband has set out on a quest, even though both endure similar hardships.

Hans's tenacity is captured in the iron shoes he uses to reach his wife, footwear rarely seen on the male protagonists of fairy tales. This dim-witted numbskull quickly becomes a fleet-footed trickster.

THE WOLVES (p. 12)

Many fairy tales begin with a childless couple, but few demonize so powerfully the woman in the couple. Often a couple can be so desperate to have a child that they will settle for a hedgehog, as in the Grimms' "Hans My Hedgehog." In this case, the princess's decision to abandon her seven boys and throw them to the wolves turns her into the most wicked of them all. The red-hot iron shoes that are fitted on the princess appear in the Grimms' "Snow White," and it is in that tale that the evil queen dances to death after seeking to murder her stepdaughter. The magic mirror that reveals Snow White to be the fairest of them all finds an analogue in the revelatory mirror, which shows the true nature of the evil princess.

In "The Wolves," the main conflict is less generational than class based, with high-spirited peasants pitted against mean-spirited royalty. Naming the boys "wolves" suggests a disavowal of the princess's maternal title and emphasizes that even wild beasts can make better parents than some biological progenitors. Class resentment and anxieties about infidelity place this tale decisively in the category of adult fare.

THE FLYING TRUNK (p. 14)

Cinderella and the magic slipper are so familiar to us that it is hard to imagine a story in which there is a search for a young man whose foot fits a boot. Flying trunks will be familiar from Hans Christian Andersen's tale about a merchant's son whose adventures end with an abandoned princess and a hero who is left without bride or trunk and has only stories to tell.

KING GOLDENLOCKS (p. 17)

Blond beauties may appear to be overrepresented in fairy tales, but their male counterparts—young men who conceal their standing by covering up their golden tresses—turn up with some frequency as well. The term *blond(e)* is most likely related to the Latin *blandus*, which means "charming," making the word all the more apt for fairy-tale princes. As fairy-tale scholar Marina Warner has pointed out, the term has a "double resonance," signifying both light coloring and beauty and thereby overlapping with the English usage of *fairy* as beautiful or pleasing: "Blondeness and beauty have provided a conceptual rhyme in visual and literary imagery ever since the goddess of Love's tresses were described as *xanthe*, golden, by Homer."

Although not a part of the European canon, this tale seems to kaleidoscopically reassemble bits and pieces of it. The opening episode, with the boy and the wild man, evokes the beginning of the Grimms' "The Frog King," with its lost ball and bargain for the return of it. And the king's decision to have his son killed closely resembles the scene in "Snow White," with the wicked queen demanding the lungs and liver of her beautiful stepdaughter. This tale reminds us that fair-haired princes, like sleeping princes and Cinderfellas, can play as prominent a role in fairy tales as their female counterparts do today. Part two of the story modulates into another canonical tale, one that is also in the Grimms' collection: "The Water of Life." In this second part, we learn about the medieval practice of branding criminals with an image of the gallows or the rack.

THE BEAUTIFUL SLAVE GIRL (p. 22)

The slave girl as heroine is something of a novelty in Schönwerth's collection. Both the princess's writing of letters and Karl's painting of landscapes are unusual motifs for a fairy tale, where there is generally not much writing or art. Karl is described as a young man of few words, but he loves beauty, dwelling in a lovely garden and falling in love with the slave girl because of her attractiveness. That he becomes a painter seems not entirely accidental. Both protagonists engineer scenes of recognition, showing that they are evenly matched when it comes to wits.

THREE FLOWERS (p. 25)

The rapid-fire narrative pace suggests that the storyteller hoped to keep his audience engaged and alert, with surprise twists and turns throughout, along with mysterious figures and events. The woman in the woods, for example, remains enigmatic, a helper who warms up milk in a thimble, understands the language of the flowers, and disappears, perhaps living on as the chirping cricket under the hearthstone.

THE FIGS (p. 28)

The figs in the title are native to Mediterranean regions, and they appear frequently in myth and folklore as a source of strength and nourishment. A tale that displays the rewards of compassion and generosity is oddly also full of class resentment and revenge plots. The first two of the hero's three tasks figure prominently in other tales. Fetching a ring from the ocean and sorting grains are conventional "impossible tasks." By contrast, retrieving a flower from heaven and acquiring a burning torch from hell are unusual assignments, with the flower representing beauty and fire standing for its destruction.

THE ENCHANTED MUSKET (p. 30)

The heroic youngest son is a bundle of contradictions in many ways. On the one hand he is a kind fellow who gives alms to beggars, but he also does not hesitate to slay giants and appropriate their property. Despite the sensitivity he shows when it comes to beggars, he is thick-skinned and indestructible in the castle when ghosts try to torture him. And, oddly, he makes no effort to prove his family identity, waiting instead for the princess to liberate him from the Cinderfella role to which he has been consigned. His serial adventures seem designed to show his humility, strength, endurance, as well as his good fortune— he seems always to be in the right place at the right time.

THE THREE ABDUCTED
DAUGHTERS (p. 33)

This story is closely related to the biblical narrative about Joseph and his brothers, in which Joseph's half brothers betray him and throw him into an empty cistern. As in "Cinderella," two same-sex siblings gang up on the principal character and are punished or forgiven in the end.

Ferocious animals in the form of lions and snakes threaten the hero with death, but in the end it is a grateful animal that enables the hero to outwit his treacherous companions and triumph.

THE PORTRAIT (p. 36)

The portrait of the sister and the mirror to which she speaks remind us of the importance of appearance in fairy tales. When the squire falls in love, it is with the portrait rather than the sister herself. And when the boy is thrown into prison, his sister's portrait is kept on display by the hearth. The girl in turn uses the mirror as an apotropaic device, intended to break the witch's spell by speaking truth to power in an indirect fashion. In typical fairy-tale fashion, the sister makes three visits to the mirror, and it is only on the third, when the squire is present, that the spell is mysteriously broken. In variants of the tale type, the act of speaking the truth has the same magical power, modeling how to do things with words without using spells. In the end, the family is reconstituted as a new kind of nuclear unit, with sister and squire "adopting" the boy and treating him like a son.

ASHFEATHERS (p. 39)

Ashfeathers is more assertive than many of her folkloric cousins. While it is true that she receives a "modest" gift, she is insistent that her father finally bring her a gift when he returns from one of his many journeys. And yet, the gentleman suitor who pursues her does not seem to need her consent. He falls in love, woos her, and whisks her off to his castle, without a word from her. Consent is coded through the display of beauty she puts on in church. We learn almost nothing about Ashfeathers' mother, and Ashfeathers plays a pious Cinderella, going to church rather than to a ball.

Everything seems scaled down in this version of the tale, with an innkeeper father, a nobleman in place of a prince, and a dwarf instead of Perrault's fairy godmother. Schönwerth's story does not dwell in detail on the amputations of the toe and heel and instead presents the mutilations in a matter-of-fact tone. The stepsisters escape the fate of the Grimms' version, in which doves peck out their eyes, first the left one and then the right one.

TWELVE TORTOISES (p. 42)

"The Princess on the Glass Mountain" has a long and venerable history, charting the trials and tribulations of a young man who must reach an inaccessible, remote place to break a curse that keeps a beautiful princess bound to a castle. The tale begins with abandonment, but the two children get into real trouble when Elias curses Caroline and his words prove to be transformative. Magical thinking, the fear that words can change reality (wishing someone dead will make it so), takes hold of many young children, and this tale enacts that anxiety.

Kissing the tortoises, the last act required of Elias, proves to be the easiest of all the tasks assigned—not at all "impossible" in the usual sense of fairy-tale challenges. "Twelve Tortoises" gives us a kaleidoscopic swirl of demands made of heroes, revealing that there is no real logic or order to the transformative energy of tasks carried out and deeds done.

THUMBNICKEL (p. 46)

Whether called Tom Thumb, Thumbling, Petit Poucet, Svend Tomling, or Pulgarcito, the diminutive hero found in this tale plays his pranks, revealing that size does not always matter. Standard features of the tale include the supernatural birth to a childless couple, the child's survival skills on a farm, and the outsmarting of thieves or of the wealthy. A distant ancestor of Pinocchio, Tom Thumb is something of a miniature picaresque hero, moving from one adventure to the next, putting his survival skills to the test. His size often seems to work in his favor, for he can hide in unlikely places (the ear of an animal), but it works against him too, for he is often swallowed by larger creatures, though inevitably regurgitated or excreted.

Tom's origins can be traced to English folklore, and in 1621 his deeds were celebrated in a publication titled *The History of Tom Thumbe, the Little, for his small stature surnamed, King Arthur's Dwarfe: whose Life and adventures containe many strange and wonderfull accidents, published for the delight of merry Time-spenders*, by Richard Johnson. In Germany, Tom Thumb was known as Däumling or Daumesdick, and he was frequently associated with the numbskull figure known as Dümmling, a full-grown man, but one seen as a simpleton until he outwits everyone around him.

HANS THE STRONG MAN (p. 48)

Most folkloric heroes triumph by keeping their wits about them, but Hans succeeds with brawn rather than brains. His literal-mindedness, on the other hand, creates difficulties for his masters, who are at their wit's end when they discover that strength and stupidity do not necessarily yield positive results for them. What is striking about Hans is that he seeks and makes no allies—even his own brother turns on him, irritated by his overbearing strength.

The scatological elements in the tale are not to be found in collections like those of the Brothers Grimm. To them it would have been unseemly to refer to buttocks being ground down or used as a weapon. Nor would they have portrayed the good-natured Hans relieving himself—in ways that create a minor natural disaster—after a hearty dish of dumplings. The series of self-contained episodes in this tale suggests the possibility that those gathered at tables, firesides, or harvesting rooms could each contribute a vignette to produce a never-ending cycle of Hans narratives, with a hero who is of two minds and moods, at times a merry prankster and at times a determined pragmatist.

LOUSEHEAD (p. 52)

In some versions of this tale, the young man is turned into an animal, but occasionally he simply befriends a foal, a horse, or, in this case, a mare. It is the mother, through her connection to nature, who enables the boy to carry out household chores expertly and to develop a green thumb.

SEVEN WITH ONE BLOW! (p. 55)

Also known as "The Brave Little Tailor," this story features a hero who decorates himself for a trivial accomplishment. He seems to stand as the very incarnation of foolishness. Yet the bravado and naïveté of the tailor are exactly what enable him to slay giants, defeat a treacherous unicorn, and win an armed battle. The initial victory over the seven flies gives an unvarnished picture of village life. In the Grimms' version of this story, flies land on jam that the tailor has just spread on a piece of bread. Here, the red flies on the dung heap make for a different picture, one less child-friendly than the Grimms' version, repulsive rather than charming and whimsical.

The tailor is something of a trickster figure, particularly in his ability to use language to vanquish his enemies. The phrase "Seven with one blow!" reveals that he knows how to use words, and when he "talks in his sleep," he also cleverly recites the story of his various feats to the conspirators. Even when he runs up against class barriers, he manages to triumph, earning not only the hand of the princess but also her love and devotion. He is a winning figure in many ways—even willing to forgive a wife who hires men to murder him.

THE BURNING TROUGH (p. 58)

Inanimate objects occasionally play a key role in fairy tales, creating surreal effects. We never learn exactly why the prince was transformed, first into a dwarf, then into a kneading trough, the exact translation for the German *Backtrog*, in the tale's title. As in "Beauty and the Beast" and "The Maiden without Hands," a father makes a deal that imperils his daughters. In this tale, however, the daughters are not at all shocked by the father's bargain, but accept it as a just price in exchange for the exquisite meals they will be eating.

THE KING'S BODYGUARD (p. 60)

In this story, a young man is the fairest of them all, and he courts the daughter of a nobleman. That the two become intimate before marrying is unusual in edited collections of fairy tales. Like Jack or Thumbling, the young man wins over the wife of the monster, and she serves as mediator, acquiring for him not only the three feathers of a dragon or three hairs from the devil's head but also the answers to the mysterious questions. Why is she so magnanimous? Perhaps her role is that of a maternal facilitator, who takes the obstacles placed by the young woman's father out of his path. The king's bodyguard is not as benevolent. His revenge on the nobleman feels gratuitous—why smash the dishes of a man who is down on his luck? Perhaps we have here an example of preposterous violence, an episode that can be told with vigorous expressions and lively gestures.

THE SCORNED PRINCESS (p. 63)

Of the three soldiers in this tale, one is unnamed, a second is a miller's son, and the third is Fortunatus, named after the hero of a chapbook that was first printed in Augsburg, Germany, in 1509 and circulated in Europe during the fifteenth and sixteenth centuries. A native of Cyprus, Fortunatus receives from the goddess of Fortune a purse that replenishes itself as soon as it is emptied. In the chapbook, Fortunatus steals a hat that enables him to travel anywhere he desires. He returns from Cairo to Cyprus, where he settles down and leaves the magical objects to his sons Ampedo and Andelosia, who fall on hard times because they are jealous of each other.

The tale begins with what appear to be small acts of kindness, but ends in an almost unimaginably brutal fashion. What initially appears to be a playful fairy-tale flirtation turns deadly, with a hero who lives happily ever after by getting even and exacting revenge.

THE TALKING BIRD, THE SINGING TREE, AND THE SPARKLING STREAM (p. 71)

The enchanted bird, tree, and stream—the forces of nature in shorthand form—reunite orphans with their parents in a popular tale that can be found the world over. Most folklore collections are short on curious men, but in this tale one of the brothers suffers the fate of Lot's wife, who is turned into a pillar (of salt) when she looks back at the city of Sodom, despite the warnings of angels. In some versions of the story, it is the water of life that the son brings back to heal his father. Nature proves to be a powerful healer, undoing the evil of the king's mother and her confidante—double forms of trouble—and dark retribution is paired with the light of redemption.

THE WEASEL (p. 73)

Weasels, as small, active predators, make unlikely candidates for fairy-tale heroes, particularly since they pose a threat to those who depend on eggs from a hen, as does the heroine of this tale. But there has never been much logic in fairy tales about animal grooms, and the beasts range from small-toothed dogs and snotty-faced goats to the more traditional bear and frog. The princess's act of compassion, her protective instincts in the face of bullies torturing an animal, singles her out as a champion worthy of marriage.

Although this story gives us purely pagan magic, with flames bursting from eggs that turn into castles and princes metamorphosed into weasels, there is a Christian inflection that manifests itself through the consecrated Easter egg, a talisman that rights wrongs and restores the weasel to his human state.

THE KNIGHT'S SASH (p. 75)

Wicked stepmothers who persecute their daughters are part of a teeming population of disruptive, scheming, evil women in fairy tales. Tales in which mothers persecute their sons are rare in the Western canon, but they are not as unusual as we once thought. "The Faithless Mother" (ATU 590) can be found in variant forms

in Estonian lore, in British collections, and in tales recorded in
Puerto Rico, Algeria, Sudan, and Croatia, among other places.

Animals, along with those outside the kinship unit, become
the natural partners and allies of the hero, while his own family
members, whom he seeks to protect and help, turn into adversaries. The most ferocious of all beasts takes immediately to
Hans, serving not only as a donor but also as a guide and the
most loyal of companions. If tales like Cinderella give us a good
(dead) biological mother and an evil stepmother, this tale type
also sets up two rival mothers: the good maternal lion who pro-
vides a gift in the form of healing milk and an evil biological
mother who seeks to undo her son's strength and serves to me-
diate the giant's own hostility to his stepson. The giant, like
many fairy-tale fathers, seems less murderously hostile than the
boy's mother, who is determined to rid herself of a son who has
shown her nothing but love and devotion.

THE GIRL AND THE COW (p. 78)

Instead of a miller with three sons, we have a miller with three
daughters, each of whom is adventurous about seeking out the
mysteries behind a wandering cow. The youngest of the three
sisters is also the most modest, preferring to look at the beautiful clothes and objects in the castle, rather than making off
with them. Unlike the myth of Zeus and Europa, in which a
girl is abducted by a bull, this story features a benevolent cow
who serves as something of a matchmaker.

THE CALL OF THE SHEPHERD'S HORN (p. 80)

This tale is unusual in taking up a theme found in Shakespeare's
The Winter's Tale, reuniting a king and queen who were separated by a false denunciation. The king's betrayal of the shepherd repeats the errors of his youth, and somehow he has the
good fortune to recover his wife and celebrate his daughter's
marriage. The exact lineage of the shepherd is not entirely clear
in the story, but the mysterious elevation to an aristocratic rank
quickly solves the problem of his social status.

THE MARK OF THE DOG, PIG, AND CAT (p. 83)

The anthropologist Ruth Benedict once pointed out that Zuni culture, which has only the rarest instances of child abandonment, is filled with stories about the evils of the practice. One can only hope that the same is true for the many tales in Schönwerth's collection about mischievous mothers-in-law, evil women who substitute animals for newborns in a plot to divide their sons from their wives. The tale type appears in collections ranging from *The Thousand and One Nights* to Straparola's seventeenth-century Italian collection, *The Facetious Nights*.

THE THREE-LEGGED GOATS (p. 86)

Much in this tale remains cryptic, from the three-legged goats to the seven candlesticks and the woman in black. Instead of three sons, we have three young men who enter a castle and are tested. What distinguishes this tale from the many variations on the theme of disenchanting a princess is the moral at the end, with a princess who asks her father's advice about whether to stay with her husband or remarry. Her choice of metaphor—the husband as a broom—makes her even more unlikable than before, when she showed disdain for her husband's social standing. Class distinctions often disappear at the end of fairy tales, but the Schönwerth collection reveals that they are crucial to resolve in explicit terms before there can be a happily-ever-after ending.

THE TRAVELING ANIMALS (p. 89)

Using their wits and physical strength, the six nomadic animals in this story create a comfortable retirement home for themselves, a place where they are no longer required to wear themselves out by earning a living for their masters. Humans are represented as torturers and thieves: They exploit the capabilities and strengths of animals, and they also try to do each other in. The animals, by contrast, form an alliance—pragmatic, to be sure, but effective in ensuring that they find a safe house.

THE SNAKE'S TREASURE (p. 92)

Extreme disappointment is enacted in this tale, with a shepherd who loses his chance at a fortune, along with a snake still desperately seeking disenchantment. Resolution, revelation, and salvation—the classic features of fairy-tale endings—are all missing. The aged shepherd succumbs to fear and greed, and the snake must wait for her liberation. The tale turns on the notion of an innocent child trumping a culpable old man as an agent of deliverance.

THE SNAKE SISTER (p. 94)

With its epic sweep and maelstrom of dark deeds, the story of the girl pushed into a lake by her stepmother and transformed into a snake can seem baggy and hard to follow at times. Yet the trajectories of the two children meet and resolve themselves into a neat happily-ever-after. Stories belonging to the "Black and the White Bride" tale type do not ordinarily include the journey of the true bride's brother. Like many other characters, he is required to chop the person he loves into bits in order to bring about her transformation in a mysterious allegory about the healing power and renewing energy of destructive actions. Redemption is born from pain and suffering.

"FOLLOW ME, JODEL!" (p. 98)

A tale initially about sibling rivalry shades into a story about the production of beauty from what appears disgusting and repulsive. The reluctant bridegroom becomes the recipient of wealth and happiness through the intervention of a toad, who is the bearer of beauty notwithstanding her appearance. Note that the son overcomes his sense of repulsion and treats the toad with compassion, remaining obedient to its commands, unlike the princess in the Grimms' "Frog King," who hurls the frog against the wall when it wants to sleep in her bed.

THE TOAD BRIDE (p. 101)

Out of the least promising materials imaginable—flax, toads, and spindles—presto! A fairy tale emerges. Reading canonical fairy tales can leave us with the mistaken impression that only young women and crones spun flax in times past. In this tale, boys compete to produce the finest possible thread from flax, and the toad in this case is not a prince in disguise but a lovely princess.

PRINCE DUNG BEETLE (p. 102)

One morning, a young man wakes up and finds himself turned into a dung beetle—that might be the kind of anti–fairy tale that inspired Kafka's story about Gregor Samsa. But in this case, the transformation is clearly motivated. Those who torture and inflict pain on animals will suffer like the creatures they've killed. Melding fairy-tale motifs with the cautionary tale that was making its way into the nursery, this story ends with the dissolution of the boundary dividing humans from animals—everyone sings and dances at the wedding, including the lowliest of animals.

THE THREE SPINDLES (p. 107)

Few of the Grimms' fairy tales actually have fairies in them, but many of Schönwerth's do, reflecting a fascination with woodland creatures and lore. This tale also reflects how stories were used to navigate problems that arose in everyday life. Heroines who run into trouble at home and are persecuted by evil stepmothers or proposed to by their fathers often find shelter in nature, using trees as places to sleep and finding accomplices in the creatures who inhabit forests.

THE LITTLE FLAX FLOWER (p. 109)

This tale pits what is described as a "beautiful" girl against an "ugly" and "nasty-looking" one. It gives us extreme polarization, in ways that ring false to contemporary readers. My translation substitutes *pretty* and *plain* for *beautiful* and *ugly*, making the contrast less stark yet preserving the narrative energy and pathos of Schönwerth's tale. In a story like this one, we see a grim process of socialization at work. Singing while you work is frivolous—best to mind those seeds and weeds or you might end up like the pretty girl, the target of insults. Never mind the promotion of superstitions about a revenge-seeking goddess who demands sacrifices (however small). The fantasy of social mobility encapsulated in the story is somewhat preposterous, even for a fairy tale, for the arrival of the prince and his cult of fine fabrics is completely unmotivated by any events in the tale.

WOODPECKER (p. 112)

The hero of this tale, half-human and half–wood sprite, has trouble adjusting to the rules of civilization, and he is so immersed in nature that others worry about his state of mind. Taken in by an impresario of adoption, the boy finds it challenging to embrace a work ethic and prefers the woods to the woodpile. Once his mother appears to help him carry out tasks and to proclaim his ancestry, he seems liberated to embrace his father's values. The tale's playful combination of chores involving chopping wood and a name that suggests a bird that drills into wood reveals the self-conscious use of language, telling a story yet also engaging in associative language games.

THE RED SILK RIBBON (p. 116)

A classic formulation of a tale type that charts the encounter between mortals and creatures of the sea, this tale reminds us of the double face of nature, treacherous and grasping on the one hand, benevolent and generous on the other. The (unwitting) exchange of a child for material riches and prosperity is a theme frequently sounded in folktales, with tales such as "Beauty and the Beast" and "Rapunzel" reminding us of two extremes, in one case providing an exchange for untold wealth; in the other, the fulfillment of a frivolous wish. The human agents in the tale, faced with the seemingly uncompromising side of nature, learn how to settle disputes fairly and make their own bargains and exchanges, with Lucas dividing up the carcass for the animals fair and square, and the princess discovering the value of exchanging material possessions for something far more valuable, thus reversing the curse brought on by the fisherman's bargain.

TWELVE BRIDES (p. 121)

The seductive power of mermaids is highlighted in this racy story about a young man who resembles Bluebeard in his lethal touch and serial marriages. Oddly he is rescued from the mermaids by the use of both magic and prayer, with one shrewd young bride who catches on that all those dead wives do not bode well. She consults a witch, who gives her good advice but also uses prayer to ward off evil spirits.

THE HOWLING OF THE WIND (p. 124)

The plaintive sounds of the wind are explained here as the lamentations of a mother and her seven sons. As in Hans Christian Andersen's "Little Mermaid," this sea creature is in search of a soul and just misses acquiring something that will remove her from her origins and settle her comfortably in the human world. As sirens and beauties that lure men to their death, mermaids not only bring danger to the mortal world but are also often driven to return to their origins.

HANS DUDELDEE (p. 126)

With the most prosaic name possible, Hans carries out a series of extraordinary feats. Grateful animals and a magic mirror enable him to disenchant a princess and restore all the castle's inhabitants to their human form. The trio of brothers behaves as scripted for fairy tales, but the golden fish as grateful animal adds an eye-popping decorative touch to the tale.

THE BELT AND THE NECKLACE (p. 130)

The heroine of this tale undergoes a startling transformation but one for which she pays a high price. Her high-stakes wager with the nixies, or mermaids, is made without a thought about its consequences or about the deep divide between mortals and merfolk. Woods and water harbor creatures that can be both benevolent and compassionate, but also spiteful and wicked.

DRUNK WITH LOVE (p. 132)

By turns ecstatic and elegiac, this tale about a mermaid and her union with a mortal is a reminder of the doomed nature of those marriages. To be sure, there is redemption of a kind for the mermaid, who is given another three hundred years of youthful beauty, but there is also loss and despair, with a husband and six children left behind once she returns to the sea.

ANNA MAYALA (p. 135)

George Macdonald, the author of many Victorian novels and fairy tales, was once asked to define fairy tales. His reply: "Read *Undine*; that is a fairy tale . . . of all the fairy tales I know, I think *Undine* the most beautiful." Stories about star-crossed lovers, in this story as in *Undine*, have a certain seductive appeal, particularly those that pair a mortal with a wood nymph or sea creature. Much as "Anna Mayala" is rooted in pagan beliefs about supernatural forces in the waters and woods, it also carries a distinctly Christian message about transgression and redemption. Veri, the daydreamer, lives in his imagination and succumbs to the forces of beauty in an underworld realm, only to return and discover that where there was beauty there was also monstrosity and horror.

IN THE JAWS OF THE MERMAN (p. 140)

Legend rather than fairy tale, this story reveals how beauty is linked with sorcery and seduction. The beauty of the girls turns out to be too good to be true, and they are turned upon by the villagers with unprecedented savagery sanctioned by the legal system.

THE KING'S RING (p. 141)

In this variant of "The Enchanted Castle Disenchanted," the three brothers show their piety by going on a pilgrimage with their mother. The princess herself is a model of virtue, compassion, and hospitality. Building the inn, beyond its goal of attracting her beloved with a sign inviting the poor to stay for free, reveals her generosity and true noble spirit. There is more than a hint of waywardness, however, in the birth of a child nine months after the two meet, even though the brother stays in the princess's arms for a "short time."

THE THREE GOLDEN CROWNS (p. 145)

The young beggars at the castle turn out to be the grooms of the missing princesses in this tale tracing a rise from rags to riches. Gnomes are both treacherous and beneficial, and the hero of the tale knows exactly how to exploit their powers. Not one to hold a grudge, he rewards his companions but not without insisting that they remain subservient to him. Much as this tale appears highly stylized and formulaic, it engages in some remarkable code switching, revealing that compassion and generosity are not always rewarded. The third in the trio is rewarded when he requires the gnomes to work for their supper, while the others are punished for sharing their food with them.

NINE BAGS OF GOLD (p. 148)

Who knew about the secret lives of children and how they manage to engineer happy endings for themselves, securing a fortune and leaving it to the grandparents to raise their child? This tale begins in a conventional manner, with two brothers and a conflict that arises between them. It then takes an abrupt turn, leading us into a world of mysterious transactions between the heroine and the elves that befriend her, teaching her reading, writing, and the domestic arts. The alliance enables the girl to practice magic in ways that secure for her a companionate marriage rather than an arranged marriage. In the end, all generational conflicts are resolved and the mills remain in the family. The magic of the household elves proves successful.

TWO BROTHERS (p. 151)

Rather than giving us a weary retread of a story pitting two brothers against each other, this tale animates the action with whips and swords, lifesaving pets, and limbs that fly through the air. Evil resides purely in the old beggar woman, whose abject exterior conceals violence and aggression. The brothers can reconcile precisely because the blame for all evils—from petrifaction to delusional behavior—is placed on her shoulders.

TRICKING THE WITCH (p. 155)

The witch who kidnaps three princesses has trouble keeping secrets to herself. The clever trio learns how to work magic, and the youngest of the three uses it to keep the witch and her accomplices (the two sisters) at bay in a chase that has the frenzied, bolting energy of a cinematic sequence. The rose and rosebush, church and priest, lake and duck are standard features of the chase in similar tales, but the girl in this tale does not throw magic objects (combs, brushes, and mirrors) in the path of her pursuers, as she does in variants of the tale type known as "The Magic Flight." Like Rapunzel, the three girls are kept captive by a witch or enchantress and liberate themselves when they come of age, in a plot that resonates with adolescent longings from times past as well as today.

THE ENCHANTED FIDDLE (p. 158)

Here is a tale that reminds us of the power of words. A mother's words, spoken in anger, turn out to work magic, with unintended consequences. That tale type, "The Dance among the Thorns," features a boy who is dismissed from work or driven away from home. He meets up with a helper/donor who grants him three wishes, usually a musket with perfect aim and an enchanted fiddle. The third wish varies tremendously, with some fellows electing a place in heaven, others forcing their stepmothers to break wind whenever they sneeze. In this particular tale, dance is aligned more with the medieval dance of death than with festive celebrations. The fiddle becomes a diabolical instrument that may release the boy from his death sentence yet also becomes a means of torturing and killing others.

THE DEVIL AND THE FISHERMAN (p. 161)

Zacharias's name comes from the Greek "God has remembered" and thus exercises a certain protective quality over the boy. His adventures in the castle turn him into a superhero who conquers not just male giants but also a female giant, who is replaced by an enchanted young woman with the power to reanimate the castle and its inhabitants.

THE EXPERT HUNTER (p. 164)

Closely related to "The Danced-Out Shoes," this tale, belonging to the category of "The Dangerous Night-Watch," presents us with the crafty youngest of three sons. When he meets a sleeping beauty, he does not awaken her with a kiss but slips away and returns home. The princess awakens and demonstrates her munificence by opening an inn that is free for the poor, thereby balancing the hunter's brutal show of expert marksmanship and craft with compassion and beauty.

A POT OF GOLD IN THE OVEN (p. 167)

Coarse in its content yet also poetic in its language, this tale gives us a self-reflexive meditation on storytelling and language. The man who discovers buried treasure claims to his talkative partner that some kind of miracle has occurred, thus ensuring that the partner will lose credibility when boasting about the treasure to others. In this case, when the soldier begins to speak poetry and work magic, his wife's prosaic words of warning break the spell and banish the little man and his treasure. Left to his own devices, the soldier was able to animate the ruins and produce the copper pot filled with coins.

CONTESTS WITH THE DEVIL (p. 169)

The devil makes frequent appearances in tales about earning a living through agricultural work. Often he is as much ally as adversary, unwittingly helping a poor farmhand with the mowing or haying and just as often sending a rich man to hell. Who is better suited than the devil for the duplicitous role of villain who enables the hero to gain worldly goods but who must also be tricked or banished in order for the hero to live happily ever after?

WOUD AND FREID (p. 171)

This tale offers a fine example of a myth transformed into a folktale, with characters based on the Norse gods Odin and Freyja. A fourteenth-century narrative in *Olaf's Saga* recounts Freyja's acquisition of a necklace. One day Freyja, one of Odin's concubines, discovers dwarfs in a cave working on a golden necklace. Freyja offers to buy the necklace, but the dwarfs will give it to her only on the condition that she spend one night with each of them. Loki learns about Freyja's actions and reports them to Odin, who then orders Loki to steal the necklace, which is returned to Freyja under Odin's conditions. The teller of this tale has turned the story into one of transgression, remorse, and the renewal of devotion between husband and wife.

THE MOUSE CATCHER, OR THE BOY AND THE BEETLE (p. 175)

The Pied Piper of Hamelin is here transformed into a mouse catcher, with a whistle rather than a pipe or flute. The German legend refers back to the mysterious disappearance of children from the town of Hamelin in 1284, an event that may have had more to do with disease, a natural catastrophe, emigration, or the Children's Crusade than with a rat catcher betrayed, if it happened at all. The tale was included in *German Legends* by the Brothers Grimm, and verse accounts by

Goethe and Browning have kept the story alive. Schönwerth adds a coda that gives the story a local flavor and transforms tragedy into "happily ever after."

PEARL TEARS (p. 177)

The girl in this tale functions as both martyr and saint, and she shows unparalleled fortitude in managing the tribulations that come her way, from the death of her mother to persecution at the hands of her stepmother, beatings from her stepbrothers, and exile after opening the door to a forbidden chamber. Especially remarkable is the use of motifs from multiple tale types: The pearls and roses are reminiscent of "The Kind and Unkind Girls," which features a girl from whose mouth diamonds drop. The forbidden chamber is the central motif of Bluebeard tales, in which the husband forbids his wife to open the door to a single room in his castle. It is a short step from the domestic melodrama of fairy tales to the realm of Christian parable, with a heroine who moves from the hearth as classic innocent persecuted heroine of the fairy tale to a place of healing, where she is saintly in both life and death. Especially noteworthy is the scene of writing, in which God the Father and his Son shape human destinies by inscribing the course of lives into a book. The description suggests something sacred about writing down the story of a life and thereby enacts what the author of this particular tale is attempting in his account of the conversion of a fairy-tale figure into a saint.

FLOUR FOR SNOW (p. 181)

Ending with a conciliatory message about the value of satisfaction with the status quo, this is a tale that endorses the work ethic and dutiful piety while renouncing the value of rebellious imagination. The worker does what few fairy-tale characters do: He dreams up a world driven by the work of his imagination, a world in which flour comes down from the heavens, making human labor unnecessary. He quickly learns that a worldly order ruled by the pleasure principle brings nothing but un-pleasure and, relieved that the new order was nothing more than a fantasy, he ceases to grumble about his lot.

HOYDEL (p. 183)

Legends about a wooden stick that grows leaves and blossoms into a tree are not uncommon. Redemption is symbolically represented by the green leaves on the dry branch the hero was carrying. The tale evokes the legend of Tannhäuser, who is denied absolution by the pope and told that his chances of being forgiven are as good as the possibility of the pope's staff sprouting leaves. Miraculously, the staff puts out green shoots. How the carpenter turned into a criminal is not clear, and it is odd that he repents only when there is no more space for notches on his staff. But his story is a reminder that grace can enter the lives of even the most hard-bitten criminals.

THE TALKER (p. 187)

"Talk" is, of course, what folktales are all about. The farmer's wife may not be clever, but she is wise to the ways of the world, knowing that a talker is likely to talk her husband into a bargain for the buyer. She is also unaware that her husband, like many of the fools in oral tradition, is a literalist, taking her advice at its word. Like many simpletons and numbskulls, he is also protected by good fortune, and in the end, he manages to fetch an excellent price for the cow, returning to his wife and to a happily-ever-after ending.

THE CLEVER TAILOR (p. 189)

The title figure of this folktale has no redeeming virtues whatsoever. He does not appear unsettled by the murder of his mother and feels no sense of responsibility, despite the fact that his ruse did her in. And he cheerfully drowns the farmers and steals their livestock. The hardworking women in the village have their bawdy side too, and mooning the tailor is the kind of move that was edited out of print collections of fairy tales. This unrepentant, happy-go-lucky lad (a tailor whose apprenticeship must have been lost when the tale moved from oral storytelling to print culture) keeps his ill-gotten gains and will continue to lie, cheat, and steal in another village.

LEARNING HOW TO STEAL (p. 192)

The hero of this tale has turned theft into a fine art. Like the "master thief" found in many different cultures, he is nimble, clever, and cunning. He not only carries out all the tasks put to him but also shows his ability to mix potions, perform physical feats, and engage in mimicry. Note that he never actually steals anything, but rather performs tricks to display the magic of his craft. An itinerant artist, he makes his way into new territory as soon as he is given his traveling papers. Mobility matters to him, especially since he is immersed in a bureaucracy that perpetually seeks to restrain him.

"DON'T GET MAD!" (p. 194)

There is a set of tale types known as "labor contracts," and one of the more interesting among the twenty-nine variants is the "Contest Not to Become Angry." A farmhand agrees to a contest with the devil, an ogre, or a priest (note the odd fellow in this trio). Whoever becomes angry first loses and must pay the other a sum of money. Often three sons enter the contest, with only the youngest winning, by using the strategy of feigning stupidity, taking idleness to an extreme, or taking an order literally. With an ending that anticipates an episode in the film *Fatal Attraction*, this tale gives us a hero who may be naive but is also ruthless about winning the contest. And it is his act of storytelling, as proclaimed in the ending, that gives rise to tales about his feats and those of others.

OFERLA (p. 198)

Belonging to the tale type known as "The Woman in the Chest" (ATU 1536A), this story has been documented the world over, with Japanese, Russian, and Chilean variants. The motif of disposing of a corpse is repeated three times, with the pastor, the innkeeper's servant, and the farmer each calling on the schoolteacher to help them out. And the schoolteacher himself finally passes the corpse off to robbers, who come up with the most obvious solution of all: burying the body. In variant forms of the tale, a mother-in-law or a wife's lover is killed by accident or on purpose, and the husband covers up the murder by leaving the body at a doorstep or putting it on someone's property. The tale itself can be seen as an allegory about shifting blame, putting the evidence of a crime or misdeed at someone else's doorstep.

Showing how a poor man can make money at the expense of the rich, the schoolteacher does not seem to mind that his newfound wealth comes at the expense of an old woman's life. His story uses burlesque slapstick to conceal what might really be at stake in this tale: the fact that an aging parent can be a troublesome burden, both while alive and at home but also even once dead, as a corpse that needs to find a resting place. The "stolen corpse" story appears today in the form of urban legends (see Jan Harold Brunvand's *The Vanishing Hitchhiker* and the film *National Lampoon's Vacation*, in which Aunt Edna inconveniently dies during an out-of-state vacation).

SIR WIND AND HIS WIFE (p. 205)

This etiological tale about the winds and their direction illustrates the kaleidoscopic structure of fairy tales. Combining the magic of fairy tales (humans turned into statues, glass mountains, and the purifying forces of fire and water), it also gives us the mythical logic of origin tales along with bits and pieces of folk humor about wind and weight. The three aristocrats must develop malleable bodies and use their height and weight to conquer the light breeziness and weighty force of the winds.

THE ICE GIANTS (p. 208)

Like many fairy tales, this one begins in a time of famine, with a woman who plans to abandon her children. The mother of the three girls, rescued by a voice that calls out to her, moves into a mythical realm, with its signature giants, frozen seas, and golden apples. In blending fairy-tale themes with mythical motifs, the tale nods in the direction of the story of Demeter and Persephone, with a mother who, in contrast to the mythical goddess, seems perfectly content to arrange marriages with titanic figures.

WHY SNOW IS WHITE (p. 210)

In a layer of snow, light bounces around and is reflected and absorbed until it is neutralized to form white. When we see all colors in equal measure on a surface, the object itself turns white. This etiological story explains not only the color of snow but also the antagonism between snow and flowers, anthropomorphized blossoms that jealously guard their colors, withholding them from the baffled and dispirited snow.

THE SUN TAKES AN OATH (p. 211)

Few etiological tales work as hard as this one to explain natural events. The story of the sun setting and rising and the moon waxing and waning becomes the opportunity for an allegory about a star-crossed married couple unable to settle differences, despite their love for each other. Sun and Moon are both at fault, the one for volatility and red-hot anger, the other for chilliness and lack of affect, but it is the Sun that takes the fatal oath forever dividing the two marriage partners. And note that star-crossed lovers can take their troubles today to the moon, a heavenly body sympathetic to their sorrows.

THE SUN'S SHADOW (p. 213)

Gods can be as temperamental as humans, and so can celestial orbs. In this concise microdrama about the origins of mourning and shadows, the Sun and the Moon gang up on Death, and Death throws a fit even after his rights are validated by the Titans. There are many mysteries in the tale, most notably the white weasel and the effects of licking the eyes of the Titans. The anthropomorphic approach to explaining natural events can be found in folklore the world over.

WHAT THE MOON TRIED TO WEAR (p. 214)

Only in fairy tales can an ordinary tailor travel with the moon. And this tailor uses his craft well, making a coat that will keep him warm in the winter, even as the moon is freezing. The moon waxes and wanes, much to the distress of the tailor, who finally gives up on the reward offered by the moon for a warm coat. Writers ranging from Margaret Wise Brown (*Goodnight Moon*) and Maurice Sendak (*Where the Wild Things Are*) to James Thurber (*Many Moons*) and Brian Selznick (*The Invention of Hugo Cabret*) have understood the literary pull of the moon, creating books for children and adults that captivate through the luminous beauty of the moon. This moon, by contrast, appears cranky and demanding to the heroic tailor, who does his best to keep making adjustments, without understanding exactly why the moon is such a tough customer to please.

THE SINGING TREE (p. 215)

Environmental themes are sounded in many European fairy tales, with rewards for those who treat animals and plants with respect and punishment for those who are careless, profligate, or cruel when it comes to other living beings. Tailors are often positioned as naive and courageous simpletons, but in this story a tailor, seduced by the sorcery of a beautiful melody, is high-spirited and curious, yet also condemned for an act of cruelty that takes the form of vandalizing a tree. Unlike the carter in the Grimms' "The Dog and the Sparrow," who is killed as retribution for running over a dog, the tailor in this story survives and internalizes a lesson about doing no harm when it comes to plants and trees. The three scenes of punishment draw on the tools of the tailor's trade. Needle, scissors, and iron are turned on the tailor, who finds that those tools can become instruments of torture—a telling commentary perhaps on the demands of his trade.

Notes on Sources and Tale Types

by NICOLA SCHÄFFLER

Below is further information about the tales, including their sources and German titles. All of the tales were recorded in the Oberpfalz, a region in Eastern Bavaria. In some cases information is provided about the specific town where Schönwerth located the tale and who related it to him. For a deeper exploration of the types of tales, supplemental literature is listed, along with the ATU number, which can be used to find further literature about the tales in *The Types of International Folktales* by Hans-Jörg Uther.

ABBREVIATIONS

ATU
Hans-Jörg Uther. *The Types of International Folktales: A Classification and Bibliography.* 3 vols. Helsinki: Academia Scientiarum Fennica, 2004.

EM
Kurt Ranke (ed.). *Enzyklopädie des Märchens. Handwörterbuch zur historischen und vergleichenden Erzählforschung.* Vol. 1-13.2 Berlin, New York 1977–2009.

KHM
Brüder Grimm. *Kinder- und Hausmärchen: Nach der großen Ausgabe von 1857, textkritisch revidiert, kommentiert und durch Register erschlossen,* 2nd ed. Ed. Hans-Jörg Uther. 4 vols. Munich: Diederich, 1996.

SCHÖNWERTH: COMPOUND ENTRY

Compound entry from Franz Xaver von Schönwerth owned by *Historischer Verein für Oberpfalz und Regensburg* at the archive of the city Regensburg. AHVOR: Schönwerthiana, Fascicle I-X

SCHÖNWERTH: SITTEN UND SAGEN

Franz Xaver von Schönwerth. *Aus der Oberpfalz: Sitten und Sagen.* 3 vols. Augsburg: M. Rieger, 1857–1859.

ZA

Zentralarchiv der deutschen Volkserzählung, Universität Marburg, Institut für Europäische Ethnologie / Kulturwissenschaft.

SOURCES AND REFERENCES

THE TURNIP PRINCESS (p. 3)

Source:
Schönwerth: Compound entry IVb, folder 21/8, envelope 1, sheet 9; ZA Marburg No. 202 057 ("Die Rübenprinzessin")

Town:
Gaisheim (Gaisheim/Neukirchen, County Amberg or Gaisheim/Moosbach, County Neustadt a. d. Waldnaab)

Tale Type:
ATU 554 "The Grateful Animals"

THE ENCHANTED QUILL (p. 6)

Source:
ZA Marburg No. 202 044 ("Die verwunschene Krähe")

Town:
Neuenhammer (Neuenhammer/Georgenberg, County Neustadt a. d. Waldnaab)

Tale Type:
ATU 432 "The Prince as Bird"

THE IRON SHOES (p. 9)

Source:
Schönwerth: Compound entry I, folder 6c, sheet 37; ZA Marburg
No. 202 993 (untitled)

Town:
Neukirchen St. Chr. (Neukirchen zu St. Chr./Georgenberg, County
Neustadt a. d. Waldnaab)

Tale Type:
ATU 400 "The Man on a Quest for His Lost Wife"

THE WOLVES (p. 12)

Source:
ZA Marburg No. 203 024 ("Die Welfen-Sage")

Town:
Neuenhammer (Neuenhammer/Georgenberg, County Neustadt a. d.
Waldnaab)

Tale Type:
ATU 762 "Woman with Three Hundred and Sixty-Five Children";
ATU 765 "The Mother Who Wants to Kill Her Children"

THE FLYING TRUNK (p. 14)

Source:
Schönwerth: Compound entry VIb, folder 21/8, envelope 1, sheet 15;
ZA Marburg No. 202 062 ("Das fliegende Kästchen")

Informant:
"Eugen"

Tale Type:
ATU 575 "The Prince's Wings"; KHM 77a "The Carpenter and the
Turner"

KING GOLDENLOCKS (p. 17)

Source:
Schönwerth: Compound entry VI, folder 24b, sheet 23; ZA Marburg
No. 202 132 ("König Goldhaar")

Town:
Katzberg (County Cham)

Tale Type:
ATU 314 "Goldener"; ATU 502 "The Wild Man"; KHM 136
"Iron Hans"

THE BEAUTIFUL SLAVE GIRL (p. 22)

Source:
ZA Marburg No. 203 027 (untitled)

Tale Type:
ATU 505 "The Grateful Dead"

THREE FLOWERS (p. 25)

Source:
ZA Marburg No. 203 528 (untitled)

Town:
Waldmühle b. Neuenhammer (Waldmühle/Pressath, County Neu-
    stadt a. d. Waldnaab or Waldmühle/Hirschau, County Amberg)

Tale Type:
ATU 451 "The Maiden Who Seeks Her Brother"; KHM 3 "Mary's
    Child"; KHM 9 "The Twelve Brothers"; KHM 49 "The Six Swans"

THE FIGS (p. 28)

Source:
ZA Marburg No. 202 294 ("Die Feigen")

Town:
Tirschenreuth (County Tirschenreuth)

Tale Type:
ATU 554 "The Grateful Animals"; ATU 610 "The Healing Fruits";
    KHM 62 "The Queen Bee"; KHM 165 "The Griffin"

THE ENCHANTED MUSKET (p. 30)

Source:
ZA Marburg No. 202 459 (untitled)

Tale Type:
ATU 314A "The Shepherd and the Three Giants"; ATU 400 "The Man on the Quest for His Lost Wife"; ATU 594* "The Magic Bridle"; ATU 935 "The Prodigal's Return"

THE THREE ABDUCTED DAUGHTERS (p. 33)

Source:
ZA Marburg No. 202 992 ("Der Wunderbeutel, das Wunschhütchen und das Wunderhorn")

Tale Type:
ATU 566 "The Three Magic Objects and the Wonderful Fruits"; ATU 569 "The Knapsack, the Hat and the Horn"; KHM 54 "The Knapsack, the Hat and the Horn"

THE PORTRAIT (p. 36)

Source:
Schönwerth: Compound entry I, folder 6c, envelope 130 (first part) a. folder 15, envelope 14 (second part); ZA Marburg No. 202 853 ("Brüderlein und Schwesterlein")

Tale Type:
ATU 403 "The Black and the White Bride"; KHM 135 "The White and the Black Bride"

ASHFEATHERS (p. 39)

Source:
ZA Marburg No. 202 249 ("Aschenflügel")

Tale Type:
ATU 510A "Cinderella"; KHM 21 "Cinderella"

TWELVE TORTOISES (p. 42)

Source:
ZA Marburg No. 202 855 (untitled)

Tale Type:
ATU 312C "The Rescued Bride"; ATU 530 "The Princess on the Glass Mountain"; ATU 814 "The Careless Word Summons the Devil"

THUMBNICKEL (p. 46)

Source:
ZA Marburg No. 202 046 ("Der Daumen-Nickerl")

Town:
Parkstein (Parkstein, County Neustadt a. d. Waldnaab)

Tale Type:
ATU 700 "Thumbling"; KHM 37 "Thumbling"; KHM 45 "Thumbling's Travels"

HANS THE STRONG MAN (p. 48)

Source:
Schönwerth: *Sitten und Sagen*, II, p. 271-75 ("Der grosse Hans")

Town:
Oberbernried (Waldthurn, County Neustadt a. d. Waldnaab)

Tale Type:
ATU 650A "Strong John"; ATU 1008 "Lighting the Road"; KHM 90 "The Young Giant"

LOUSEHEAD (p. 52)

Source:
Schönwerth: Compound entry VII, folder 1, sheet 61; ZA Marburg No. 203 559 ("Die Waldfrau")

Informant:
"Eugen"

Tale Type:
ATU 314 "Goldener"; KHM 136 "Iron John"

SEVEN WITH ONE BLOW! (p. 55)

Source:
ZA Marburg No. 203 020 ("Sieben auf einen Schlag")

Town:
Radwaschen (Pleystein, County Neustadt a. d. Waldnaab)

Tale Type:
ATU 1640 "The Brave Tailor"; KHM 20 "The Brave Little Tailor"

THE BURNING TROUGH (p. 58)

Source:
ZA Marburg No. 202 963 ("Des Bauern 3 Töchter")

Tale Type:
ATU 425 "The Search for the Lost Husband"; ATU 425B "Son of the Witch"; KHM 127 "The Iron Oven"

THE KING'S BODYGUARD (p. 60)

Source:
ZA Marburg No. 202 247 ("Der Leibhusar")

Tale Type:
ATU 461 "Three Hairs from the Devil's Beard"; KHM 29 "The Devil with the Three Golden Hairs"

THE SCORNED PRINCESS (p. 63)

Source:
ZA Marburg No. 202 992 ("Der Wunderbeutel, das Wunschhütchen und das Wunderhorn")

Tale Type:
ATU 566 "The Three Magic Objects and the Wonderful Fruits"; ATU 569 "The Knapsack, the Hat and the Horn"; KHM 54 "The Knapsack, the Hat, and the Horn"

THE TALKING BIRD, THE SINGING TREE, AND THE SPARKLING STREAM (p. 71)

Source:
ZA Marburg No. 202 290 ("Die armen Königskinder")

Town:
Tirschenreuth (County Tirschenreuth)

Tale Type:
ATU 707 "The Three Golden Children"

THE WEASEL (p. 73)

Source:
ZA Marburg No. 203 489 ("Das Wieserl")

Town:
Neuenhammer (Neuenhammer/Georgenberg, County Neustadt a. d. Waldnaab)

Tale Type:
ATU 444* "Enchanted Prince Disenchanted"; ATU 554 "The Grateful Animals"

THE KNIGHT'S SASH (p. 75)

Source:
ZA Marburg No. 202 258 ("Hans mit der Löwin")

Town:
Neukirchen St. Chr. (Neukirchen zu St. Chr./Georgenberg, County Neustadt a. d. Waldnaab)

Tale Type:
ATU 590 "The Faithless Mother"; KHM 121 "The Prince Who Feared Nothing"

THE GIRL AND THE COW (p. 78)

Source:
ZA Marburg No. 203 000 ("Die Prinzessin und die Kuh")

Tale Type:
ATU 444* "Enchanted Prince Disenchanted"

THE CALL OF THE SHEPHERD'S HORN (p. 80)

Source:
ZA Marburg No. 202 064 ("Die Prinzessin und die Kuh")

Town:
Neuenhammer (Neuenhammer/Georgenberg, County Neustadt a. d. Waldnaab)

Tale Type:
ATU 444* "Enchanted Prince Disenchanted"

THE MARK OF THE DOG, PIG, AND CAT (p. 83)

Source:
ZA Marburg No. 203 205 (untitled)

Town:
Neuenhammer (Neuenhammer/Georgenberg, County Neustadt a. d. Waldnaab)

Tale Type:
ATU 707 "The Three Golden Children"; KHM 3 "Mary's Child"

THE THREE-LEGGED GOATS (p. 86)

Source:
ZA Marburg No. 202 137 ("Märchen")

Town:
"Kulm" (Town unknown)

Tale Type:
ATU 400 "The Man on a Quest for His Lost Wife"

THE TRAVELING ANIMALS (p. 89)

Source:
ZA Marburg No. 202 338 ("Die wandernden Thiere")

Town:
Tirschenreuth (County Tirschenreuth)

Tale Type:
ATU 130 "The Animals in Night Quarters"; KHM 27 "The Bremen Town Musicians"

THE SNAKE'S TREASURE (p. 92)

Source:
ZA Marburg No. 202 287 ("Die weiße Frau")

Town:
Tirschenreuth (County Tirschenreuth)

Tale Type:
ATU 760*** "Salvation in the Cradle"

THE SNAKE SISTER (p. 94)

Source:
Schönwerth: Compound entry VI, folder 24b, sheet 1; ZA Marburg No. 202 111 ("Die Kaufmannskinder")

Town:
Waldau (Vohenstrauß, County Neustadt a. d. Waldnaab)

Tale Type:
ATU 403 "The Black and the White Bride"; KHM 135 "The White and the Black Bride"

"FOLLOW ME, JODEL!" (p. 98)

Source:
Schönwerth: Compound entry I, folder 6c, sheet 33; ZA Marburg No. 202 991 ("Jodl, rutsch mir nach")

Tale Type:
ATU 402 "The Animal Bride"; KHM 63 "The Three Feathers"; KHM 106 "The Poor Miller's Son and the Cat"

THE TOAD BRIDE (p. 101)

Source:
ZA Marburg No. 203 600 ("Kröte")

Tale Type:
ATU 402 "The Animal Bride"; KHM 63 "The Three Feathers";
KHM 106 "The Poor Miller's Son and the Cat"

PRINCE DUNG BEETLE (p. 102)

Source:
Schönwerth: Compound entry IVb, folder 21/8, envelope 1, sheet 12;
ZA Marburg No. 202 053 ("Prinz Roßzwifl")

Town:
Neuenhammer (Neuenhammer/Georgenberg, County Neustadt a. d.
Waldnaab)

Tale Type:
ATU 444* "Enchanted Prince Disenchanted"

THE THREE SPINDLES (p. 107)

Source:
Schönwerth: Compound entry VI, folder 8, envelope 2, sheet 6; ZA
Marburg No. 202 415 ("Hulzfral")

Town:
Seitenthal (Seitenthal/Speinshart, County Neustadt a. d. Waldnaab)

THE LITTLE FLAX FLOWER (p. 109)

Source:
ZA Marburg No. 203 079 ("Das Holzfräulein")

Town:
Neuenhammer (Neuenhammer/Georgenberg, County Neustadt a. d.
Waldnaab)

Secondary Literature:
Lüthi, M.: Belohnung, Lohn. In: EM 2, col. 92–99

WOODPECKER (p. 112)

Source:
Schönwerth: Compound entry I, folder 1 No. 15, sheet 23, p. 6
("Windspecht")

Secondary Literature:
Blum, E.: Geschicklichkeitsproben. In: EM 5, col. 1131-34; Horn,
K.: Fleiß und Faulheit. In: EM 4, col. 1266–67

THE RED SILK RIBBON (p. 116)

Source:
Schönwerth: *Sitten und Sagen*, II, p. 219–25 (untitled)

Town:
Dimpfl (Dimpfl/Georgenberg, County Neustadt a. d. Waldnaab)

Tale Type:
ATU 316 "The Nix of the Mill-Pond"; ATU 554 "The Grateful Animals"; KHM 181 "The Nixie in the Pond"

TWELVE BRIDES (p. 121)

Source:
Schönwerth: *Sitten und Sagen*, II, p. 203–6 (untitled)

THE HOWLING OF THE WIND (p. 124)

Source:
Schönwerth: *Sitten und Sagen*, II, p. 194–95 (untitled)

Town:
Dimpfl (Dimpfl/Georgenberg, County Neustadt a. d. Waldnaab)

Tale Type:
ATU 425E "The Enchanted Husband Sings Lullaby"

HANS DUDELDEE (p. 126)

Source:
Schönwerth: Compound entry I, folder 6c, sheet 32; ZA Marburg
No. 202 990 ("Hans Dudlde")

Tale Type:
ATU 303A "Brothers Seek Sisters as Wives"; ATU 554 "The Grateful Animals"; ATU 922 "The Shepherd Substituting for the Clergyman Answers the King's Questions"; KHM 62 "The Queen Bee"; KHM 152 "The Shepherd Boy"

THE BELT AND THE NECKLACE (p. 130)

Source:
Schönwerth: Compound entry VI, folder 24b, envelope 1, sheet 2; ZA Marburg No. 202 068 ("Die Wasserfrauen")

Town:
Vilseck (County Amberg-Sulzbach)

Secondary Literature:
Horn, K.: Schön und häßlich. In: EM 12, col. 153–61

DRUNK WITH LOVE (p. 132)

Source:
Schönwerth: *Sitten und Sagen*, II, p. 200–3 ("Der Wasserfräulein Liebe")

Town:
Neuenhammer (Neuenhammer/Georgenberg, County Neustadt a. d. Waldnaab)

ANNA MAYALA (p. 135)

Source:
Schönwerth: *Sitten und Sagen*, II, p. 213–19 (untitled)

Town:
Neuenhammer (Neuenhammer/Georgenberg, County Neustadt a. d. Waldnaab)

IN THE JAWS OF THE MERMAN (p. 140)

Source:
Schönwerth: *Sitten und Sagen*, II, p. 177–78 (untitled)

Town:
Neuenhammer (Neuenhammer/Georgenberg, County Neustadt a. d. Waldnaab)

Secondary Literature:
EM "Wassergeister" (in prep.)

THE KING'S RING (p. 141)

Source:
ZA Marburg No. 202 050 ("Die drey Riesen und die drey Jäger")

Tale Type:
ATU 304 "The Dangerous Night-Watch"; KHM 111 "The Skillful Huntsman"

THE THREE GOLDEN CROWNS (p. 145)

Source:
ZA Marburg No. 202 985 ("Die drey Königstöchter")

Tale Type:
ATU 301 "The Three Stolen Princesses"; KHM 91 "The Gnome"; KHM 166 "Strong Hans"

NINE BAGS OF GOLD (p. 148)

Source:
ZA Marburg No. 202 199 (untitled)

Town:
Neuenhammer (Neuenhammer/Georgenberg, County Neustadt a. d. Waldnaab)

TWO BROTHERS (p. 151)

Source:
Schönwerth: Compound entry I, folder 6c, sheet 51-52; ZA Marburg No. 202 255 ("Das Hexenschloß im Walde")

Tale Type:
ATU 303 "The Twins or Blood-Brothers"; KHM 60 "The Two Brothers"

TRICKING THE WITCH (p. 155)

Source:

ZA Marburg No. 202 256 ("Die drei Königtöchter")

Tale Type:

ATU 313 "The Magic Flight"; KHM 51 "Foundling-Bird"; KHM 113 "The Two Kings' Children"

THE ENCHANTED FIDDLE (p. 158)

Source:

Schönwerth: Compound entry I, folder 6c, sheet 87-88; ZA Marburg No. 202 691 ("Die Zaubergeige" and "Von einem Knaben, dem seine Mutter wünscht, dem Teufel zu dienen")

Tale Type:

ATU 475 "The Man as Heater of Hell's Kettle"; ATU 592 "The Dance Among Thorns"; KHM 100 "The Devil's Sooty Brother"

THE DEVIL AND THE FISHERMAN (p. 161)

Source:

ZA Marburg No. 202 577 (untitled)

Tale Type:

ATU 400 "The Man on a Quest for His Lost Wife"

THE EXPERT HUNTER (p. 164)

Source:

ZA Marburg No. 202 958 ("Hans und die Riesen")

Town:

Neukirchen (Neukirchen b. Hl. Blut, County Cham; Neukirchen-Balbini, County Schwandorf; Neukirchen, County Schwandorf; Neukirchen/Hemau, County Regensburg or Neukirchen b. Sulzbach-Rosenberg, County Amberg)

Tale Type:

ATU 304 "The Dangerous Night-Watch"; KHM 111 "The Skillful Huntsman"

A POT OF GOLD IN THE OVEN (p. 167)

Source:
Schönwerth: Compound entry I, folder 15, sheet 31; ZA Marburg
No. 203 080 ("Der Landsknecht mit dem Schatz")

Town:
Neuenhammer (Neuenhammer/Georgenberg, County Neustadt a. d.
Waldnaab)

Tale Type:
ATU 1381 "The Talkative Wife and the Discovered Treasure"

CONTESTS WITH THE DEVIL (p. 169)

Source:
ZA Marburg No. 202 854 (untitled)

Tale Type:
ATU 820 "The Devil as Substitute for Day Laborer at Mowing";
ATU 1063 "Throwing a Club"; ATU 1084 "Screaming or Whis-
tling Contest"

WOUD AND FREID (p. 171)

Source:
Schönwerth: *Sitten und Sagen*, II, p. 312–14 (untitled)

Town:
Neuenhammer (Neuenhammer/Georgenberg, County Neustadt a. d.
Waldnaab)

Tale Type:
ATU 590 "The Faithless Mother"

THE MOUSE CATCHER, OR THE BOY AND THE BEETLE (p. 175)

Source:
ZA Marburg 202 765 (untitled) and 202 241 ("Der Knabe mit dem
Käfer")

Secondary Literature:
Uther, H.-J.: Rattenfänger von Hameln. In: EM 11, col. 300-7

PEARL TEARS (p. 177)

Source:
Schönwerth: *Sitten und Sagen*, III, p. 311–17 ("Von A. L. Frauen")

Town:
Neuenhammer (Neuenhammer/Georgenberg, County Neustadt a. d. Waldnaab)

Tale Type:
ATU 710 "Our Lady's Child"

FLOUR FOR SNOW (p. 181)

Source:
Schönwerth: *Sitten und Sagen*, II, p. 137–39 (untitled)

Tale Type:
ATU 759 "Angel and Hermit"

HOYDEL (p. 183)

Source:
ZA Marburg No. 202 229 ("Der Höydl")

Town:
Wildenreuth (Wildenreuth/Erbendorf, County Tirschenreuth)

Tale Type:
ATU 756C "The Two Sinners"

THE TALKER (p. 187)

Source:
Schönwerth: Compound entry I, folder 6c, sheet 50 ("Der däppische Bauer")

Tale Type:
ATU 1643 "Money Inside the Statue"

THE CLEVER TAILOR (p. 189)

Source:
ZA Marburg No. 203 003 ("Der kluge Schneider")

Tale Type:
ATU 1536 "Disposing of the Corpse"; ATU 1539 "Cleverness and Gullibility"

LEARNING HOW TO STEAL (p. 192)

Source:
ZA Marburg No. 203 009 (untitled)

Informant:
"Katherl"

Tale Type:
ATU 1525 "The Master Thief"

"DON'T GET MAD!" (p. 194)

Source:
Schönwerth: Compound entry I, folder 6c, sheet 45; ZA Marburg No. 203 002 ("Nicht zornig werden")

Tale Type:
ATU 1000 "Contest Not to Become Angry"

OFERLA (p. 198)

Source:
Schönwerth: Compound entry I, folder 6c, sheet 60; ZA Marburg No. 203 048 ("Geschichte")

Town:
Neukirchen (Neukirchen b. Hl. Blut, County Cham; Neukirchen-Balbini, County Schwandorf; Neukirchen, County Schwandorf; Neukirchen/Hemau, County Regensburg or Neukirchen b. Sulzbach-Rosenberg, County Amberg)

Tale Type:
ATU 1536 "Disposing of the Corpse"; ATU 1537 "The Corpse Killed Five Times"

SIR WIND AND HIS WIFE (p. 205)

Source:
Schönwerth: *Sitten und Sagen*, II, p. 109–12 ("Warum der Wind vom Meere her weht")

Town:
Tiefenbach (Tiefenbach, County Cham; Tiefenbach/Nittenau, County Schwandorf or Tiefenbach/Kemnath, County Tirschenreuth)

Secondary Literature:
Ward, D.: Glasberg. In: EM 5, col. 1265–70

THE ICE GIANTS (p. 208)

Source:
Schönwerth: *Sitten und Sagen*, III, p. 362–64 (untitled)

Town:
Neuenhammer (Neuenhammer/Georgenberg, County Neustadt a. d. Waldnaab)

WHY SNOW IS WHITE (p. 210)

Source:
Schönwerth: *Sitten und Sagen*, II, p. 136–37 (untitled)

Town:
Neuenhammer (Neuenhammer/Georgenberg, County Neustadt a. d. Waldnaab)

THE SUN TAKES AN OATH (p. 211)

Source:
Schönwerth: *Sitten und Sagen*, II, p. 57–59 ("Sagenkreis von Sonne und Mond")

THE SUN'S SHADOW (p. 213)

Source:
Schönwerth: *Sitten und Sagen*, III, p. 9 (untitled)

Town:
Lind (Lind/Oberviechtach, County Schwandorf)

Secondary Literature:
Lox, H.: Tod. In: EM 13, col. 696–712

WHAT THE MOON TRIED TO WEAR (p. 214)

Source:
Schönwerth: Compound entry I, folder 2, sheet 27; ZA Marburg No.
    202 932 ("Mondsage")

Secondary Literature:
Meinel, G.: Mond. In: EM 9, col. 795-802; Neumann, S.: Schneider.
    In: EM 12, col. 140-45

THE SINGING TREE (p. 215)

Source:
ZA Marburg No. 202 056 ("Der Schneider im Baum")

Secondary Literature:
Neumann, S.: Schneider. In: EM 12, col. 140-45

Printed in the United States
by Baker & Taylor Publisher Services